DEMONIC RESONANCE THERAPY

DEMON HOOD

AMY HENDRICKS

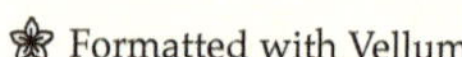 Formatted with Vellum

CONTENT WARNING

While this book may have an occasional joke and gaff, the content inside focuses upon serious topics.

This story features triggers such as blood, self harm, parental abuse, violent transformation, mental health, and more.

In the table of contents, you'll notice a "Trigger Index." This will contain a list of triggers per chapter, along with an intensity rating.

If you need a heads up, feel free to check it.

If you're wondering why the hell a "Trigger Index" exists and consider this a bad thing, please get some empathy.

Thanks!

Dedicated to square pegs in round holes…

…to those who hate the status quo…

…to the soft, tough, and weary souls…

…and those who need a little space to grow.

Godspeed you hellions.

PART ONE
THE FABULOUS FOLD

CHAPTER 1
TACO HELL

A woman is in the middle of a makeup livestream. Today's topic? Eyeliner.

Her golden halo eyes look away from the camera as she speaks, words flowing from a digital tablet as spotted in her mirror. The metal halo above her head flashes a glow, wings shrink as she stumbles over a line. It's only when she applies the eyeliner does her wings gently expand. A perfect application brings a perfect smile.

This angel seems nice, gonna follow her just in case I get back into makeup.

Like. Swipe.

The Celestinauts are once again showing off a recruitment ad. They've established humanity's first base on Phobos while preparations are being done for the first space-built shuttle.

Don't get me wrong, huge fan of space. What I'm not a fan of is a trillionaire with a blank check ignoring the rest of us in the twenty first century. There's a lot of mouths that need feedin'.

Swipe.

A group of sea canoers cheer in excitement at the Great Barrier Reef. The person recording can't stop shaking, pointing the camera face down into the water spotting the iconic blue glow of mermaids. Their fin-esque hands placed upon the coral as it shifts from a dead white to many vibrant colors.

Hell yeah. Like and Swipe.

Doomscrolling is bein' kind to me tonight.

Biting into a cheese wrap, it gives me something to do while lookin' through the fingerprint-smeared window. The forest outside is covered in snow, flakes adding to the collage. A lone light pole illuminates the country road that connects this place to the rest of society.

That's what I love about this Taco Hell. Outside of the occasional delivery driver it's dead silent. That dead air is my comfort; only thing keeping me sane after a late night shift. Allows me to swipe through the world on my lil' phone screen, pretending what's around me doesn't exist.

If that can happen for at least half an hour, I'll be fine. I need to be fine.

Closing my eyes as I breathe in deep—my battery almost ready to go for tomorrow's sensory assault.

Was doing pretty good on that front, but screeching tires drag me back to Earth.

A hatchback screams into the parking lot, huge fella sticking out of the rear sunroof. The thing's a pure rustbucket with more parts missing than remaining. Panels with mismatched colors, probably bought in a pinch. It's amazing how little a car needs to run, especially retro-lookin' models like that one. Is it from the nineties? eighties?

The contraption halts, metal exterior no longer vibrating as the only working taillight fades. When the doors pop open, some humanoids pop out. Their kind are rare 'round the town of Comfort, but it's always cool to see some variety. Can the tall one can even get through the doors? The hatchback's suspension is begging for release as the they climb out of the sunroof, metal grinding loudly before the quiet returns.

As they walk into the Taco Hell's lighting, they got the colors of a crayon box—a wine red, deep blue, and warm yellow—their horns shoot into the sky, threatening god.

They defy my expectations as they successfully slide inside the joint, employees scurrying away from the front counter. The group stands there, red one shrugging at the sight as they toward the digital screens. The red one taps away at the display.

"Look sister, all I am asking is that you stop getting us trespassed." The blue one speaks up. "It's not even midnight, and you already punched someone."

"They were bein' feckin eejits." the red one responds with a slight defensiveness. "You saw the girls bein' afraid. They weren't wanted, so I took care of it."

The blue one rubs their temples, "Yeah, you're right, but—*ugh*. Can you wait long enough to take it outside next time?"

"I will, yeah." the red one says mashing the screen with her finger, the amount of hot sauce packets skyrockets on the display. The blue one sighs as the tall yellow fella' snickers at them both.

My brain continues the variant guessing game, horns being the main hint. They ain't animal horns, not even close to cow, goat, whatever. Gotta be something more mythical. The colors and patterns are cluing me in—the red one has glowing gold lines spiraling around theirs, definitely demonic in some fashion but—

Oh shit! Demonic! They're fucking demons! Play it cool. Demons are awesome, but I don't wanna piss 'em off. Gotta distract myself.

Pulling out my phone, gotta scroll for new dopamine fodder so I can distract myself.

Wait, they have tails?

Shit, look away. I need to stop. It's the first time I seen their kind in a while, and despite how cool they look I feel like a stalker.

It's hard to have chances like this since demons are isolationists. It's probably due to the fact that our society demonizes, well, demons. They tend to stick to the shadows as a result, who's gonna bother them in a dead-end fast food joint? Sure as hell not me.

Food's gotta distract, right? Tossin' a cinna-snap in my mouth, there's that big puffy crunch of cinnamon, but it didn't help. The urge is still there.

Ok, fine. Let's make a deal. One more glance, then I'll stop forever. Cool, let's do it.

The plan fails as the red one stares me down. golden glow in her eyes, devious twinkle in her toothy grin.

Shit! Shit shit shit.

"Oi! You enjoying the show over there?" The other two break away from the screen as the order goes through, blue one rolls their eyes as they notice the situation unfolding.

Gotta look away, be harmless. They won't see me as a threat, right? I'm a boring human eating a boring meal. Gonna look at my phone, look busy.

The red one crashes into the opposite booth seat at my table. "I'm talkin' to you, lil' human."

Guess I'm as good as dead, and she'll be the one dragging me to hell.

She smirks at me, like I'm some toy to play with. Red skin is littered with black freckles and designs; A tattoo-like choker stamped on her neck in the form of a fancy knot, with a huge black trinity symbol right on her chest. The crackling glow on her chest matches her eyes, pulsating with a calm rhythm.

Her long hair has a braided crown, but further down blow out like a roaring fire. Long pointy ears pop out the sides; golden earrings with tiny black bird feathers attached. Her thick tail rolls off the booth chair as she stabilizes in the seat, short enough to hover over the ground.

Despite the baggy military jacket covering their tanktop, the temperature around the table went up by a few degrees.

"Please excuse my sister Morrigan." The blue one rushes in, looking worried. "She's—"

Morrigan puts a finger up and they go quiet, watching the situation from the distance. What's goin' on here?

"C'mon, I ain't a biter—" she flashes her fangs at me, "—yet."

Gulp.

"What interests ya?" She's staring directly into my soul now. Do I have a soul? Do demons see souls?

Gotta say something at least. "Sorry, I meant no offense. Thought you all looked cool and—"

"Ahh, an admirer, eh?" She cut me off, putting her hands behind her head as she leans back in the booth seat. "Though we ain't really cool. Kinda hot actually, am I right Sam?" She points a finger gun at the blue demon, pausing for a laugh.

Sam returns a monotone stare, eyes reminiscent of blue china plates with golden trims old people love collectin'. While Morrigan dresses for rugged utility, Sam looks ready for a comfy lo-fi music stream. She's the only one that has a singular horn—A blade of blue, flowery designs of white and yellow decorating the sides, and a gold trim to line the edge, ready to strike. Her thin tail flows through the air as her unamused stare continues.

"Ah, she gets it." Morrigan says to the dead silence, gently waving her off before turning back to me. "Tell ya what, new admirer. You seem harmless, and I'm a generous kinda demon tonight—"

She pulls a carton of cigs out of her jacket, placing one cig in her mouth. "—Since you're such a big admirer of us demons, and we're waitin' on the grub, I'll let ya ask three questions about us." One snap of her fingers and flames shoot out, lighting the cigarette as it begins to smoke. "No tricks, no judgment, no anger. Ask honestly, and you get honest answers, understand?" She goes for a drag, breathing in deep.

Never really had a chance for credible information before. Internet is a black hole for humanoids, let alone demons. The only things that exist are a few fan pages and humanoid theory forums. Sure I signed up for a few of them, but it was a bunch of humans making up things or AI-generated garbage hallucinating facts. The only other source are academic text-books that I can never afford. Local library doesn't carry them either; I triple checked.

My one chance to get some actual info is staring right at me. I genuinely want to understand what makes them so unique, so *cool*.

Can't mess this up though, so what do I even ask? Something about their horns? The awesome tails? Those cool designs stamped across their body? So many questions, but I'm forced to fit it all into three small sentences.

I should think about this opportunity carefully, but my dumb heart throws a question out on impulse.

"Is it hard to wear hats with those horns?"

Morrigan's eyes widen as she looks slightly taken aback. Then she cracks a grin, bursting into a giggle fit. Smoke pours out of her mouth with her forked tongue, making me cough.

"Really?" She asks as she calms down.

God, smite me now.

"Well...I ain't a hat enjoyer, but I assume it would be a bit difficult due to me horns." She feels her forehead at the base of her horns, double checking to make sure.

"...I guess one of those fancy tennis hats might fit. Bud over there has side horns so they can wear normal hats and things." She points to the big yellow demon behind Sam currently wearing a beanie.

Thought they were tall outside, seeing them this close makes them gigantic. Sitting in that hatchback's gotta be a nightmare if they go through the rear sunroof. Surprised they got clothes that fit—black, shaggy and cheap—coming straight from a punk concert.

Their knees and arms have brown rocks shooting out of them, with their horns sharing the same shade. While everyone else's horns shoots out the front, theirs juts out the sides, sitting right behind their ears like a cow. Their tail is long and strong, a big puft of hair at the back as it gently swooshes through the air. Bud gives a polite wave, hair covering their eyes with a fang filled smile.

Besides that, they don't utter a single word.

"Two more questions." Morrigan says.

Gotta think of a serious one to balance things out; not look like a scared child. Don't wanna die from demon-induced embarrassment.

As my mind plays memory pinball, I remember there was a demon kid or two in elementary; never had the chance to talk to them. Mom wasn't a fan of me hanging out with humanoids, so I was too anxious to even say hi. Growing up a demon can be a cool question, right?

"Was it hard being a demon growing up?" I ask. "I mean, people probably picked on y'all at school or somethin, right?"

Her playful demeanor simmers down to more of a stern vibe. She takes a long drag of her cigarette, blowing smoke towards the no smoking sign.

"I wasn't always a demon, ya know." she speaks up.

That's a thing? My head tilts to the side, trying to process what she meant.

"Oh, you didn't know about that part?" She says after a bit of silence. "I'm one of the demons who took injections; descended, they call us. Was a weak lil' human like you at one point—cringy lil' shite. No identity to grab onto, military will do that to ya after grindin' ya up and throwin' ya away."

Another drag and puff. "One day at a community vet meetin', notice one of the usual guys came in entirely demonized. Big buff lad; deadly as hell. Horns as big as me arms—handed me what little resources there is to get started. There's these clinics ran by some big medical company—"

"Lailah Pharmaceuticals." Sam interjects.

"Yes yes, leelah pharma or whatever." Morrigan continues as Sam delivers an annoyed sigh. "They have a program where ya get these energy injections. When your body starts to generate enough of it, ya give some back."

"It's called Energy Injection Therapy and Recovery, or EITR." Sam interjects once again, sliding her glasses up. "Morrigan is specifically talking about the variant called DRT, or Demonic

Resonance Therapy. In simple terms medical and scientific professionals cannot artificially create these energies in a lab, as using non-consenting animals for such a thing is tantamount to cruelty due to physical and mental alterations. Consenting humans turned humanoid with EITR are able to provide a surplus of resonant energy easily. It's like donating blood or plasma, but you get turned into a variant of your choice before it begins. It's relatively harmless, and allows research and development of these energies to continue across labs nationwide. It has lead to some incredible results, such as clean energy and renewable fuel sources. You can thank us for your gas prices going down drastically while keeping the climate from getting hotter."

Us? We? Gas Prices? What?

"Don't mind her info-dumps." Morrigan chimes in, "She works for a big health foundation thing and—"

"I *run* the Circe Advocacy Network, Morrigan." Sam glares at her, her expression becoming neutral when moving back to me. "The only healthcare foundation in the USA built for folks like us. We make sure that folks can get the proper care, mutual aid, and legal protections we all need."

Sam smiles at herself, prideful pose included. I mean, she is apparently helping a lot of people. That's awesome.

"Health execs, am I right?" Morrigan said leaning in closer, giggling at her own joke. Sam's pride shatters as she glares at Morrigan once again.

"But ya, she helps lots of folks get help where there isn't any. We demons and other folk have 'special needs' that apparently are 'unnecessary'. Extremely valuable work she does, but we gettin' off track ain't we?"

Morrigan lays back in her seat, arms behind her head, "Anyways, I went to one of those lira pharm clinics to get me a new pair of horns. A few signatures, physical, and other fancy legal documents designed to scare ya later, I walk out with a few vials of demonic energy, becomin' the deadly demon ya see now." She smiles with her eyes closed, playing with the cig in her mouth, seemingly content with her life.

Meanwhile, a door opens.

Injections—that's where humanoids can come from? You're saying I could *be* a humanoid? Inject some stuff, become a demon? That's... Why do I feel so giddy? Is that optimism? Hope? I haven't felt that in, well, I don't know how long, if ever. What is that? Where did it come from?

"Ok admirer! Last question—be smart with it." Both her and Sam are looking at me differently. Is that curiosity? Anticipation?

Gotta focus. One more question. Nothing impulsive, has to be serious and well thought out. Problem is the previous answer keeps bouncing in my head. Is it easy? hard? What happens?

My mind becomes overloaded with those strange feelings, and before I knew it, my brain loses the race as my mouth begins to improv.

"So, if demons can be, uh, 'made', and, um, let's say someone wanted to…" I trail off, should I really ask? I look towards the group, and now they're definitely curious.

Gotta push through.

"…wanted to be a, uh…"

It's so hard to speak. I swallow my nerves, then finally throw it out in the open.

"…If I wanted to be a demon, is that a good idea? Is it worth it?"

My brain catches up too late. Want to be a demon? Really? My heart spoke that, but the shame fades in. Why did I ask that? What will these demons think?

God, I'm an idiot. Closing my eyes, I put my head in my hands, ready to be laughed at again.

But the laughter never came.

After a few seconds of silence, I open my eyes and look around. Morrigan's roughness became softer. Sam went from being annoyed at her sister to looking at me with a gentleness. Bud looks, uh, excited? Hard to tell with their face half covered by hair.

Morrigan takes one huge drag of the cig before putting it out on the table, leaving a burn mark and ashes. Her tone becomes softer as she speaks up, "Look, what's your name again?"

Oh god, I didn't even introduce myself yet.

Don't want to use my legal name, but at the same time I don't want to leave them hanging. I try my best to filter it out whenever I hear it, but the first letter always comes through. That'll do for now, I hope.

"Uh, call me E. I'm still workshoppin' a name…" Here comes the rejection, for real this time. Who has a name that's a letter?

"Well E, it wasn't an easy process." Morrigan starts off. "Sure, the medical side is simple. A weekly injection, a few new cravings for a growin' body, check-ups to make sure you're doin' grand—all that. That isn't hard."

She closes her eyes, seemingly quick in thought, then opens them back up with a hint of seriousness. "The hard part of it is what goes on around you. Rejection is common. Stares you get from those both familiar and new are annoying. Those important relationships ya thought were unconditional? Turns out they might be conditional."

She then looks towards the other demons of her group, smile forming. "Ah, but the bonds you build with so many demons; such beautiful souls that humans could never comprehend. The hot bod that these injections gave me, and for the first time in my life I felt grounded, loved, alive—*that* is what was worth it to me. Why I got my pair of horns."

She pulls out her phone as her thumbs tap across the screen. "Here…" She places her phone on the table before sliding it to me, an invite code visible on the screen. "…Unfortunately, can't stick here all night with ya. The employees don't seem to be fans of us, and the last thing we need is peelers poppin' up." The three human workers are cowering in the kitchen. Yeah, looks like a crowd that would call the cops on any oddity.

"This code invites ya to the group chat that we're a part of, our 'fold' as it's called in demonic circles." Morrigan continues. "If ya join it, we can help you make a decision that's right for you. Fill you in on some tips and tricks if ya want to continue down the path of demonhood."

I scan it with my phone, and an invite for a group chat called "The Fabulous Fold" pops up, numerous demon and fire emojis surrounding the title.

"Now, here's the important part—you have to make that decision yourself." Morrigan says boldly. "This ain't no peer pressure shite. If you're fine with being a human, then so be it. You have some more time talking to us demons before we possibly part paths. If ya wanna go all in though—shed your humanity and join us other folk—the community will welcome you with open arms."

I join the chat group as she gets up from the table, Bud's in the back carrying the many bags of fast food they ordered with one arm, drinks with the other. Morrigan walks to my side of the table and immediately puts a hand on my shoulder, a very warm heating pad to my cold skin.

"And potential hellion?" Morrigan eyes seem to flicker like fire. "Good luck."

A what?

She walks off before I could even ask. Sam gives me a polite wave out the door while Morrigan goes for the sauces. She jabs her hand into the packet box, the spiciest sauce packets imaginable in her grasp as some fall to the ground. She pushes the exit door with her shoulder as she turns to me, gesturing demon horns with her free hand while creating a breadcrumb trail of packets to their car.

They all felt and look so confident. They looked so fuckin' bad ass too. Happy. Content. Cool.

I want that.

Am I allowed to have that?

Heck, I'm a twenty-five-year-old livin' with my parents. Mom's religious as hell, and Dad religiously watches right-wing news. I really don't want to make them angry.

At the same time, these demons gave me answers I didn't know I needed. Hints as to why I lose my mind staring into a mirror. New feelings.

When's the last time that's happened? I can't remember.

All that I know is that out of everything in my life so far, those demons made the most sense. I want to jump in, but it sounds scary.

Do I go for it?

CHAPTER 2
THE HUMANOID AISLE
BARTER BOB'S GROCERY

Gazing at the destruction wrought upon the shopping aisle—trusty mop in one hand, toolkit in another—all I can do is sigh.

Spent hours restoring this aisle over and over—day after day—and all it takes is one loser to wreck it in seconds. The metal shelves are surfing around the oily mess on the floor, labels stuck to broken glass and plastic that once held whatever this newfound concoction is. They even put a fresh coat of spray paint up, delivering a lovely message.

"Humanoids leave, or you're next."

With this big grand mess before me, only one thought comes to mind—It's time to clean shit up.

Sliding my earbuds in, letting fancy algorithms control tonight's music as I get myself into the rhythm. Sounds like an album my dad would listen to, but The Avalanches sound pretty nice.

The wet mop slides across the floor as pools of used car oil, seashell chips, grass shreddies, and crushed charcoal swirl together into a complete mess. This kinda situation happens every month— shitty humanists come in, aim for the aisle, and trash the place. Every time, I'm the chosen one of the employee roster, cleanin' it up once again.

Lots' of the people I work with get to do a variety of tasks: deli workers, cashiers, cart pushers—heck—even storage. Unfortunately, Derrick the store manager always puts me on clean-up and repairs. Mentioned off-hand that I liked tinkering with electronics, and that sealed my fate.

Wiping down yet another collection of sticky nectar infused with clay smeared across the floor, my mind drifts to the absurdity of this whole situation. Why do people even hate humanoids so much, anyway? Sure, they don't look like us— some have fish scales, fluffy tails, bug antennas, even some unusual ethereal qualities—but what's the problem with that? With the way the bigots yell about some replacement theory of the week, you'd think humanity was gonna go extinct tomorrow.

Doubt it.

From those I met, they don't wanna take over the world— They just wanna be themselves. Shouldn't have to punish them for being a lil' funny lookin'.

You'd think they'll install some more security cameras around the aisle, catch whoever is responsible; but for some reason evidence never manifests. Police come, takes first-hand accounts of the situation, extremely detailed face sketches, everything. Wouldn't matter if they had Sherlock himself, the culprits don't turn up. Derrick jokes about how we should get rid of this aisle if it causes so much chaos, but we're the only major retailer in the area with humanoid products. Too much profit to tear it down.

Whatever people feel about the aisle, I hate cleaning this shit up. Charcoal and nectar mixed in oil? That will be a few hours of mopping up and wiping down easily. I don't even know how they use this stuff. Is it like skin care or something? Is that why it's right next door to hygiene? You'd think I'd get a hint at this point with the amount of times I restore the space, but I got nothin'. Maybe with their unique needs they have special regimens or something that—

"Hey, E████!" Derrick yells at me from behind. Really hate that name.

"Yes sir?" I ask, a lowly peasant staring at a feudal lord.

"Did ya catch the game last night?" he asks. "Those nasty Angels from Paradise swindled victory from our Cougars once again. Real shame what those humanoids are doin' to the good ol' American ballgame. They gotta regulate that shit, y'know?" Don't even know what ball sport he's talking about, but I'm not interested.

"I didn't catch it." I respond.

He sighs, "Oh yeah, right, ain't a baseball fan. You're more into reality shows or girly stuff like that, right?" Another repeat of this kinda questioning. He's still trying to find out my gender, but for some reason using TV shows as a metric?

"I don't watch TV." I say firmly.

He stares at me weirdly. "...Sure. Also, once you're done with the humanoid aisle, I need you to check out the freezer in the meat section. It's been going on the fritz again. Consulted Metatron, told me those fish people are probably shootin' too much water in it when browsing, shorting it out."

He's talking to that chat bot again. Not like he listens when I tell him it's wrong. Guess I gotta find the actual reason.

"Yes sir." I reply.

"Great! That's why I like ya kid!" Hate that stupid smile on his face—so happy he doesn't have to call a proper repairman with me around. Wouldn't mind it if he paid me more, but he gives me speeches about how our team is all "one big family" and how "we should be happy with the emotional pay our job provides."

Good feels don't pay for good meals, asshole.

Gotta hold that back, job market sucks right now. I don't have a single degree or certification to leave this place, so I put my earbud back in and return to the rhythm—the aisle must be cleaned.

Hours pass, and the sticky crumbly mess took some effort. Cleaning chemicals got me coughing up a lung due to a lack of working masks. Gotta be a violation for that somewhere, but who cares about a country town like this?

Next up was putting up the shelves again. Seems like they finally got around my huge bolt idea; they were mounted right above the shelves to keep em from moving. For some reason though, the bolts are gone. Didn't see them broken or lying around everywhere. Where did they go?

Would mounting tape do anything? Doubt it, but hey it's worth a shot. Can't move them up and out if they can't move, right? Time to slap it on.

With the final shelf modified and placed back on the wall, the aisle is restored. I can complain about cleaning all I want—once I look upon my handiwork across the restoration, can't help but feel pride.

No matter how many humanist bigots try to terrorize this grand Barter Bob with vandalism, I'll always be there, toolkit in hand, warding off the evils of this land.

I'm going overboard, right? Making myself sound like a silly knight or somethin'. Even got me gigglin'.

It's just a shopping aisle. Let's get back to reality and fix that freezer.

I place the toolkit down in the meat section, flipping the switch on the unit to shut it off. I lift open the electrical panel with the help of a good ol' fashioned screwdriver. With one trusty multimeter and a service manual downloaded onto my phone, it's time to test connections.

Tapping grounds around the board and checking some cables to see where the issue was—Nothing out of the ordinary. Swapping to different modes and voltages, same story.

Now I'm confused.

Wait, no. There's no way. Grabbing the power cable and out of curiosity give it a tug—it's loose. Following the cable to its socket, and there's a plug laying on the floor. A quick slap into the wall then flipping the power switch once again, and the freezer revs up without a single issue.

Did someone trip over the cord or something? Whatever, it's "fixed". Onto the next task.

Rest of the night was full of mind-numbing tasks stacking up. Clean another aisle here, fix the shopping cart wheel there. I was busy trying to fish a broken plastic card out of a trading card machine when the speakers announces we're closing.

I'm tired, it's time to go home.

Sneaking my way into the employee area, there's a few small groups trying to relax from the long shift. I wanna grab my messenger bag and hoodie then peace out. Sliding the hoodie on, My ears are forced to pick up a conversation.

"That's great Jason! No wonder you look so happy lately!" One employee chirps.

"Thanks!" Jason replies. "I know it's gonna be a lot of homework, but I feel like moving into social work is something that I wanna do. Not to mention the grants I get smooth out costs. I wanna help people, you know? Always been my calling."

He then looks straight at me. Shit, I don't want to be perceived right now. My nerves shoot up as I mess with my bag; an attempt to ward off conversation.

"Maybe when I'm done, I can finally help E█████ over there get out of his shell!" Confusion hits his face, "…her shell?"

No one really gets it, do they? I don't even really know my gender, nor do I care. Not like my body helps in this department. Brown hair is always short yet shaggy, bangs are covering my eyes, and body is flat as a board. Not a soft curve or chiseled edge in sight.

Honestly, I'm me—whatever that means.

I don't really give a verbal response to Jason, but I throw a silent thumbs up before walking to the door. His grin looks genuine, probably thinkin' he already made progress. Hope his social work goes well, but don't drag me into it please.

One cold walk through the parking lot snow as flakes dance in the parking lot lights, I slide into my mom's silver car. Ain't no luxury, but the seat warmers are a blessing as I turn on the car then back off again to let the battery run. Gives me time to relax for a sec before I drive home. Closing my eyes and embracing the warmth, my mind drifts to last night.

Were they serious about that humanoid stuff? Injections turned them into demons? Sounds too good to be true. How would a process like that even work? They said to message them if I had questions, but I've never been one to initiate contact with others. I feel my body stressin' up thinking about it.

My phone pings me out of my anxiety. Opening up, a notification in their group chat. Guess I didn't need to make the first move.

———

FIREMAIDEN - 10:30PM

hey @ToyTinkerer its morrigan

wanna hang out with the fold tonight

———

They wanna hang out with me already? When's the last time someone asked me to hang out, High school? No, middle school? Hell if I know.

There's the anxiousness again, shit. Would Mom be okay with it since I got her car? Can say I went to a fast food joint again, right?

———

TOYTINKERER - 10:32PM

if it isn't a problem...

FIREMAIDEN - 10:32PM

lad

if it was a problem i wouldnt have asked

anyways u know that castle bar food place

SAGESAMMY - 10:33PM

Cabinet Castle Barcade.

FIREMAIDEN - 10:33PM

yeah that

were already there

whatever ya decide no pressure

if ya dont show have a good night

———

Are they being too friendly? No clue. It's strange to have people inviting me out, but it's also nice. Searching up the name of the restaurant, according to the map it's the opposite way home. Is that worth it? Whatever I choose, gotta turn the car on and get movin'.

Driving up to the exit intersection, it's time to make a decision. Looking to the left, the dark street heading home. Would be back in my room in a half hour, ready to melt the midnight solder on my camera project. To the right is the town of Comfort, illuminated by streetlight. People ready to hang out just a few minutes away.

Why is making a choice like this so hard? It's talking to a few people. That's what a simple hangout is, right? It sounds simple, but whatever my body is going through is clouding my judgment. What the hell is this feeling? What does it want?

A gentle knock on the car window jumps me out of my seat as I grab my chest.

Oh, it's Jason.

I tap the window button, cracking the window open. "Uh, whats up?" I ask, trying to regain my composure.

"You good dude?" He replies with concern in his voice. "You've been at the stop sign for a few minutes now." I look down at the clock and it's been five minutes. What the hell? I only just notice the headlights from his truck blaring through the rear windshield.

Guess I gotta ward him off. "Yeah I'm fine, thinking things through. Sorry for holding ya up." I say.

He smiles with a gentle nod, "That's great. See you tomorrow E█████." He walks off, sliding back into his truck as he slams the door shut.

God, I hate that name.

Turning on the right blinker, I start heading towards the light.

CHAPTER 3
THE FABULOUS FOLD
CABINET CASTLE BARCADE

The name wasn't lying, this place looks like a weird ass castle. The building looks like one of those pizza joints, but the corners have weird structures that masquerades as watchtowers. Clearly decorative additions, not actually usable. Gotta admire the craftsmanship though. You can see the paint is chipped showing the plywood construction below, but it's made with love.

That's all that matters, right?

Closing the car door, a group of rednecks stare at me for a few seconds before redirecting their attention to their group. Wonder what their deal is.

Pulling open the front door, a blast of warm air greets me. Cold white nothingness becomes warm orange-red, accompanied with the sounds of people. Wooden flooring, stained glass windows and lamps hovering over booth tables—Yep, definitely an old pizza joint. What's different though is the round tables line the floor with an interesting mix of humans and humanoids.

A bar in the back has a mouse humanoid, serving another glass of whatever alcoholic mixture to a deer. A dog is doing a horrible karaoke rendition of some pop song. Haven't seen anything like this in Comfort before. Thought such a blend of the two would be an impossible sight in these lonely woods, but I guess I'm wrong. Wonder how hard it would be to spot the demons in this mass of people.

"Once again, the queen reigns supreme!" A familiar voice shouts from the arcade cabinets.

Not that long I guess.

The fold is standing in front of a big-screened cabinet with "THY GRAND VICTORY!" emblazoned on the arcade's CRT. Morrigan's hands are on her hips, looking smug towards an annoyed Sam.

"That's because you keep button mashing instead of having actual skill." Sam responds.

Morrigan smirks as her demonic tail wags, "If slamming buttons beats your advanced fighter skills then they weren't advanced, were they?"

Bud manifests from the crowd, their huge stature splitting the two apart. They cross their arms, staring them both down like a disappointed parent. Their argument cools as their aggressive stances turn soft.

"Sorry sis." Morrigan rubs the back of her head with her hand.

"I'm sorry too, sister." Sam responds, looking away embarrassed.

What happened there?

Bud smiles at them with a nod, before they spot me from a distance. Their smile becomes a wide grin. The other two look up at Bud with confusion, then straight at me. They begin to share Bud's happiness, Morrigan making first contact with their approach.

"See, told ya they would come!" Morrigan says to the others before turning back to me. "How ya doin lad? Ya seem stressed."

I shrug, "I'm doing fine. Showing up cause ya asked." That answer sucked, but what else could I say?

Morrigan stares at me for a sec, looking me up and down, before the smirk reappears. "We're glad ya did. Say, are you a fighting game fan?"

"I've played a few." I reply. "Not sure if I'm any good at it though."

She lightly chuckles, "Don't worry, we're all shite at it. Say, let's get a game going—iron out those nerves of yours with an ice breaker fight."

The arcade cabinet fits the theme of the castle—Knights clashing swords on the side of the machine, the demo looping on the screen showing a guy getting tossed across the stage, low poly graphics stretched across a old tube TV. That's when I spot logo above the screen in a big golden fancy font—Knight Night Fight.

"Say, E, You ever heard of The Knights of The Round Table?" She asks, throwing a few quarters into the machine.

"Barely." I reply, "Dad got me and my mom to watch a movie with them years ago. They kept smacking coconuts or whatever but it made me laugh."

"Ahh, *Monty Python's The Holy Grail!*" Morrigan replies as she slides the final quarter in. "Great film, weird way to get introduced to the legends. Need to get ya on *Green Knight* ASAP."

The machine screams with noises of swords clashing as a giant block of text on the screen demands us to press start. Morrigan leans back up as Sam and Bud take a step back, giving me room. A gentle smile from both of them as I grab a hold of the controls.

"Anyways, this game is full of knights from those legends, but in this they're a bit more serious compared to those coconut knights." Morrigan says.

She presses the two player start button on the machine, and the game screams at us both to select characters. A quick glance at the controller on the cabinet, huge stick with a set of six buttons. Sure beats the keyboard on my laptop, but gotta get used to this plastic and metal. Grabbing the stick, I look up at the screen and god damn—There's got to be at least forty knights here. What the hell do I pick?

Morrigan already shoots down the list and instalocks a character. "Morgan Le Fay!" The announcer of the game shouts.

A woman with a pair of wings and two daggers appears, her armor coated in black metal feathers, almost like some sort of dragon scale armor. Morrigan gives me a silly smile, "Dunno if you can tell, but I'm a big fan of hers."

Is that a joke? I don't get it, but I try to return a smile.

Moving the stick around for a bit around the roster, every knight here seems alright at best. That guy has a fancy mustache, another dude is too golden. The first girl I come across that isn't Morgan is too scantly clad with bikini armor. Sure is a nineties game.

There's too many choices, but zero information. What's the play styles? What's their mobility like? What about—

"Make your choice lad, or the game will do it for ya." Morrigan interjects, pointing to the timer on the screen.

Ten seconds left, shit. Might as well leave it to chance. I close my eyes, move the stick a few times, and then slam the button.

"Tristan!" The announcer shouts. A fancy looking knight appears, donned in chainmail with a shield of yellow, flowing cape and quiver on his back.

"Ooh, Tristan! A grand choice!" She says.

"I kinda picked at random." I shrug.

She chuckles, "Ah, don't we all?"

"Stage Select!" The announcer screams again. She holds the stick to the right as it spins through the stages—a countryside with a strange tower on a hill, a bridge running across a creek, Stonehenge even—she continues to slide past all of that, slamming the select button down with the side of her fist out of nowhere.

"Camelot!" The announcer says once more, a loud clash of metal blares from the old speakers as the arcade machine loads in the stage.

A big cobblestone castle appears in the distance, a big dirt road becoming the battlefield. Both of our characters walk in from the sides, Morgan brandishing some daggers while Tristan pulls out a sword while placing the longbow to their back, posing at each other trying to intimidate the other.

"Good luck." She says with a grin.

I'm about to get my ass beat, aren't I?

"Round One, Fight!" The announcer shouts with golden text on the screen, and Morrigan charges after my guy.

Yep, I only had twenty seconds.

Morrigan's been playing before I got here, so she's warmed up to smash my character to pieces, and round one comes to a close.

"Morrigan always charges in head first." Sam chimes in, I forgot she was even watching. "She smashes any attack without reason. Barely dodges. Use that to your advantage, and you'll break through her simplistic strategy."

"Don't be givin' away my secrets, sis!" Morrigan replies with her tail straightened.

Sam giggles. "Should have thought of that before making fun of my advanced fighter tactics."

Round two starts up quick, and now that I figured out the controls I'm holding my own. Tristan is slower than Morgan, but his weapons hit harder. The match goes on for a bit longer, but when she charges at me again, I jump right over her, followed by a slash of my sword across her back. Her character falls, and round two comes to a close, one point between both of us.

"There's that spark!" She says. "Now, since you got a proper understanding, I won't go easy on ya."

Felt something inside me take the wheel. "Don't worry Morrigan—I'll go easy on you." I respond.

She's surprised, tail speeds up it's sway as the fiery glow crackles in her eyes. "Big words for a potential demon!" She jests. "Just remember—don't miss."

It felt nice being called a demon, even a potential one.

Round three begins, our knights dance back and forth with our fingers flowing amongst buttons and sticks. Morrigan suddenly switches tactics, once charging in, now taking the back corner of the screen as she begins throwing an endless amount of daggers my way.

I jump over the knives before pressing a few buttons. Wanted to see if air attacks were a thing. My reward was Tristan pulling out a bow and arrow, aiming directly at Morgan before it flies across the screen. A huge chunk of her health bar vanishes in an instant as the arrow lands, Tristan landing in front of her. Time to sword em'.

As Tristan's sword slashes, Morgan suddenly rolls off the ground, creating distance as a weird sound effect goes off for the first time.

"Sorry E, but I gotta bring this to a close." Morrigan says, jamming the stick straight down then right, holding down a combo of buttons.

I looked at her health bar, right below three notches are filled up, all of them flow with a rainbow. Oh shit, She's prepping a special attack.

The screen darkens, and Morgan shoots across the screen as a loud blinking noise erupts the speakers. I hold the stick back, and Tristan responds with his shield. If you blinked, you would've missed her dash before a loud clang is heard. Even the arcade lighting shut off for a split second.

Somehow, the block persists.

Morgan keeps wailing on the shield, my defense holding up, yet my health bar keeps chipping away bit by bit as she keeps pushing me further across the stage. These seconds felt like minutes as she kept her barrage on me.

Then her attack is spent and Morgan halts, but the damage has been done—both of us a sliver away from death. She's looking at the screen with a slight bewilderment—she didn't expect me to block that.

That's my opening.

Initiating a ground slide attack, I launch her up in the air, followed by a few upper sword attacks, juggling her before swapping to a heavy hit. It throws her high into the air, and it's time for the fatal blow. Tristan's bow aims to the heavens, her flying body entering his eyeline, and the arrow flies through her cleanly as the screen goes black and white. Morgan screams in defeat as the game goes into slow motion, her body slamming into the ground.

"THY GRAND VICTORY!" The announcer shouts, golden

text covering the screen as what I can only assume is a theme for Tristan playing through the speakers.

Morrigan goes dead silent, looking away from me and the arcade machine before making some weird noises. Did I do something wrong?

Those noises get louder, becoming cackling laughter as she places a hand on my shoulder. "Someone's finally done it! Ya dethroned me! Excellent showing, lad!"

I was gonna gloat, but hearing praise defused me and my smile returns, her hand radiating that demonic heat into me.

Behind us, one person is clapping. It's Bud, cheering me on while Sam gives a smug look.

"Seems like we found your counter." Sam says.

"For now." Morrigan replies, taking her hand off my shoulder. "Maybe I'll restore my title with a bit of grub. To a booth!"

Our destination in the restaurant was a circular cushiony booth chair wrapped around a table, bits of colored glass and wood lining the seats fitted into the wall. As we slid in, I found myself in the center of the group—Morrigan on my right, Sam on my left. Bud picks up a chair from one of the open tables and sits down at the corner. Are they too big to slide in? Wouldn't they like a comfier seat?

"So lad, you watch movies?" Morrigan asks. "The Monty Python thing got me curious."

I shake my head, "Nah, I mainly watch online vids. Every time I try to look up a film that sounds interesting, there's a bunch of people that seem irrationally angry about them. Why watch stuff people hate? The movies my Dad watched were pretty cool though."

"Oh? Like what?" She asks.

"He likes watching old stuff. The one that I liked the most was the one where the kid was doing karate?"

Morrigan giggle-snorts, "Yeah, that's *Karate Kid*. Prime eighties cheese that is even though it's a bit aged. You seen any other eighties films, like *Highlander*?"

"Uh, no?"

"What about *Dark Crystal*? *Bill and Ted*? *Neverending Story*?"

No idea what any of those are.

"…not even *The Best Boys*?"

"*The Best Boys*?" I ask.

Morrigan's eyes light up. "Oh, lad—it's feckin gas. They made it right after us folk first started poppin' up! An alt-history tale about a ragtag group of soldiers in World War Two huntin' down Hitler. The best part is the entire squad is all dog folk. The bunker scene is unreal! Gotta get you over to our place and—"

"Oh goddess no…" Sam sighs. "We're starting it up again, aren't we?"

"You're damn right Sam!" Morrigan responds.

"Starting what up?" I ask.

"Movie night!" Morrigan replies. "You are the excuse I've been needin'—A fresh face to experience em' all over again."

"Only if the entire group can pick films this time." Sam responds. "If you make us watch weird tapes again…"

"That was an accident, Sis! Those tapes had no feckin label!"

"What?" I ask.

"Don't worry, it's sorted." Morrigan replies with a stern look at Sam, before switching to a bit more cheerful vibe. "Okay look, here's the new movie night idea—we pick movies we wanna watch, then we vote on the choice. Tie-breakers decided by rock paper scissors. We grand?"

Bud nods yes, while Sam sighs, "Deal, but no unlabeled media, and E has to agree to it. You want to introduce them to films after all."

The group turns to me. Oh god.

Sam and Bud stares with a curiousity, while Morrigan stares at me with some sort of excitement. They're all waiting on my decision.

"Uh, sure? But—"

"Feck yeah! I—wait, but what?" Morrigan cuts herself off.

"I'm not sure if I can use my Mom's car to go anywhere. She doesn't let me borrow it whenever, only for work."

"I can drive ya over. Ain't no bother." Morrigan shrugs off my concern.

"Wait, are you sure? I don't wanna inconvenience you. Also my parents are—"

"E, lad, let me resurrect movie night. Please." Oh god, she's super serious about it. I guess a few movies could be nice.

"Uhm, Okay." I reply.

Morrigan ramps back up to full energy, "Feck yeah! Movie night is back! Sam, send the calendar invites! I gotta plan the themes and—"

"E should pick the first movie." Sam says, cutting off Morrigan.

"But I don't know any movies..." I reply.

"Nah, she's got a point!" Morrigan says. "Get to our house, got shelves of media as tall as Bud! Ya find one that interests ya, and we'll have opening night!"

I look Bud up and down again, towering over us despite sitting down. That sounds like a ton of movies, a ton of fun.

"Yeah, sure." I reply.

"Hello and welcome to the Cabinet Castle!" A voice chirps as a figure approaches the table. She's another humanoid— brown fluffy fur around her neck, big black bulbs for eyes right below her fuzzy antennas, and big brown wings flickering occasionally screams "moth." Other than that, she's your average cheery waitress wearing a brown diner dress.

"Have you big hungry demons decided on what to get?" She stands next to Bud as she flips open a notepad, looking around the table before spotting me. "Oh! and your new human friend too!" That's a weird feeling I got from that. Not a fan of whatever that is.

"Demons is fine Maisie." Morrigan says. Now that weird feeling is gone, replaced with something positive. What is that? The waitress tilts her head in confusion, looking back and forth at me and the rest of the demons before her eyes light up

"Ooooh! Okey dokey Morrigan!" Maisie responds. Even notice Morrigan staring at me for a second as she rummages through her jacket.

The menu is small, so we all agreed on a "Camelot Burger"— a BLT with crispy onions, along with fries and "Honor Sauce", whatever that is. When drinks orders came through, Morrigan ordered whatever "Black Stuff" is, Me and Bud got soda, and Sam asked for sweet tea.

Maisie writes it all down as Morrigan pulls out a cig, snapping her fingers as she gets ready to light it.

"Uh, Morrigan?" Maisie locks onto her. "You can't smoke in here. There's…a rule for…" She begins trailing off.

Morrigan stops right at the edge before it's lit, but notices something as she smirks. She slides the cigarette back into the pack, but moves her lit hand back and forth. I look to Maisie and, uh, she's following the fire?

Sam sighs, "Sister, please stop distracting the waitress." Morrigan went from amusement to annoyance as she puts out the light.

Maisie snaps out of her hypnotic daze, a few seconds of processing before trying to hide herself behind her notepad in embarrassment.

"Please excuse her, she's always been a curious one." Sam says, Morrigan sighing as she takes the hit.

"Ah, okay! I'm still getting used to my moth quirks and—" Then, realization hits Maisie's many eyes. "Wait, haven't I seen you on TV?" she asks.

A smile forms on Sam's face. "I've been on the news a few times, yes." The moth tilts her head, before her wings expand in realization. "Oh! Oh my god! You're Samantha! The Circe Samantha! Huge fan! The grants your network offered helped me and my friends become our buggy selves! Can I get a picture of us together? I'll only share it with them!" Her second set of arms dig through her pockets as Sam slides out of the booth.

"It would be a pleasure, Maisie." Sam replies, walking around Bud.

Maisie pulls out her phone as they take a few shots on the selfie-style cam, cracked screen showing them both happy,

Maisie's antennas curling in joy as she seems extremely giddy.

All the humanoids here look so happy.

A few snaps later, Sam slides right back in.

"I'll make sure your burgers come right away, thank you so much!" Maisie says, rushing off to the kitchen with happiness.

"So E, do ya want your own pair of horns?" Morrigan asks, a stare that puts me in her crosshairs. About jumped out of my seat from that question.

"Morrigan! Sister! You can't be that direct!" Sam says. "You should let them figure it out on their own!"

"Sam, you've been feelin' the same stuff I've been feelin." Morrigan Replies. "E's clearly enjoying all the folk stuff here. Gotta give a lil' push sometimes, get em' past the finish line."

I gulped, "What do you mean? I haven't said anything?"

Morrigan sighs, "You don't need to say anything E—It's been hanging over ya since ya got here. Feck, it's been there since Taco Hell. It's clear ya wanna be one of us demons, so why not ask for help?"

Did I really want to be that? I look around at the demons— Morrigan looking determined, Sam looking concerned, Bud smiling—I look down at myself in the reflection of the table.

Ugly, unkempt hair; bangs lifting revealing my hazel eyes for the first time in months. Yeah, I'm a scrawny little thing, but did I want to shed my humanity over it? Staring at that reflection is twisting something in me. I hate that thing staring back. Need to look away.

"I mean it sounds nice, but I'm kinda worried about how my family would feel about it." I reply.

Morrigan shrugs, "Yeah, I get that. Lot of folk got family issues."

"That's because Humankind has a hard time with change." Sam chimes in, sliding her glasses up to her face. "Folks—or Humanoids as the legal system calls us—are all about change. The issue is that Humans love putting up guard rails and regulations to make change harder. It just confuses me as to why they're so hesitant about such things."

"Cause they're human, sis." Morrigan responds. "Look at history, feck, look at the news today. Humans taught themselves to be afraid of anything that doesn't look or act like em'. Gender, ethnicity, religion, what's goin on in your body or brain, heck, even something as small as pink or blue color choices are a big deal to em. Ain't no wonder their brains have been short circuiting since the eighties."

"Has it really been that short of a time since they popped up?" I ask. "Humanoids—uh, Folk I mean—have always been around since I was growing up. Feels weird to even think there was a time before all that."

"The beginning was tough." Sam replies, a bit of stress fading into her monotone speech. "When me and Morrigan were kids, folks started becoming a thing. Didn't matter if you were team red or blue, they all voted for the legal humanoid classification and we became lawless entities for years. 'Laws are for humans' was the justification, allowing them to terrorize our communities with no legal recourse." Sam slams her back into the chair, clearly upset with the historical recap, "It was disgusting."

"But it's better now, right?" I ask, a bit of nervousness rising up. "Cause, like, if I decide on this demon stuff, y'all are making it sound like I gotta prep."

A plate containing a piece of buttered bread slides in front of me. Across the table, Bud gives me a thumbs up. "Uh... thanks?" I say, taking the piece off the plate. They're sure quiet about things, but they seem nice.

"Ah, right." Morrigan says, picking up on my curiosity. "Bud can't talk. Been like that since we met em'. Not even sure Bud's their actual name, but they love it."

Bud agrees with a gentle nod.

"Don't bother trying to learn sign language either. They don't, uh, how do I put this...participate in human languages."

"You mean like, speaking in general? Then how do they socialize?" I ask.

"They like posting emoji's, along with physical movements." Morrigan continues, Bud nodding with a smile. "It's one of those things where the more you hang out with them, the more you just 'get' it, y'know? Hard to elaborate in human terms without soundin' a bit mad."

Bud throws me a thumbs up before I take another stress-filled bite of bread.

"Anyways, you don't really need to fear all that much nowadays, E." Sam chimes in. "With national protests and organizations encouraging better laws—"

"And a little vigilante persuasion." Morrigan cuts in.

Sam sighs, "...Yes. Activism—and occasional vigilantism— forced the government to pass laws to restore basic rights. That doesn't mean we stopped there, now we're trying to plug any loopholes and counter any attempt to roll them back. It's a reason why I fly cross-country every few weeks to help clients and push legislation. Need to make sure folks not only survive, but thrive."

All this history talk is makin' me anxious. On one hand yeah, they seem to suffer a lot, and Sam seems to be cleaning up the mess. Makes it seem ridiculous to want to toss away my humanity and sign up for a pair of horns.

But then I look down at my body. Pale white, formless, baggy clothes covering it all up. Ever since the possibility was revealed to me that I could change this, make it better, I feel like there's a fire in me that I can't seem to stomp out.

Why do I have to stay stuck like this? Why do I want to stay stuck like this? None of the reasons left made sense when there's a way out of it. I don't feel anything in life when I'm like this. A cold, dull, grey rock.

The demons are even warming me up. When Morrigan corrected Maisie, that was a good feeling, right? That's me wanting to be a demon, right? It sounds so nonsensical, but it's lodged there in my head, potentially forever.

A light warmth grows on my left shoulder. It's Sam holding my shoulder with her hand. "E, are you alright? You became quiet."

Oh great, I was roaming around in my head again.

"Yeah! yeah...thinking about choices is all." I reply, breathing in deep, slightly calming me. "It seems like it's a lot from what you all said, but at the same time it feels so enticing."

Sam ponders for a second, before an idea pops up on her face. "Look, here's an idea—you know how I run the advocacy network, right?"

I nod quietly.

"One of the things we do is help people like you pay for their EITR appointments. Maisie over there is one example." She points over to her as she's taking the order for a few deer and bear folk, laughing at what one of them said. She's so happy and carefree.

"Let's say we plan an appointment for you right now in a month or two. At any point—even if you're in the clinic minutes before your appointment—you decide to abandon the idea, we'll cover the costs."

"Wait, how much does it cost?" I ask.

"Don't worry about that, E. That's what the grant is for." She replies. "The point is you should have the opportunity to decide what you want in life, risk-free with zero debt. That's what every person in the world should have, human or folk. That's why I founded CAN, so you, well, can."

Huh. "That...that sounds great, but I don't want to be a burden on your network and—"

"This is what the network is for." Sam replies. "We do what I'm giving you for thousands of people a year. Consider it a drop in the bucket."

No risk? There's gotta be a catch somewhere, right? People can't be this nice and actually mean it, right? The offer is too irresistible though.

"...Okay." I reply, to which Sam smiles, "Great. I already got your contact info in the group chat. I'll get things ready for you."

"Thanks, Sam."

"Us demons have to look out for each other, right?" She pulls out her phone, unfolding it to a big screen as she clacks away.

There's that positive feeling again. I take a bite of the buttered bread. God damn do I need this right now.

"Well, now that we got all the serious talk outta the way, I think me and E here can get another game of clashin' knights in before food arrives, right?" Morrigan says. "Besides, I want my crown back."

I almost choke on my bread from a giggle. Swallowing it down, I only have one response. "Let's do it."

As we get up from the booth, something seemed to peak Morrigan's interest down the row. There's a group of humans Maisie is tending to, but she looks uncomfortable.

"No thanks fellas! I need to get back to work." even her voice is shaky.

"C'mon, lady!" One of the guys spoke up "We're just trying to be nice, least you can do is give us your number to talk. Maybe we'll even show ya the light later tonight." The rest of the guys at the table chuckle.

"Think about it Mothy, Four hands, four guys, how bout it?" another says, which causes the table to erupt in laughter.

What pieces of shit.

Looking over to Morrigan, she vanished. Looking back to that table, Morrigan is already beelining towards the situation.

"Sister, please!" Sam says. Morrigan turns to the group, "No worries, Sam! Just a lil' chat about class is all!" She says as she continues her trek to the table.

"Hey cunts!" She loudly starts off, "Mind leavin' the lass alone? It's clear she want's nothin' to do with ya."

The group of guys looks over, one spits into his cup some weird brown stuff. "Fuck off, devil. Mind your own business." He says, Morrigan balling her hand up into a fist as she walks up closer.

She walks up to Maisie, pointing back to our table. "Hey Maisie, can ya please get us some refills? Our drink's are gettin kinda empty." Maisie looks as confused as me—only drank a few sips—but then her face lights up as she quietly nods, walking off.

As Morrigan watches Maisie distance herself, the guy speaks up, "What's your fucking problem, devil bitch?"

Did the room just get hotter?

"I'm tired of fuckboys like you thinkin' ya can just harass anyone ya want and get laid for it." Morrigan replies. "Learn some feckin' respect for those around ya."

One of the other four stands up from the table, "This is a free country, us human citizens can do whatever we want! What are you gonna do about it?"

She emits a long sigh, "Ya really wanna do this?"

"I'm gonna knock you out, bitch!" The guy shouts at her.

Morrigan snorts, "You will, yeah?"

The man throws a sucker punch directly at her chest. Morrigan doesn't budge an inch, but the guy screams in pain, holding his hand as the rest of the bar looks over.

"Was tryin to warn ya, gobshite. Sit the feck down." Her eyes flicker brighter as he shrieks in fear, shooting right into his seat, his right hand turning red as he tries to rub it.

Morrigan then looks across the room to the bar. "Hey, Boss man!"

The mouse guy from the bar looks up through his glasses while pouring a pint, face full of disappointment. "What now, Morrigan?"

"Gonna need to call a paramedic. This guy didn't know what he was messin' with." Morrigan responds, devious grin in tow.

"Fuck you!" Another one responds "We just wanted good ol' country hospitality with that moth girl and you came in and fucked it up!"

Morrigan sighs. "Guess they still don't get it."

The mouse looks at the group, and now that disappointment swaps out for anger.

"Okay, you humans need to leave." The mouse says.

The entire human group looks befuddled. "What for? We did nothin you stupid rat! She's the one that—"

The mouse takes one hand under the bar, before placing a double-barreled shotgun on top.

"I said get out." He says in a louder, more aggressive tone.

The human group looks aggrivated, before one of them sighs. "Fine." one guy starts off. "Fellas, let's get out of this trash heap."

They got out of their seats aggressively, staring at Morrigan with pure malice as they head towards the exit.

"Good call there Boss man, They were—"

"Stop calling me Boss man. My name's Boss. You don't even work here." The mouse responds as he puts the gun back under the bar.

"And stop fucking around with assholes in my bar. We got good customers here who don't deserve seein' that shit. Take it outside next time."

"Got it, Boss!" Morrigan says with a smile. Boss rolls his eyes as he grabs a whiskey glass and the good vibes start back up.

Morrigan turns back to me, walking back with a big smile on her face. "Sorry for that, E. Let's get to clashin' swords!"

By the end of the night, she took back her crown.

CHAPTER 4
HOME JUST HOME
E'S PARENTS HOUSE

After a few days of grocery store bombardment, my reward is a day off. Tonight's inaugural movie night and Morrigan is gonna swoop me up later in that rustbucket of hers. For now though, it's time to get out of bed.

Sliding some new clothes on for the day—simple shirt and jeans—one of my rituals to orient myself is glancing at tinkering projects lining the walls. Silly little things, doubt anyone would care about them. Who would buy a servo controlled action figure with wires all over? Don't think anyone would want a TV remote disguised as a school calculator either. Prank items at most.

I don't make these things for cash anyway; only to figure out if it's possible. There's been a few yes's, way more no's, and even a resonant-lithium battery fire, but that's the joy of it all —explore what's possible and push it to the limit.

I pick up my phone for my morning reality check and see a text from my dad.

———

DAD - 8:30AM

Love ya! Don't forget the camera!

———

Oh, right the camera! I gotta get on that.

That leads me to my workshop table. That's a generous description to be honest; more of a flip-up TV table with a heat-resistant soldering pad. Sits next to my small desk with a laptop, some photos, and tools I managed to acquire. Everything else in my room are supplies, clothes, or projects that are either complete or in endless work-in-progress. Don't need anything else right now, got too much in flux, not to mention I'm covered in it too.

On the table right now is the aforementioned camera. It's one of those fancy instant print ones where you shoot a photo and it spits it out on paper in seconds. This thing was built in the seventies—easy foldable design, silver and black with a hint of leather brown with a neck strap, takes some obscure film that costs like twenty bucks for eight shots nowadays—a janky analog camera.

That's kinda the fun of it though. You can take thousands of shots on a smartphone within seconds. On this thing you gotta make sure that shot is worth it.

Grew up with it as my Dad passed it down to me like some family heirloom. All it took was one tumble on a camping trip in my teens and it broke.

Refused to throw it out despite how much my mom wanted to. Wanted to repair it, but didn't know how to start. After years of buildin' up my skills for tinkering, and recently gettin' done helpin' Dad with an automated sprinkler system, he finally challenged me on it. Wanted to see what I do with it.

Challenged accepted, Pop.

There's a variety of issues with the cam—resistors on the PCB are aged and inefficient, The shutter is jammed, rollers need cleaning, viewfinder misaligned and cracked. Online is kinda spotty about how to go about it, but that's what this challenge is all about, right?

I tend to be silly with my tinkering, modifying the hell outta everything in a nearby radius. For classics like these though, I wanna keep it original. A restoration if you will. A modern mod or two tops. Sometimes you gotta ensure the thing shoots well without changing the entire idea of the thing, right? None of that digital conversion shit though. I want it to be fun, not sterile.

Before I lay a hand on this bad boy, a more important matter is at hand—breakfast. Can't resurrect tech if I'm dyin'.

Cracking open the door to my room, no one is in the house right now. Walkin' by the small couch and TV to the right, walled off kitchen on the left. No sign of life over here either.

Ah, peace and quiet, gonna make some pancakes and sausage.

Opening the cabinets, I pull out my auto-mixer. Those store brand mixers cost too damn much back when my Mom wanted one, so I made one with an eggbeater attached to A RC Car motor. Swapped out the hand crank for a few gears, connected the whole thing with a rubber belt. Sure, Mom's been afraid of it since the chocolate cake mishap, even got a fancier mixer to replace it once money started flowing, but I'm proud of my work. I'll use it any damn chance I get.

I pour pancake mix into the mixer, along with a few eggs and water, heck, even snuck in some chocolate chips and blueberries. I tune down the speed dial, ensuring it's at the slowest speed and flip it on. Turning the speed back up a lil' bit to ensure it's stirring well. It's safe if you know what you're doing. Should be good in a minute or two, at least the package says so.

"Hey E█████." I cringe at my name as Mom pops out of her room, work clothes on. Guess her jewelry store shift is today, so fancy looking suit and skirt with a pair of gold earrings and a golden cross necklace. We both embrace each other in a hug.

"I'm heading off to work and Dad's already working—" She went silent, which means she spotted the mixer. "Oh gosh, E████. You're still using that thing? You know we bought a better one a few years ago. You don't have to use that death contraption anymore."

"You know me, ma. I trust whatever I make over those corporate things. Cheap, effective—"

I hear a loud pop, and the mixer stops mixing. Shit.

Inspecting it, a wire got tangled in the mixer. Quick untangle, unscathed from pancake batter as I jam it into the hole it belongs to, and it thankfully starts up again. I'll replace and solder that wire back once I'm done. "—And it's easily repairable, see? Don't have to call tech support for hundred dollar service bills when ya got me around!"

Why does she look concerned?

"I'm glad you're good with tech things dear, but please be careful okay?" She replies. "Just know we have a mixer that's proven to work."

But I don't want to use someone else's mixer, I want to use mine. Ugh, whatever; no sense debating it.

"Okay Mom." I reply.

A smile appears on her face, then her eyes widen.

"Oh! You know church is tomorrow, right? Want to join me and your father again? They're going to have the broadcast from the angel event tomorrow and—"

"Nah I'm good. Thanks for the offer though." I reply. If God created us in their image, then I'm gonna create, y'know? Not really a fan of idling in one spot every week hearin' about headcanons. I'd rather read the manual instead.

"Then I'll be sure to pray for you, E███." Mom says with a sigh.

Thank God.

"Thanks, have a good day at work." I reply.

She nods, heading to the door before turning to me once more.

"I also got a HOA meeting tonight. It's gonna be tough work tonight as the board decides what colors the garbage cans need to be—I'm personally pushing for denim blue—feel free to order pizza or something!"

Ah right, she does that too. Not sure why she does that stuff, but I'm always up for free pizza. "Thanks, Ma. I'll be sure to get a stuffed crust supreme."

She laughs, "You're so funny, E███. Just a regular cheese pizza is fine, and be sure to save me a few slices if you do! See ya later, alligator!" She slides out the front door, and I'm alone again. Not a big fan of plain cheese to be honest, but back to breakfast.

With the sausage and pancakes cooked, I munch down in my room while my laptop is playing a video of some angel creator talkin' gaming news. Today's video was sponsored by that Metatron AI thing again. The one time I tried it was terrible. Tested it with basic info about resistors and it thought I was talking about capacitors. Who'd trust that shit?

While the guy blathers about token limits or whatever, my mind trails off to the barcade meetup. Been a few days, but any attempt to delve deeper into all that talk is hitting a mental wall. It's a huge decision to just change who I am, not to mention the risk of uprooting my whole life.

But at the same time, it felt so nice to be identified as one of them. It felt correct. It should be an instant yes, but what if I make the wrong choice? What if I regret it? The moment my Mom hears I go humanoid—or, uh, folk—she'll be angry unless I go the angel route. Problem is I'm not in the mood to make a down payment for those angelic looks.

Oh god I just realized—demons, angels. demonizing is the direct opposite, right? She'll fuckin' lose it. No clue how my Dad will react, but it probably won't be any better.

The demons I befriended are so nice though. Tons of stories claim that demons have a way to grab you if you aren't prepared, twist your mindset into something that they can control. There's a few religious books and tons of fiction everywhere that scream it loud and proud. Don't let them control your heart. Don't let them use you.

But these demons don't feel like villains. The most aggressive one of the bunch is a huge movie nerd. The smartest one runs an organization that helps people, which I guess includes me. Bud is, well, acting like a buddy—looking out for me when I got too stressed.

The only answers that made sense were from them, and something inside me starts burning again. The hell is that? Where do I go with this? What the fuck do I do with it?

Well, puttin' that in a box for now, gotta go back to the real world.

Oh, my meal vanished off my plate. Guess that means the camera beckons for me.

Pickin' the PCB up off the table, this board is one of the older variants. Didn't know they made chips like this in the seventies. Had to deal with low res photos from old dusty internet blogs, but I got my list of resistors to grab and throw in. After flippin' the fume extractor on to solder a few things, I test the circuits and it seems to connect. Now for the rest of the camera—Let's roll.

Got to gently wiping down the rollers for film when my phone vibrates with a notification. Should be used to how much time passes when I have fun, but how the hell is it almost four?

———

FIREMAIDEN - 3:45PM

hey

almost near ya

ready for me to pick ya up

———

Oh, shit. I almost forgot the security cams exist outside. Dunno how my mom would feel about demons just existing on our lawn, so I gotta direct a detour.

———

TOYTINKERER - 3:46PM

hey, can you park down the road?

mom has cameras and she isn't the biggest fan of humanoids.

shit, sorry, i meant folk.

demons would probably terrify her.

FIREMAIDEN - 3:46PM

uh

sure

guess im already here then

TOYTINKERER - 3:47PM

ill walk over now.

———

Givin' the dish a quick wash, throwing on ye classic hoodie and messenger bag, I once again enter the outside world. One block down, that rusty wagon awaits.

"Hey E. Ready for the movies?" Morrigan asks through the window while I opening the car door, the whole thing shaking as I sit down.

"Yeah! Sounds fun." I reply with a little enthusiasm.

She smiles, "Grand. Let's get to it then." I try to roll up the window for her with the hand crank, but it doesn't budge.

"Ahh don't mind that. Think of it as free air conditioning." She speaks up, sliding on some silver aviators as she presses play on her phone, rock music blaring across the cabin.

She jams the clutch as she shifts the gear, the rusty hatchback squeezing me into my seat as we shoot out of the neighborhood.

The car gets comfier as we speed past the infinite forest. The seats are well built, nothing really ripping or tearing on them. Morrigan's seat is swapped out for a bucket seat; huge hole carved out the back to fit her thick tail.

The speakers seem modified too, big booming music coming from the phone in the cup holder, wired up to the…cassette drive? Is she using one of those adapters? She could afford good speakers but uses a cassette adapter?

"Ya eyein' up my shitbox?" Morrigan speaks up, turning down the volume.

"Oh uhm, yeah, sorry." I reply.

"Nah, it's alright." She says with a grin "Been a while since my beauty's driven with someone new. Meaning to fix it up, but every time I take it to a mechanic they say some stupid shite like 'It's a death trap' and 'it would cost more to fix it then buy a new car.' Real cowards talk if ya ask me. Sides, I got memories with this thing—Ain't gonna give it up for something newer."

Can't find a single sign of the manufacturer in here. Modern steering wheel combined with old wooden dashboards and beige plastic. Most definitely a eighties model of some kind. "Do you know who made your, uh, shitbox?"

She chuckles, "Bought it a long time ago, forgot the exact model name, but I know it's a Trinity hatchback of some kind. You younger lot can probably figure it out faster then I can."

"I might be good with hardware, but cars are an entirely different ball game; at least, I think so?"

She shrugs at that. "Anyways, what ya pickin' for movie night? got anything in mind?"

"My palette isn't really big. Would've brought one of the films on the shelf but it's mostly kids stuff." I say.

"Even the kids stuff can be fun." Morrigan responds. "Would hand ya an assist, but good ol' Sammy would find out if I suggested some obscure thing."

"So we're limited to superhero movies then?" I joke back.

"Nah. The moment ya pick *Darkman* or *Birdman* off the shelf, the gig is up."

No clue what that is, but we laugh as she turns up the tunes; shitbox shooting us down country roads to the rebirth of movie night.

CHAPTER 5
MOVIE NIGHT
THE FABULOUS FOLD'S HOME

Forgot how much the forest surrounds us in Comfort. When you're driving all the time you're always focused on the asphalt, worried about the cars around you. Never really have much time focusin' away, keepin' watch for the occasional deer.

In the side seat though, you have nothing to do but look around. I'm forced to stop and smell the flowers—or in this case, fast food long gone in Morrigan's shitbox. The forest looks calm today, and with the stress of socializing returning, I hope it stays calm. Need to stim on something to keep it that way.

Pulling my fidget out of my bag, I begin messing around with it. It's built from a dead music player from the early two thousands. Screen and motherboard were dead on arrival, so the entire top is retrofitted to house four keyboard switches of various kinds. Red, blue, yellow, even modified it to include one of those new magnetic switches. The joy of pressing each key individually— different actualization points and clicks—it helps me stay sane.

I also kept the dial from the music player, spinning and clicking on something tactile is hard to beat. Why doesn't today's tech have stuff like this? The combo sensory experience on this thing is what keeps me sane, especially when I'm deciding about that potential demonic transformation.

"Is that a calculator or something?" Morrigan asks as she's watches the road.

"Ah, no. Just a fidget I built." I reply. "It keeps me calm."

"Yeah, I see that." She replies. "So are you a tech wizard or somethin'?"

"More of a tinkerer, honestly. Though tech wizard has more of a fun ring to it. I like repairing old tech and modding things."

"So you're the one to talk to when the VCR breaks?"

Is there one that's broken? "Uhh, yeah I guess but there's a lot of variables like—"

"I'm just feckin' with ya lad." She says while holding in a giggle. "To be real, the ability to fix things up sounds pretty grand. Big fan of people like ya goin round restorin' the past, even if it's lil' gadgets I barely understand."

Huh, that's a way to look at it. I just like messing with old stuff, but now I got this silly smile on my face.

Now we're really in rural territory, the forest occasionally breaking apart, revealing trailer houses and small homes, random empty lots of grass and parking lots, then a huge fenced area full of garbage. Is that a junkyard?

The road becomes a single lane as she turns onto a dirt road, feeling every bump in her car as it shakes. The forest grows thicker, and right before it closes in on us, I start to see smoke in the distance. The trees begin to distance themselves as they release the road from their clutches. That's when a home pops up.

It's single floor, white paint shedding on the corners, a few windows letting what little sun exists in this forest inside. It has an elevated presence, a wood porch with a set of stairs; along with a ramp on the right side that seems pretty long.

The front yard has a bonfire pit roaring on, patch of grass surrounding it as the snow melts from its flames. Bud and

Sam are sitting next to each other, their own grass patches where they sit. Sam seems to be talking about something, showing Bud a notepad. Bud grins and nods before grabbing it and…writing something? I thought they don't write. Maybe they're drawing?

They notice our arrival as we roll up, Bud giving us a gentle wave as Morrigan parks next to the house. As we get out, Morrigan shouts over "I got our final piece of the puzzle, and now we can setup Movie Night! C'mon Bud, lets get to it!"

Bud gets up, handing the notepad to Sam as they hug Morrigan, then giving me one too. They feel like a nice heating blanket, great for a cold day like this. They look me up and down with a smile, before following Morrigan inside, getting ready for the big event as the snow at their feet becomes wet grass and dirt.

"Glad you can make it, E." Sam says, offering a handshake to which I return.

"Doin' the best I can, I guess." I keep messing with the fidget in my other hand. Sam glances at it for a second, before looking back up at me.

"You want to sit at the bonfire with me for a second? The other two will probably take a bit of time." She asks.

"Oh, uh, sure." I reply. How hard is it to set up movie night? Should be just flippin' on a TV, right?

Sitting down at the log Bud was sittin' at, it's still warm from their presence. Sam sits back down in her same spot.

"So are you doing okay with everything?" Sam asks, "You seem rather stressed."

God, are my feelings that obvious?

"I mean in today's world, who isn't stressed?" I try to deflect.

She lightly giggles "E, It's okay if you wanna talk about anything with us. This is a safe space to explore and figure things out."

Maybe I should test that.

"I am curious about one thing. Y'all say Bud doesn't read and write, right? Didn't they just write in your little notepad?"

Sam nods, flipping a few pages around on her pad as she slides her glasses up, a bunch of fancy looking shapes on each page. "Yes they did, E. As Morrigan said the other night Bud doesn't participate in 'human languages'. This notepad isn't for human languages." She stops at a certain page before turning it towards me. "Let me introduce you to Demconica."

The page has a pentagram, various shapes and characters on the sides with different languages. Looks fancy and exact, like they drew it with one of those compasses we had in school.

"Looks cool" I say, "Is this pentagram the logo for the language or—"

"No E." She replies with a gentle, yet corrective tone. "This is a sentence. Also, it's a pentacle."

"Oh, pentacle. Okay."

It looks like something I would see on a high school desk, but it's so much cleaner and nicer than other pentagrams—I mean —pentacles are.

She takes a pen and points to different parts. "There's a lot more nuance to it, but each point of the star indicates part of the sentence. See this one Bud wrote?"

Looking at each point, it seems like complete gibberish. There's words from languages I've never learned—one looks like a spanish word, another seems russian-looking. What's stranger is that there are shapes involved, why is there a symbol for a heart here? Is that the logo for Taco Hell? What do corporate logos gotta do with their language?

"It's incomprehensible to me, sorry." I respond.

"That's okay!" She responds. "It's because the other half involves our demonic resonance. I don't wish to dive too deep, but due to non-demonic individuals and technology having a lack of resonance alignment, it's indecipherable to anyone but us. It's why you will only see this language in physical spaces. Never digitized."

That…makes sense?

"Ah okay, was curious since I saw Bud scribbling is all."

Sam slides the notepad into a pocket on her long brown skirt. "Of course! don't be afraid to ask questions. Answering them is one of my favorite things to do."

Seconds pass as quiet befalls the forest. the rustling of the trees flows through as the fire crackles with warmth. Seems Sam is in the moment too, closing her eyes, taking a deep breath, and exhaling. She looks peaceful.

"The sounds remind me of Georgia sometimes…" She speaks, looking up at the sky. "…The pines are different up here. Helps you get a better view of the stars."

Despite the winter sun setting an hour ago, I barely see anything up there. Maybe the little dipper at most. Must be a cloudy night.

The winds shift around us in the forest, and the bonfire decides I should partake in some smoke as it smacks me across the face. I'm uncontrollably coughing and—fucking hell, I remember why I stopped camping. This is the worst.

"Oh goddess! E, are you okay?" Sam gets on her feet in the cloud of smoke. "Quick, let's go inside where you can get some fresh air." She offers her hand, which I gladly grab as her quick pace rushes us inside.

Still clearing my eyes, I feel us turning a left before she sits me down on a soft couch.

"Thanks Sam." I say, rubbing my eyes as I look up and—

Jesus fucking christ. That's a lot of movies.

I know Morrigan said shelves as tall as Bud, but these are definitely taller. They even wrap around the room. The only thing disturbing that harmony is the big white screen on the wall with sound equipment and five types of disc and cart players. I don't know how the shelf is categorized, nothing seems alphabetized.

"Impressed with me collection?" Morrigan asks as she sets up the projector; Sam sitting me on the couch in the center of the room.

With the smoke subsiding, my coughing stops and I'm able to utter a response. "I've never seen so many movies before."

"Hell yeah!" Morrigan says with a bombastic pride. "Spent decades buildin' it up. Raided every rental store, garage sale, thrift store, supermarket, anywhere to amass this collection."

"Did you watch everything here?" I ask.

"Maybe I have~" Morrigan replies with a smug tone.

"No, she hasn't." Sam barges into the conversation. "She comes home with ten movies just for the sake of putting them on the shelves."

"You don't know that." Morrigan shoots back. Sam sighs.

"…Anyways, you get first pick E." Morrigan starts back up as she slams into the couch, gesturing to the walls of movies. "It's time to begin the glorious reboot of Movie Night!"

Coughing out the last bit of smoke, it's time to get up and look at the choices. Scrolling the shelves, there's thousands of choices, dozens of formats, tons of genres, she wants me to pick just one. God, that's a lot.

Pulling out one movie, this cover's not interesting, so I slide it back in. Another pick, what's a UMD? Whatever, place it back. There's a huge rack here with huge discs, looks like vinyl records. Why are they called LaserDisc? All discs use lasers.

Shuffling through films, Bud enters the room with hands full of snacks—popcorn, drinks, candy, the classics—acting like our personal concession stand. Sam gently picks a pack of chocolate and water, while Morrigan grabs a few buckets of popcorn and a can of some weird energy drink. "Moto Oil"? Never heard of it.

"Thank ya, Bud." She says to them, to which Bud returns a gleeful grin.

I've never been so picky, but none of these movies are grabbing me. Pick up high, and it's some romance comedy, not in the mood. Pick down low, and it's a random superhero film. Probably need to watch thirty others to understand it, so back in the archives it goes.

Every time I pick something up, I'm just not sure if it's right for me. Even worse, what if they make fun of that choice?

"Do ya want a recommendation?" Morrigan speaks up "Just say a genre, we can toss some your way."

"No, no. I'm fine." I reply. "It's just so much at once."

"Don't worry, E. Take your time." Sam says in a gentle tone.

"Don't want to waste this decision, but need to make sure the choice is right." I say, continuing the scan. Jumping to another shelf, Sam is staring weirdly at me, arching her eyebrow. Just gotta keep shuffling through a new set of discs and tapes.

Slide out, slide in. Another bunch of movies checked, nothing. Ugh. next shelf.

"Here's an idea E; a leap of faith." Morrigan chimes in again. "It's just a movie, pick one for the feck of it."

"But what if it's a bad choice and the movie sucks?" I say, sliding another movie into the shelf.

"Then we can swap to a different one. Ain't a big deal." Morrigan says before taking a sip of her drink.

"Is this about movies, E?" Sam speaks up again.

I freeze up, "Of course it is. Why would it be about anything else?"

"Yeah Sammy, what else would E care about right now?" Morrigan says with confusion, looking at me, then back to her, then realization hits her eyes. "Oooh, right."

"Right what?" I ask again.

"Cutting to the chase, E—I am talking about the demonization." Sam's monotone fades in a little bit of concern. "You haven't said a thing about it since the Barcade, either in person or in the group chat. How are you doing with that decision?"

Oh god, not this right now please. I got enough choices to make as is. "I am deciding. Lots of deciding." I manage to squeeze out of my mouth.

Sam's concern on her face starts to grow, and she slides over on the couch, patting an empty cushion. "E, please come sit."

I push the movie back into the shelf, and slowly walk over to the couch, softly sitting next to her.

"Any worries you wish to discuss?" Sam asks.

I look down at my boring human self, then up at the glass bowl of candies on the coffee table in front of us. Its reflection has three demons and one indecisive idiot.

Breathing in deep, I sigh before getting the energy to speak. "I worry about what happens next—whether I make the big choice or not."

Sam gives a nod, "Yes, it's indeed a big decision. That's why if you have any concerns or questions now is a good time to discuss."

I feel a heavy tap on my shoulder, and it's Bud. They're offering me a bowl of popcorn with candy in it, along with a soda. Yeah, I could stress eat right now.

Grabbing it from them, I throw a few pieces in my mouth as the peanut butter bits combine with the saltiness. It's nice.

"Thanks, Bud." I say with a mouthful, and they give me a smile before fading into the background.

I swallow, and with a bit of fuel in me, I can talk. "Feels like this is starting too fast, y'know? I've only just met y'all, and the niceness y'all keep giving is confusing me. I was taught that situations like this are too good to be true, but like, is it? I can't tell, and my brain is just a whirlwind whenever I think about it."

I shut my eyes, awaiting my anxiety to prove me right, that this is all just a bit and the veil will be lifted right now. I hate this; just laugh at me, tell me to leave, and to get over it like everyone else.

"I completely understand." Sam says. Staring at her with shock, she parries it with a grin. "You remind me a lot of myself before I demonized; A silly college student getting a MD/MBA. You wouldn't believe the amount of homework they gave me." She giggles at her little joke before continuing.

"Well, my girlfriend at the time was a demon, the one who got me into resonance injections. I picked up some knowledge in an elective class, and had doubts if demonizing was right for me. 'Was I doing it to impress her? Did I really want this, or was I irrational?' Never could understand my feelings well, but my nervousness was clear to me. She noticed it too, and after I explained my thoughts, she told me one thing that rid my confusion."

"What was it?" I ask. A hand hits my shoulder, and it turns out Morrigan is just as interested in this watching on beside me.

Sam blushes a little, "She said something simple, yet important. If I repeat it back though, you'll have to excuse my cursing…"

"If E can handle me, they can handle you saying feck." Morrigan responds.

"Thanks sister, but it wasn't that one." Sam says, before she closes her eyes and breathes in deep. Is she trying to get into an acting space? Then, after the exhale, she opened her eyes, and a sense of determination appears on her face.

"She calmed me down, looked me in the eyes, and said 'Bitch, I don't love you cause you're human or demon, I love you because of *you*." Sam said, changing her tone. Is Sam trying to emulate her voice?

She starts blushing again. "The, uh, use of 'bitch' was jokingly affectionate, of course. I probably didn't need to say that now that I think about it, sounds a bit misogynistic out of context, but I wanted to keep the message authentic…"

I chuckle a little, Morrigan laughing with me. Sam's turning out to be a silly nerd.

"So are you saying you enjoy my company whether I'm human or not?" I ask.

"E." Morrigan chimes in, "You were the decidin' vote in resurrecting movie night. You gave me the opportunity to make Sam watch all these cheesy films again. I don't give a feckin shite whether you're human or demon, you're good in my book."

Sam sighs at her response.

Bud then pokes Sam on the shoulder, showing the food in their hands. "Oh, of course Bud. They say they'll invite you to their famous summer picnics too, no matter what you choose."

"Wait, so you all like me for me?" I ask. "I barely showed y'all my interests or anything. We've only met in person twice."

"We got a good vibe off ya." Morrigan replies. "That's all that matters." Sam and Bud nod in agreement.

That's weird, but everyone in this room is weird. Sam's gentle nerdiness, Morrigan's chaotic and proud, and Bud is quiet yet kind.

The doubt begins the clear, and I start to smile. Seeing the faces around me light up, and now assured that my relationship isn't depending on my demonization, it's clear as crystal.

"I wanna be a demon." I say.

Oh god, that felt good.

"Feck yeah!" Morrigan replies. Bud's giant hand pats me on the head, and Sam is just smiling quietly with a nod.

I get up from the couch, "…and I don't care what I pick from the shelf anymore, it's time to watch something." I end up at one corner of movies, close my eyes, and jab my hand into the selection, grabbing one and pulling it out.

"Grand pick, E!" Morrigan cheers, Sam nods, and Bud gives a little quick clap. All I could do was smile.

CHAPTER 6

SIGNING THE CONTRACT

LAILAH PHARMACEUTICALS RESONANCE THERAPY CLINIC

It's appointment day, and I can't seem to open the car door.

Outside is your usual lookin' clinic. White walls, big windows, and a bigger logo for the company running the whole thing at the front door. Lailah Pharmaceuticals—even the name is intimidating. Why is it so intimidating?

Could be due to the property being surrounded by a big metal fence with a gate leading out to the main road? Wondered about why they would have such a thing, but then I remember Sam's talk about folk history. Is the proper term folklore? I don't know, I'm distracting myself from the goal.

God, this is really happening isn't it?

A warm hand lands on my shoulder. It's Morrigan in the drivers seat.

"You ready for this, lad?" She asks.

I sigh, "Yeah, but also I can't shake the stress. A major change is behind those doors, but am I ready for such a thing?"

"I get it." Morrigan responds. "The first time is always the hardest. Fear of the unknown and all that shite, y'know? Know that in those doors there are people who want to help ya become yourself."

She pats my shoulder a few times, "Don't mind the anxious-ness cloudin ya or fearin' what others might say about ya.

Feck, don't even listen to me. Instead, listen to your heart and follow it. It's that simple."

"Thanks." I say, looking to the clinic doors again.

While all that anxiousness pops up, the main feeling continues to flow within me—I want to do this. I have to. Otherwise my body will burn itself from the inside out. This anxiousness needs to get over it.

Slamming the car door, Morrigan gives me a big grin. My walk down the snowy parking lot begins.

Inside the clinic is as sterile as I'd thought it be—white linoleum floors, bright tube lighting, white walls with random art pieces from artists no one's ever heard of. Down the hallway is a door, and when I open up, it's an average waiting room.

Passing a few wooden chairs, There's an attendant sitting there to greet me. Signing my name in, handing the attendant a card Sam gave me with a bunch of numbers on it, I'm told to sit at the chairs and await my fate.

Got here on time, but it seems like the doctors aren't ready yet as it becomes five minutes past the appointment. My leg is vibrating like a jackhammer while my phone isn't doing anything to help. Looking around, it seems like one or two people are here who don't want to be bothered. There's a coffee table in the center, a few magazines strewn about random topics.

One is apparently *Off-Road Unlimited Monthly*. It's ATV month, with otter folk riding one. They're blazing through a river in a forest for the cover photo. Looks fun.

On the walls behind the potted plants, there's a few posters lining the walls. One has some folks—one cat and dog person

— hugging each other in glee. "Over one hundred and fifty ways to be yourself!" The text said. Is there really that many kinds? How many have I seen already? With the R&D department Sam mentioned, how many have we yet to see?

Another poster shows a pig person helping a human off the ground, giving anyone who looks at the poster a thumbs up. "Can't get help for humanoid situations? Yes you CAN! Contact the Circe Advocacy Network today for FREE financial and legal help!"

That's the place Sam runs. Must be super successful to have posters like that in here, right?

The last poster on the wall has a mermaid is sitting on the beach, bikini top and straw hat with sunglasses on. "Get Beach Bod Ready! Mermaid Resonance is BACK for a limited time!" Seasonal Resonance? What?

Across the posters and magazines though, the common thing I see across every folk person pops up—they're happy. After all this, will I be happy too? There goes the jackhammer again. Back to doomscrolling. Gotta figure out how to relax.

"E█████, Come in please." A voice says pulling me from my phone. It belongs to a dog person who works at the clinic. A dogtor?

Fuck, don't giggle at puns you made up in your head, idiot.

They're tilting their head giving me a weird look as I try to stop, leading me deeper into the clinic's back rooms.

First stop—physical exam. Had me lay down on a long chair table thing, checked my body for pretty much everything. I'm your average human body, or, uh, I guess demon body soon. Green light in that department.

Then they moved me to a smaller doctor's room. There's a bunch of reference posters all across the room, referencing average body temperatures depending on humanoid. Damn, a Demonic body's average temp is six thousand Celsius? My soldering iron can only go up to like what, four hundred? Guess that explains why my demon friends are always so warm. How do their clothes not burn off?

That's a weird thought. Never mind.

A few minutes of silence, the door opens and the doctor comes in. A spotted cat with a mountain of paperwork in one hand, tray in another. Don't think she's a cheetah, but I'm too nervous to ask.

"Hello E███! I'm Doctor Imani Mohlala, but call me Imani." She sits down in the chair at the desk as her tail gently flows behind her, spinning towards me with the pile. "This is all the paperwork for informal consent, acknowledging you're going to revoke your human identity and adopt a humanoid one." She says as she places it on the desk, handing me a pen. "Since you're going for demonic resonance—which includes major augmented mental and physical faculties—It also will add you to a national public database for specialized humanoid citizens."

God, that's a lot of paper. Wait, I'm gonna be on a database?

"O-okay." Is the only word I can only push out of my throat.

She sighs, "I don't like stressing out my patients any more than I have to, but unfortunately it's the legal process us folks adhere to. Sorry for the inconvenience, E███. Let me know if you have any questions or when you're ready to move on."

I look up at her as I take the pen, "...Thanks, Imani."

She smiles, tail twirling as I stare at the mountain of paperwork before me.

Well, here goes nothin'.

Informed consent there, energy info sheet there, page after page asking for acknowledgment. There's some strange ones too, such as a "Energy Transfer Agreement." Apparently at some point I build a concentration of excess energy, which then can be donated back to Lailah for "Resupply, Research, and Reimbursement."

Whatever that means.

Then I reach the paper voiding my humanity. There's so much legalese on this paper my mind can barely enter a paragraph without taking a break. For something that seems so complex, it's batshit it can be executed with a single pen stroke.

God, this is scary. Is this genuinely something that would be beneficial? Is this the best choice I could make? Should I sacrifice my humanity to become something more?

Then I caught myself—Of course I was making the right choice. I had all this time building up to the appointment to say no and back out, but I didn't. The checkups, the doctors, the papers, it's all theater to stress me out, to back out and leave. Is my "humanity" the part that's anxious about this?

If so, it needs to shut the fuck up. It had its chance.

A scribble with a pen, and legally I'm one of the folks.

"Thanks for filling that out. Now you're one of us!" Imani says with glee. "Now for the final part—injection training." They pull out needles and syringes, moving a vial of water, and a pair of oranges off a tray to place between us. "Here's how this works..."

She shows me how to pull the fluid into a syringe, along with the best way to break the skin to inject. I follow along on an orange, but my hands were shaky as I try to twist the needles on, then the needle danced on the peel as I tried to push it in.

"It's okay, E███. Everyone's nervous their first go around. Even me!" Imani says with optimism. With her support soothing my nerves, I try it again, hands stable, and my reward was a prescription.

"In case you forget, the instructions will be placed in the bag. Go to the front desk, they'll take care of you." She says. "Once done, go to the opposite side where you'll find the resonance pharmacy. This is the only place to get specialized resonant energy in Comfort, so be sure to come back for refills. Enjoy being a demon, E███!"

Whatever it takes to stop hearing that name.

We leave together, Imani breaking off to another room with her cheery introduction while I approach the front. Gotta say the check in n' out is the smoothest part of this process. Apparently Sam hooked me up on whatever this CAN stuff is, only needed to pay a few bucks. I sigh in relief that it's not a quadrillion bucks like every other piece of American healthcare.

Walking to the other side of the building, this side is a bit louder than the other, a variety of folks waiting in seats for their number to be called. A few fit the country themes around here, like cows, horses, prairie dogs, so on. There's also there's some fantastical ones here too, like this one person who looks like a tree, apples slowly growing on branches from their head. I had a friend like them in Elementary school before my mom found out. I think they call em' dryads? Dunno.

There's a touch pad to sign up, and with a code for the reception desk, I was given my own set of digits to wait with. Sitting down in a quiet corner away from everyone else, I'm already on edge and I don't wanna take it out on anyone else. Pulling out my phone, and the stress starts to leave me little by little as I scroll through today's social feed.

It's a boring day on thine digital scroll—average news, average shitposts, average puppy videos. I like average puppy videos. The little fella is slowly ripping apart some old shirt, which in turn rips apart my stress.

Before I knew it, my number is called and I get to the pick-up window. It's a whole rainbow of vials back there behind the plexiglass. So many shades and colors lining the white shelves, almost like one of those fancy paintings with the dots.

A room full of choices, but only one that's right for me.

"Here's your next steps to your new life!" The pharmacist says with a smile, pushing a white plastic bag to me. "We also have a few refills setup for the next few months. Stay safe, follow the instructions, and best of luck!"

The price went into the hundreds, but then "CAN" pops up next to the medication and it drops to a few dollars. Guess they CAN help me out.

Okay, last pun of the day. Gotta get outta here before I die from anxiety-induced puns.

I speed walk through the hallways, pushing the door to the outside world before slamming right into it.

Oh, right—it's a pull door.

I take a deep breath, and open it properly this time. Morrigan's leaning on her car, chugging another one of those cans from movie night while wearing her silver aviators. When she spots me, she puts the can down and opens her arms up for a hug. I rush into them, gladly accepting it as I begin to break down.

All of this was so intense, but Morrigan's warm hug being was a melting it all away. No idea how many seconds we were like this, but I wouldn't mind it lasting a few more minutes.

After awhile, she pats me on the back, and says one thing:

"Welcome to demon hood, E."

CHAPTER 7
THE JAB
COMFORT SUBURBIA

On the way home I couldn't stop crying.

Keys to a brand new me in a little white plastic bag, and all I could do is cry. A life of foggy confusion and nothingness, but after talking to my new friends over the past few weeks I finally got proper directions to where to go in life. Ain't no wonder why I'm nothin' but tears.

Almost took the injection right then and there in the car, but Morrigan grabs a hold of my hand.

"Don't stab yourself in my shitbox." She says with a stern tone. "Last thing we want is a single bump turnin' ya into a bloody mess."

Oh, right. The roads are nothin but bumpy cracks across Comfort. Last thing I need after a clinic visit is a trip to ER. I close up the bag.

She smiles as she turns down the car radio, "Y'know, It's gonna be fun watching this all happen again."

Again? Looking at her with curiosity, she got the hint.

"I remember being in your place, so excited to take on the world as me new self. While it'll take ya a few months to see any demon bits pokin' out, it's all worth it."

"A few months?" I respond. "Seems a bit long for whatever magical energy stuff is in these bottles, right?"

She shrugs as the car turns into the neighborhood. "Yeah, it's for good reason. You could take it all at once—know of a few DIY-ers who were followin' whispered tales of the Folk Mothers. The main problem is that no matter the variant, that much energy through the human body could level a city block mid-transformation. Injected energy is still energy, y'know? Excess gotta go somewhere."

"You mean I could explode taking this!?" I hug the bag in an attempt to keep the vial stable.

Morrigan blankly stares at me before breaking into laughter, "Lad, that's the point of those little bottles! Ya ain't gonna blow up Comfort with that small thing!"

"Oh…" I reply, loosening my grip on the bag.

It's interesting that it's an option, but not really a fan of blowing up. Doubt forest rangers would be excited about leveling the wildlife round here.

"Despite how deadly that kinda transformation is, you don't wanna be deadly to others, y'know?" She reasons. "Besides it's all at once, or a gentle flow. Take that whole tiny bottle in one go, it's gonna do nothing and be outta your system before ya can get the next. Best to keep it stable for now."

She rolls up a block away from my parents house once again and puts it in park. As I get out and close the door, she waves me back, "One more thing…" She says

Leaning down to the car door, She seems to be thinking, concern fading in.

"At some point your horns are gonna pop in, and you're not gonna be able to hide it anymore." She starts off. "If your parents aren't the biggest fans, drop a SOS in the group chat. If that doesn't work, call me. I'll make sure you'll have a safe place to call your own."

Woah, what?

"But Morrigan, we've only known each-other for a month and—"

"So feckin what?" She cuts me off. "Us demon folk need to keep an eye on each other in this shite world. Besides, we got a guest room collectin' nothing but dust. Say the word and it's yours. If it's really a big deal, keep it till ya find stability."

It's such a big offer out of nowhere, but don't wanna intrude. "I don't think my parents would be that bad, but—"

"E." She cuts me off again. "You've had me park a block away every time, just so your folks don't go off on ya for bein' *near* demon folk. You're probably gonna need the room."

I sigh, "Yeah…thanks, Morrigan."

She politely waves me off "Ahh, don't mind it…" before pointing to the bag in my hand "Now, take your meds ya silly hellion."

Oh, right!

Moving away from the shitbox, Morrigan slides on her sunglasses, turning the volume up deafeningly loud as she shoots down the street, leaving skid marks in her wake.

Morrigan sure is something. What that something is, who knows.

Walkin' the sidewalk, I'm hearin' Mom's voice in my head grading everyone's lawns to HOA standards.

"Garage doors must be closed during the day!"

"We don't allow garden gnomes outside of gardens!"

"The only flags we fly are all-American!"

Okay, that last one I made up. Taking a quick glance around though, there's nothing but stars and stripes fluttering in the breeze. I might be right about that.

My parents beat me home today, both their cars are in the driveway. Can't stop walking now cause the cameras will notice, Mom will ask me about it. Gotta make up a thing for this bag of demonic magic I'm carrying.

There isn't a gas station for miles, can't say I went to get some snacks. Maybe a friend took me to a game store?

Shit, I don't have any human friends either.

Ok, new plan: She won't check the cameras if I'm not suspicious. I'll put the bag behind me, and slip through before they ask anything. Easy. Smooth.

Cracking open the front door, and the first thing I hear is the TV blaring down the hallway. Yep, Dad's in the living room watching news again.

Gonna be honest, "news" is a strong word for that channel. They're discussing the same topic that's all the rage these days: Should folks have rights? If so—how many? Judging that the hosts are fresh from the crypt and unable to express a positive emotion, the answer is easy to guess. Sounds like they are talking about another national bill, some sort of humanitarian act thing. Whatever, I tune it out.

"E███? Is that you?" Mom calls out.

Welp, there goes my stealth run.

"Yeah Mom, I'm home." I reply, hiding the bag behind my leg.

Right on time too, as she rushes around the corner, giving me a big hug; a faint warmth.

"Have you heard the news?" As we let go I kinda silently shrug in response. Is she talking about the humanitarian thing?

Her eyes light up at my indifference, "There's going to be a group of angels at church this Sunday!"

Oh, regular news.

"You should come this time! Maybe they can help ya get out of your shell! Maybe talk to them about the angelic ascension plan?" Nah, I picked my flavor of folk already. Gotta think of a good way out of this.

"Thanks Mom, but I'm working that day at the grocer." Her smile slowly lowers, but doesn't vanish. "Oh! Well, uh, maybe we can get you one of those holy blessings for you when you get home! I know you've been feeling better lately, but it won't hurt to have some of Jesus' love. Would help you get to one hundred!"

There's the attempt at slang, eh.

"What's with the bag?" she asks looking down at it. Shit. She's gonna be invasive about it.

"They're uh, trying out plastic bags at the grocer again. Bigger bags will be paper, but small purchases will be plastic. Employee test runs, y'know?"

I'm a terrible liar.

"Are the snowflakes crying about it?" Dad asks while turning down the TV. There's that weird political side again. He ain't usually like that, but I guess the TV channels his inner right-winger to pop out. Should feed into it, see if it gets them off my trail.

"Yeah. Real angry." I reply with a monotone voice. They both laugh at that, Mom giggling while Dad chuckles.

"Ahh don't worry kiddo!" He says while calming his laughter "Just giving ya a hard time for the fuck of it. How's the camera going?"

Oh right, camera!

"Pretty good, pop! I was planning to work on it right as I got home. Viewfinder ain't gonna adjust itself, yknow? Gonna head to my room now, gotta start workin' on it while I'm in the mindset."

He smiles at me, "Ahh yeah, I understand. Good luck fixin' that old thing! I want photos of Superman by next week!"

I giggle, twisting the knob to my room "Dad, it's Spider-Man."

Stars sparkle in his eyes, "Correct! You passed the test for now." There's my dorky dad.

"Dinner will be ready in a few hours!" Mom says as I slide into my room "Thanks, Love y'all!" and the door shuts.

Finally, some peace and quiet.

Time to let the demon out.

With a clean surface, the meds hit the soldering pad and I open it up—A box with a vial, some injection equipment, along with the instructions and a symptoms sheet—Lots of words, but glad I got the service manual. Can always ask Sam in case things get a bit too confusing.

pulling out the injection instructions, I read them once more. Seems simple enough—Sterilize, check for air bubbles, stab my leg at the right angle, push the meds in, and throw a bandage on it.

It's so easy. So very very simple. Done in a few minutes.

…So why haven't I started on it yet?

I'm staring at the vial for what seems like an hour as the fear and anxiousness keeps crawling inside me. I keep re-reading the prescription in the meantime.

Demonidial, 20 MG/ML.

Inject 0.5ML once a week.

Yup, same text since I got it. Reality isn't warping and this is really happening.

The goal is literally in my grasp, but my body is not co-operating. I keep watching the swirls of liquid and energy at play. Clear red liquid, orange sparks. It's calming, a weird lava lamp of pure power.

My phone buzzes me out of my slight zen, and I pull it out.

It's the fold.

———

FIREMAIDEN - 3:50PM

hey @ToyTinkerer r u demon folk yet

TOYTINKERER - 3:51PM

no, not yet.

FIREMAIDEN - 3:51PM

y not

TOYTINKERER - 3:52PM

i'm really anxious.

its a whole new start and i'm overthinking it.

SAGESAMMY - 3:53PM

Do you want us to come over?

It's always good to have friends nearby if you do something nerve-racking.

BUDDY - 3:53PM

TOYTINKERER - 3:53PM

no, i think i can handle it.

need to hype myself up.

thanks for asking though.

FIREMAIDEN - 3:53PM

just stab yourself with a needle, ez

SAGESAMMY - 3:54PM

That isn't helping.

FIREMAIDEN - 3:54PM

sometimes it does tho

SAGESAMMY - 3:54PM

...

FIREMAIDEN - 3:55PM

look my first stabs at energy injections were pretty shite

hurt a lil n got blood all over

but after a few times I got the hang of it

there's was even less blood

I kno u can do it

SAGESAMMY - 3:55PM

Morrigan, you're not supposed to bleed more than a drop when you take injections.

FIREMAIDEN - 3:55PM

rly

damn

well uh

dont do what i did then

lol

BUDDY - 3:55PM

SAGESAMMY - 3:56PM

@ToyTinkerer, As long as you follow the injection instruction booklet given to you, it should be smooth sailing.

I promise it's easy, and it will get even easier as time goes on.

Also, please don't bleed all over yourself. That means you're doing it incorrectly.

TOYTINKERER - 3:56PM

uh, okay.

thanks guys.

i'm gonna try now.

————

With encouragement from the fold, it's time to commit.

As predicted, the process was easy. Air bubbles are annoying, but with a little fiddlin' my syringe is bubble-free. The paper says it's okay to have little bubbles, but I don't want to fuck anything up, y'know?

The hard part is stabbing yourself.

Not afraid of needles, but the idea of putting something through my skin has always been weird. Probably the self-defense mechanisms at work. Wasn't necessarily the best at all those shots I got growing up either, arm always hurting afterwards. As anxious then as I am now.

Wiping down the skin with an alcohol wipe, pulling back the skin on my leg with two fingers to keep it tight as the needle begins touchdown. As it gets near my skin, I close my eyes and anticipate the pain as I lightly push.

Is it going in?

Opening my eyes, I'm shocked—it's already pretty deep. I don't really feel it at all, but the needle is gone. Usually when you get a cut or bruise it hurts, but this is nothing. How do I not feel it?

I push down on the syringe plunger, and as the liquid vanishes I don't feel that either. Within a few seconds, it's already done. I pull it out quick, and all that is left is a tiniest droplet of blood. A quick mini bandage slapped on and problem solved.

I'm basically a demon now, right? It makes me feel a bit giddy inside. For the first time in a while, I feel a little bit of hope. It's time to let the fold know.

———

TOYTINKERER - 4:05PM

it finally happened.

i took my first injection!

FIREMAIDEN - 4:05PM

HELL FUKN YEA!!!!!!!!!!!!!!!!

BUDDY - 4:05PM

SAGESAMMY - 4:06PM

Congrats, @ToyTinkerer!

Currently on a business trip right now, but when I get back we can setup a little celebration dinner for you.

TOYTINKERER - 4:06PM

you don't have to, Sam.

you seem busy so i don't wanna make you plan something extra.

SAGESAMMY - 4:06PM

Do not worry, E. It's not a bother at all.

Besides, you made a major life change today. We should always celebrate such things.

I'll message you later about it.

TOYTINKERER - 4:06PM

well, okay.

thanks y'all for being so kind.

SAGESAMMY - 4:07PM

It's what us demons do best. 

FIREMAIDEN - 4:07PM

lets take e to where we met them, taco hell

they gotta get that deadly demon diet jump-started with a ton of spicy burritos

lol

SAGESAMMY - 4:07PM

...

No.

TOYTINKERER - 4:07PM

lmao

———

I can't believe how fast things are moving. Here I was, a little grocery store worker that didn't want to be near anyone. Now? My anxiety took a backseat thanks to a new group of friends. How did this happen so quickly? Has it seriously been a month?

I don't know, but this is nice.

PART TWO
GROWING PAINS

CHAPTER 8

WINNER WINNER, CHICKEN DINNER

BARTER BOBS GROCERY

The first month or two of demon injections felt like nothing. Stuff was, well, normal. Maybe I slept a bit warmer, but winter was becoming spring, so nothing out of the ordinary.

When I wasn't with the fold, cruise control flips on and I coast through life. When you're awaiting your life in the future, everything in the present becomes a dreamy blur.

Then it wakes you up with a sledgehammer.

One employee perk at Barter Bobs is a monthly allotment of pre-prepared meals. Free for us, which would allow you to offer recommendations for a customer when they ask. It's a win/win really.

I bring my own meals cause I ain't a fan of the selections— rather have safe food than a rotating list of seasonals. Today was one of those days where I forgot to pack something, so I'm forced to pick something out.

One sniff is all my body needs—Everything smelt *wonderful* in the deli aisle. Cold cuts, fried foods, anything made of meat was delectable.

Walking by the rotisserie chicken shelves, my body was screaming for it. Never felt so ravenous over grocery store chicken, but it's on the free menu list today so I grab one. Garlic herb is alright I guess.

Going to the back, I sat in my usual spot behind some boxes from today's shipment. Seems the fancy yellow capped sodas are back. Not sure what the difference is, they seem to be the same as the others.

I like hiding back here. Not really a fan of talking to people while eating, and don't want people watching me eat. Quiet is great too; rather spend the social energy for customers when they ask me for something.

Grabbed a fork and knife along with some napkins. The plan is to eat some of it now, more later tonight, and if there's extra in the morning, finish it then. Easy.

But then I crack open the top plastic, and the smell hits me once again. My god, have these always been so incredible? Oh, there's drool on my chin. There's no way these are so good.

Cutting into the breast meat, I get a nice forkful, and bite down. The chicken flavor explodes in my mouth—absolutely incredible, gotta have another bite.

Another one.

One more.

More.

I need **MORE.**

Cutting isn't fast enough—these plastic things are holding me back. I threw them in the bag as I started using my hands. Wedging my fingers into the breast, my fingertips light up with pain as I get my chunk of burning hot flesh and shove it down my gullet.

The chicken must be consumed at all costs.

My hands became too slow, so I dunk my head into the basket. A predator chewing down on its prey. Flesh and sinew flowing through my mouth. A river of meat. It felt natural. It felt correct.

Just because the meat is gone didn't mean I stopped. The bones were there too.

Crunch.

The haze takes me, and when I come to, there's bones on the floor. Bits of skin, meat, and fat stuck in my hair in front of my eyes. The plastic bag that once held rotisserie is now ripped apart, juices all over the floor.

What the fuck?

My greasy hands drop the bag on the floor while shooting out of my chair. There's no one around back here, no cameras spotting me, thank fucking god. Wouldn't have an explanation for what the hell occurred.

What the hell is wrong with me?

Throwing the remnants of rotisserie in the trash, I pull my phone out using its black screen to look at myself. Its reflection is dark enough to hide my face, but bright enough to spot any strangeness that remained. It's better than a mirror.

A white blob of a human being that stares back. My gender dysphoria stabs me, with the strange chicken feast putting me on the verge of a panic attack. I have to look away for a second; need to build up the energy for this.

Need at least a a quick five second inspection with the darkened phone screen, then right off to the bathroom to do a quick wipe down.

Sigh. Okay, Let's begin.

One—Freckled cheeks have a bit of grease on them smeared around. Need to wash that down with water.

Two—Unkempt hair around my face has pieces of bone and chicken across the front. Disgusting.

Three—Green eyes look shocked, another few bits of chicken surrounding them.

Four—The poultry debris reached my ears. A piece of bone stuck right inside its curves. How the fuck did that even happen?

And Five—Dysphoria begging for release.

Pulling away with my objectives marked, I slide my phone back in my pocket, and the dysphoria begins to vanish.

This demonizing needs to kick in faster, but if this is what it entails, I gotta be careful what to wish for.

Washing myself down in the bathroom the best I could, hands, arms, face, whatever had a trace of grease on it. Wasn't going to take any chances. Despite no prying eyes, I feel so embarrassed.

Once out of the bathroom, throwing the remaining pieces into the garbage, my phone comes out. I need answers.

———

TOYTINKERER - 12:45PM

uh

guys, something weird happened.

FIREMAIDEN - 12:45PM

did u get your first craving or something

TOYTINKERER - 12:46PM

i don't know.

i destroyed a grocery store chicken in a hunger frenzy.

felt weird and like i had no control.

i'm glad no one saw, but what the fuck?

FIREMAIDEN - 12:46PM

ya

thats a craving

was real unsettling when I first got em too

means ur doin it right

becoming a deadly demon

SAGESAMMY - 12:47PM

It's nothing to fear, E. Demonic individuals tend to enter a state of cravings early into their transformation. Demons usually have horns made of bone, bodies with increased muscle mass, and other non-human attributes.

Can't make something from nothing. Your body needs an excess diet of fats and proteins, along with other nutrients in a bigger capacity than the average human.

If you don't eat the required amount, your body will let you know with intense cravings.

FIREMAIDEN - 12:49PM

welcome to the most fuked up keto diet lmaoooooooooo

u can totally calm it down tho by adding more meat n stuff to ur diet

jerky n bone broth n shite on-hand when ur not eating meals

prob lot o milk too, calcium n shite for them horns ur gonna get

BUDDY - 12:49PM

TOYTINKERER - 12:49PM

so your saying this is normal?? I have to eat like this forever???

SAGESAMMY - 12:50PM

Not forever, only long enough for your body to complete the physical transition. Once your body is more aligned with your true self, then those cravings will reduce greatly.

FIREMAIDEN - 12:50PM

there's better stuff to eat when ur a demon anyway

don't fear the cravings, theyre good 4 u

enjoy not being human lol

TOYTINKERER - 12:51PM

look, I knew the timeline symptoms sheet mentioned cravings, but I didn't expect them to hit this hard.

SAGESAMMY - 12:52 PM

The first effects of demon-hood in your transition are going to be...unsettling at first. Everyone in this group chat has been through it themselves. I remember when my first craving meal hit. I made myself look foolish in a mall with a box of chicken teriyaki.

The best you can do for now is adjust your diet, and keep an eye out for any weirdness. You always got us if you have any questions.

FIREMAIDEN - 12:53PM

also humanity is boring af lol

ur gonna be a deadly demon E

i have a feelin bout it

BUDDY - 12:53PM

TOYTINKERER - 12:54PM

thanks guys. Im weirded out by all this but uh, I guess I gotta eat more burgers or something.

FIREMAIDEN - 12:54PM

good shite

———

This is now a normal part of my life? Eat more meaty foods so my body can demonize, or enter a frenzy? Strange, weird as hell, but it makes sense.

Wish it didn't feel so uncontrollable when it hits.

If my body needs fat and protein, guess I should get one of those protein powder things from the fitness aisle. Eat some more beef or something. Got an excuse now to get those burritos at Taco Hell now, maybe even a combo pack.

Time to let the changes flow.

CHAPTER 9
POWER DYNAMICS
BARTER BOB'S GROCERY

"Sir, please leave the customers alone."

There's this strange guy that started following a family of bunnies across the store. The bunnies tried to avoid him, but he kept getting closer and closer. Not sure what his deal is, only noticed it a few minutes ago. Kept an eye on them to prove my suspicions. With the stranger slowly escalating and the rabbit folk becoming more intimidated, had no choice but to step in.

Helping customers is apart of the Barter Bob code, after all.

The guy turns to me, lookin' like he could get his own cancellation comedy special. Red hat, brown leather jacket, denim pants and a pair of boots. Even sports a confederate flag pin. The loudest dog whistle of the pack though was a Vitruvian man tattoo.

It's that one Da Vinci piece with the guy in a circle. What was once a cool piece of art, humanists co-opted it and made it their trademark. They think it expresses pure humanity at its finest. All these cues let me know they were pure danger.

I need to stop it.

"Kid scram. This doesn't need to involve ya." He says. Probably wonders why a human is stopping the situation. Little did he know, I ain't human no longer.

"Sir, you've been following this family around for quite awhile. Either take your shopping elsewhere in the store or I'll call security."

He's annoyed at my response, but he needs to fucking deal with it. Take the one peace offering I'm giving him.

"Why should I leave them alone? Look at em! Y'all don't allow pets in the store, so why the hell do y'all allow these humanoids in here? Can't ya see their kind stinks up the place? Makes everything unsanitary for us humans!"

Clenching my fist, there's those emotions again. They've been getting easier to feel the past few weeks. So much easier to laugh, cry and—in the case of this dipshit—get mad.

"Sir, now you're being incredibly rude. Please leave the store, or I'll have you trespassed." He stares at me dumbfounded, before smirking. "And who's the security guard today? Is it Kevin? How about Lester? I know everyone, and they know how I'm such a great human citizen. Now I'll ask ya again kid —leave. Turn around like you ain't seen nothin'."

A few lucky guesses with the security detail. Doesn't mean he knows jack shit.

His attention diverts, waving at someone. "Hey, Derrick! Can I get some help over here?" he shouts.

Turning around, and it's my manager. What the hell, they know each other?

"Is there something going on here Greg? Anything I can help with?" Derrick asks.

"Yes you can!" He says, pointing to me. "This, uh, *person* right here was interrupting my duties with the neighborhood watch. Y'know how important that is around these parts, ensuring criminals aren't shopliftin'."

Greg shrugs his shoulder towards the rabbits, cuing Derrick to look over. Derrick nods, "Ahh, of course. I understand sir."

This is a group act, isn't it? Was I really surrounded by this? I understand my social compass is a bit off, but now it explains why I haven't seen a single humanoid on staff here. No fucking way I'm gonna report my status now.

Derrick lays a hand on my shoulder, cold to the touch. "Come on, E█████. Let the man do his duty for the good of humankind."

Fuck this, I rip his hand off my shoulder. "Derrick, He's clearly intimidating our customers! We need him out of the store so he stops bothering people!"

Greg snorts, "Kid, you need to understand one thing—those things over there aren't people. They're fucking animals. They might have had that grand gift of humanity at one point, or they might have been born like that. Doesn't fucking matter. Them or their ancestors took that beautiful gift of humanity and tossed it away like trash; tempted by the devils that were born out of that pit in Paradise. As soon as you and those other libs understand that, the sooner this society can be restored to its former glory."

My heart commands me to charge right at him, so I listen. Problem is Derrick grabs a hold of me, locking me in place.

"E█████! What's gotten into you?!" He asks.

I try to fight him off, but his grip wins out as he keeps me in place. Looking around for the rabbit family, they seemed to scatter.

Good, at least they got away.

Looking over to Greg, his grin only got wider. I want to wipe that shit off his stupid fucking face. In my state though, Derrick has control.

Derrick swings me away from Greg, pushing me off as he points to the back of the store. "E█████, Go to my office. Cool off, and we'll talk about this in a minute. I need to discuss something here with Greg." He lightly shoves me towards it, not enough to fall over, but enough to send me tumbling. He's staring directly at me, waiting for me to do what I was told till I'm too far away to hear their conversation. Fuck him.

I sat down in his office fuming, small ass white box that could only hold a desk and a chair. I knew there was something off with this place, footage of the anti-humanoid vandalism and shit going missing constantly when they trash the aisle, but I didn't realize it was this embedded into the grocer. Have I been supporting this shit the whole time by working here? Fuck. I hate this.

I have to yell about this to someone, so I pull up my phone, and scream into the group chat.

––––––––

TOYTINKERER - 5:10PM

i'm so done workin here guys

this place is crawling with bigots

FIREMAIDEN - 5:10PM

at barter bobs?

yeah

those people are real cunts

thought u knew

SAGESAMMY - 5:11PM

Did something happen?

TOYTINKERER - 5:11PM

there was this guy harassing a family of rabbits.

stalked them around the store.

> for some reason, felt like i had the energy for once to step in and tell him to fuck off.

> guy told me that management and security has got his back, and then my manager comes up to stop me from interfering.

> almost hit the fucker.

BUDDY - 5:11PM

FIREMAIDEN - 5:11PM

damn

shame ya didn't get to hit a bigot today

its fun

SAGESAMMY - 5:12PM

Morrigan, please don't promote violence.

FIREMAIDEN - 5:12PM

is it really violence when its towards a eejit punching down

SAGESAMMY - 5:12PM

This isn't the best situation for it.

If what E says is correct, then they are surrounded by bigots with power.

It could make such solutions un-viable, especially if E has no back-up plan.

FIREMAIDEN - 5:12PM

whatever

SAGESAMMY - 5:13PM

Anyways...

@ToyTinkerer, if what you are saying is true, highly recommend one thing.

Record everything.

If they see you as a problem, they will try to show you are an incompetent worker, regardless of your actual performance.

Journal your days, email or text your manager everything you did that day, everything you can do to catalog and leave a paper trail.

Since we are in a one-party consent state, record every conversation between you and your manager.

This is important as your demon identity becomes more prominent.

If they find out, they could easily fire you with a made up reason.

After what you told us, this is entirely possible.

Even though this is a at-will state, doesn't mean you can't sue if they fire you for a discriminatory reason.

You just need to build the paper trail to prove it.

TOYTINKERER - 5:14PM

What if I don't want to work here anymore? The manager keeps using me to clean and fix up everything here without paying properly. It's annoying.

————

"Get off your phone, E██. We gotta talk." Derrick slides right past my seat as he operates around the small room, sitting down right at his budget throne of an office chair. With Sam's advice, I switched my phone to record audio, the screen facing my lap.

"So, E██. Your conduct today was pretty off-character. Is there something going on in your life lately? You tend to be pretty quiet about things, sticking to your tasks like a good human worker." Derrick looks concerned. He'll figure it out soon enough, but for now, I'll play along.

"I saw customers getting followed across the store. They didn't do anything wrong, but that guy kept tracking them down. I wanted to be sure that customers were safe. It's part of our code of conduct too."

He lightly shrugs as he waves me off "Yeah yeah, Barter Bob's code—you love that rulebook. Look E██, even though you live in Comfort and work here, I know you don't tend to get involved in local politics. That man over there was from a, uh, 'neighborhood watch' of sorts. His goal along with others in that org is to ensure we all stay safe. If he was tracking down those rabbits, they probably had done something suspicious."

"It's a family of four. They had their kids Derrick. Who commits crimes with their kids in tow?" My snappiness surprising even me once again.

He raises an eyebrow, "There's that off-character attitude again. Gonna need you to be quiet for a sec while I explain the situation." I feel something building up inside me. It's a foreign thing. Hot. Explosive. Is this anger, or is it something more?

"So, you were basically interfering in a neighborhood watch matter, and you managed to let the suspects get away. Since this is your first time doing this, and I know you tend to be the quiet little worker we need around here, I'm gonna let you off with a verbal warning. Don't interfere again."

"But, he isn't police or anything, right? Why should I give him special leeway when he's stalking customers in the store? Shouldn't we make all customers feel comfortable?"

Derrick looks unamused, taking a deep sigh. "E█, I like you. Sure, you got some weird problem with pronouns or sex or whatever. Not to mention your silly little mind has some… eccentricities. We both know that you tend to be one of my most productive members on my team. Your custodial duties along with your repair skills are extremely valuable to our big family we're prepping for."

He fiddles with a pen on his desk, "Here's the thing though— These forces you're messing with? Way above both of our paygrades, even bigger than Barter Bob's. Our mission is not only to ensure Comfort is ready for what's next, It's about the fate of humanity as a whole. You get that, E█?"

Dude. You're the manager of a grocery store. What the fuck are you talking about? How do I even respond to that?

"Judging by your usual silence E█, I'm going to take that as an agreement." Derrick responds. "Seems like you got some anger pent up still, so let's vent it shall we? I know you've been wanting to do some more around here then fixin' stuff up, so how about organizing? The back needs some more hands. I know you had problems lifting when you first started workin' here, but those sweeping skills helped gain some muscle by now, right?"

He wants to cut me off from the store so I can't interfere— piece of shit.

"Go take your 15 minute break E█. When you're done, report to the back. Jason will be glad to have help." Oh, now I have to interact with co-workers too? This truly is hell.

"Okay." I throw out with pure monotone.

"Okay what, E█?" He asked with a tone as I got up, a smug smirk across his face. There's that anger.

"Okay, Sir." I respond begrugingly.

"Good." He nods.

I fucking hate this place.

Ending the recording, I rush out the office door. Already hear him babbling to that fucking chatbot on his phone. At least I got him admitting what I need.

Getting to the front of the supermarket, setting a timer for my break while slamming my ass onto the bench. God, I hate this feeling of rage, but it's boiling in me, wanting to exhaust somewhere.

This resonance injection stuff is clearly the cause of that. Normally I would feel muted, roll over and take it. Now I want to burn the whole store down. Good idea until I realize the humanoid— I mean folk aisle would go with it. No way some rival grocer would open up here, that would hurt people in town more than Derrick. Gonna' let my rage stew and bubble instead.

I unsheathe a stick of jerky from my pocket and bite down, ripping it to shreds. Guess it's time to check what the fold's been posting since I was gone:

———

FIREMAIDEN - 5:14PM

I mean

ur becomin a big buff demon right now

opens up a huge amount of jobs you can get

if ya want, i can try to see if there's slots
open at the fire house i work at

they always willin to train demons like us

SAGESAMMY - 5:15PM

Note that despite demonic strengths, it's still a dangerous job.

FIREMAIDEN - 5:15PM

yeah

of course

but judgin by what e said here today, they seem like they got the firefighter spirit

savin the innocent and all that

e???

TOYTINKERER - 5:18PM

sorry, manager was talking to me.

got a convo recorded, @SageSammy. said i was a important and valuable employee basically.

SAGESAMMY - 5:19PM

That's great!

That will help a ton in case they fire you out of the blue.

TOYTINKERER - 5:19PM

they're also moving me to the back to move boxes.

manager claims i interfered with a supposed "neighborhood watch" and should stay back next time.

I think hes trying to put me there to cut me off from the customers.

claimed it was "for my good" basically.

FIREMAIDEN - 5:20PM

can i promote violence yet

SAGESAMMY - 5:20PM

No.

E, make sure you keep documenting your experiences.

The more evidence you build up, the better chance you have to legally expose what's going on.

FIREMAIDEN - 5:21PM

also e

what do ya think about the firefighter thing

TOYTINKERER - 5:21PM

i don't know.

never really been the kinda person to jump into raging fires.

not to mention its a big change from grocery store worker.

i guess today was the first time i did jump into a situation like that.

it felt nice to help them get away at least.

let me see where stuff goes first before i give you a answer.

FIREMAIDEN - 5:21PM

of course no rush

i got a good feelin bout it

———

"Hello?" A voice calls out from the real world.

I look up from my phone, and what greeted me was the rabbit family—two adults, two kids. While the adults sported white and brown fur, their kids were covered in spots of both shades. "Oh, hey! Y'all alright?" I asked.

The brown rabbit nods, "Yeah, we're good now. wanted to thank ya for helpin' us back there. That guy was bein' real intimidating."

"Yeah!" The white one chimes in after. "There's so many kinds of those people around these parts, and we want to live a simple life, you know?"

"Yeah, I feel that." I respond. "With the amount of anti-folk stuff goin on round here, not sure if I will be workin here for much longer."

"Ah…" the white one says, looking solemn at my response, before perking back up. "Oh, but where are our manners? I'm Inaba, my husband here is Peter. Our sweet little kids hiding are Jack and Luna." I look down at their kids, Jack is brown fur with white and grey spots, while Luna is white with grey and brown spots. Cute looking family.

"Pleased to meet y'all." I said, getting up to shake hands with the adults.

"Say, you're the human that keeps cleanin' up the aisle when those losers hit it, right?" Peter asks.

Oh, right. I look human.

"I am, yeah." I reply. "About that human thing though, I've recently been getting energy injections, so becoming apart of the folks."

The rabbits perk up, "Well, congrats to ya!" Peter responds. "It's a complicated process no matter what brand ya take, but it's always great to see more faces enter the community. Let me guess: Dog? Elephant? Maybe one of those fancy lookin' ones like a fairy or, shucks, even one of those nice angels?"

"Demon." I reply.

They look taken aback by that response. "Oh! That explains it!" Inaba says with a gleeful grin.

"Explains what?" I question.

Inaba looks slightly shocked at my response, with Peter coming to her defense "Oh nothing bad, promise! Us non-demon folk love y'all. You standin' up to that guy? That's what demons are famous for!"

The timer went off on my phone. My break is over—time to go back to my own personal hell.

"Well, sorry to cut this short, but I gotta go back inside." I speak up.

They gently nod, "Take care in there, friend!"

"Bye demon friend!" a voice says from below. It's Luna, hiding behind one of their parent's legs. We all share a laugh, going our separate ways. Now for my descent into the grocery dungeon.

Approaching the back storage room, and lo and behold, Jason is already there, placing boxes on shelves. He's another face in this store—average gym dudebro—but lately he's been looking a bit different. Adopting more of a gold and white color scheme lately. A bit of an interesting glow to him. Barely know anything about the guy other than his apparent social work thing, but honestly I don't talk to anyone here by choice.

"Sup, E⬛? Derrick said you're gonna help me?"

I'm done cringing at that name.

"Yeah. Hey, can you call me E for now? I'm trying to work-shop a new name."

The loading bar in his head took a few seconds, but eventually he responds, "Oh, sure E⬛! Uh, I mean, E. Oops." F for effort, but at least he's trying?

This next part should've been terrible. One of the reasons they never put me back here is due to being too weak to move heavy things, Derrick probably saw it as a fit punishment for today's performance.

Too bad, these boxes felt like nothing. Even Jason was surprised as I lift a fifty pound box by myself. "Dang. Been doin' workouts, girl?" Jason asks.

"Nah, probably some performance enhancing drugs." I respond.

He chuckles, "Yeah, guess you need those to pick up the mop."

The joke was so stupid it got me to laugh. It's getting a lil' chill back here.

Wonder if it will stay that way when the horns pop up.

CHAPTER 10
NIGHT TERRORS

Slamming into the wooden floor, it provides the boost of energy I need to vanquish this foe. I quickly stand, pulling my sword out for a counter attack, but my hand can't seem to find it.

Huh? Pajamas?

Wait, my hands are pasty white. The memories fading claim they should be wrapped in leather. Where's the battlefield lit aflame? The threat who was upon me with wings of white, piercing me with their golden lance?

I close my eyes, time for a reset.

Okay yes, this is my room for sure. My phone is blaring white noise on my night stand, and I'm not a strange knight. Just a tinkering nerd.

Ok, that's it. I definitely need to stop playing Night Knight Fight.

These dreams are getting too messed up from that game. Morrigan can keep her title as the queen of the cabinet for now, all I want is a better night's sleep.

The symptom sheet warned me about this, but all it said was "Restless nights, night sweats, and possible night terrors." didn't know what a night terror was, but with these dreams getting fucked up, guess I got my answer.

Demonic energy is harsh on the human body. Who knew?

As my night of terrors continue, waking up from a few more dreamy stabbings, the sun begins to shine into my room. Fast forwarding yet another boring work shift, tonight was dedicated to hanging out with the fold.

It's movie night. Tonight's theme was animation.

Bud jiggles a DVD box between their hands called *Interstella 5555*.

"I love that movie Bud." Morrigan responds. "But I think we can go more modern. Look, got a copy of *Wolfwalkers* right here. Couldn't even buy it in-country, had to import the damn thing. Excellent folklore, beautiful art style, perfection."

"I'm in more of a Sci-fi mood to be honest." Sam says, holding a copy of *Paprika*. "This was Satoshi Kon's final work, and it's timeless."

Morrigan chuckles. "It's cause you find the main girl hot, right?"

Sam cheeks grow darker, "...Yes? And?"

"If we talkin' sci-fi, *Wall-E* would be a great choice!" I say, breaking up the accusation.

Despite my small movie palette, I grew up with Disney and *Wall-E* has been my favorite out of the set. Not sure what a Criterion Collection is, but that version was on Morrigan's shelves.

"It's Sci-fi and has a cute little robot couple saving the earth. It's great."

"Okay, look. Here's the deal." Morrigan speaks up. "We're all dead-set on our film choices. Votin' is outta the picture, so we gotta break a tie. How's about rock paper sissors? Best of three."

We all look at each other and nod.

War has begun.

It starts with Bud's betrayal. Their rocks take me out quick, followed by Sam's sissors delivering the final blow.

Bud pats me on the back, giggling as they take on the sisters. They didn't last long either.

The two sisters go to war, Morrigan trying to get under Sam's skin, but Sam is too levelheaded as the battle escalates.

Rocks thrown, papers tossed, scissors cut. As the smoke settles, the champion stood proudly in her blue splendor.

Sam with paper. Tonight's showing was *Paprika*.

A bit into the film, the dream sequences kept being super trippy.

"Reminds me of my recent nightmares." I said offhandedly, expecting a laugh. Sam stares at me, grabbing the remote to pause the film.

"E, did your doctors talk to you about The Night of Passage?" She starts off.

"Uh, no? They gave me the symptom sheet and that's about it." I respond.

She looks off to the side. "Of course." She grumbles. "These doctors need proper training."

She gets up from the sofa. "Come with me E, we need to discuss something." The rest of the fold stares on as she leads me to a quieter space.

In a empty guest room, we sit next to each other on the bed. Sam slides her glasses up, turning the safety off for another blast of info. "So, E. Your dreams have been quite erratic lately, right?"

"Yeah, the other night I was apparently some knight? Thought it was due to the arcade game so I stopped playing that on my laptop. Didn't stop the dreams about being stabbed though."

"Uhm. Uh…" She mutters before going quiet. Guess I said too much. Oops.

She closes her eyes for a reset, then continues "…So, dreams tend to be influenced from real life, but there is an enhanced realism from the resonance attunement."

She looks around the guest room full of dust, before pointing to an old piece of tech on a shelf.

"Imagine your brain is that FM radio, and the resonance flowing through your body is the tuner." She starts off. "The resonance in you is currently shuffling through the frequencies, getting nothing but static and random channels from unknown spaces. This results in night terrors, like the one you mentioned earlier."

"Like the stabbing?" I ask.

Sam sighs. "…Yes. That."

She coughs to herself. "…Moving on. For the sake of analogy, every one of us, demon or other folk, have a unique wavelength of sorts. Once the resonance tunes in to the right frequency, that's when it begins the major transformation. That final attunement comes in many forms, but for demons, it comes in the form of a dream."

"Like a lucid dream?" I ask.

"Hmm…sort of. You will be 'lucid' in this dream; the main difference though is that it will *be* real. Pinch yourself all you want, it will hurt, and you won't wake up. No one's really sure of why this dream exists, or how much of it is a dream, but it's a gateway to the next stage of your attunement."

Huh.

"So if this dream is a gateway, I'm sent somewhere?" I ask, trying to figure it out.

Sam puts her hand up to her chin in thought, "In a sense, yes. Physically, your body will remain where it rests. A deep sleep that CAN research says is a borderline comatose state. Mentally, you will be a participant in the passage. There's reports of demons who have slept for hours, then wake up claiming the dream lasted for weeks. Current technology can't detect any major changes at all other than the comatose state, it's so strange yet so fascinating."

Sam goes quiet for a second, deep in thought, before a smile appears. "...Isn't it wild how we had forty years to decipher this newfound energy, seeing life-changing discoveries every day, yet it's like we are kids playing with toys? Every new discovery makes it feel like we're at ground zero. Recently we figured out that demonization of the brain leads to an enlarged insula and frontal cortex. Such a unique change, but it hints at why the dreams feel so real..."

Ah, the famous Sam tangent pops up, let's get her back on track. "So, when I find myself in the Night of Passage, what's the goal?"

She blinks a few times, like she needs to re-calibrate her train of thought, before starting back up. "Ah, right. The Night of Passage for every individual comes with a test. Your interests, fears, things you didn't realize about yourself, all wrapped up in a dream designed to push you to the limit. Your main concern now is needing to make sure you're emotionally and mentally stable for it."

"Uh, why? Is it bad or something?" She starts to look a little bit concerned, "Well, the passage is designed to push some buttons. If I tap into my more spiritual side, I would say it's a test of your soul."

Well that's calming.

"So, what happens if I fail? Do I die for real or something?"

She gently places her hand on my shoulder, "You won't die, E. If it fails, it will loop over and over again until you pass or —goddess forbid—be forced by those uninformed doctors to detransistion. Please stand strong, and know we are cheering you on. You will make it."

"Tell E about the weird voice while you're at it." Morrigan says, crashing the conversation with a devious grin on her face.

Sam looks quite annoyed as she turns to her, "Morrigan—sister, I've told you many *many* times. Demons don't always get a 'weird voice' when they complete their passage. The percentage of that occurring is low. Do not give them that expectation."

I shrug, "Dunno, a weird voice sounds pretty cool."

Morrigan shoots finger guns at me, "Now we're suckin' diesel!"

We giggled as Sam stared at us. "Are you two done?" She asks.

"I am, not sure about Morrigan though." I reply.

We both look at Morrigan, posing triumphantly once again with her grin of chaos.

"Yeah, nah, she's never done." I continue.

A big yellow hand grabs Morrigan's shoulder, startling her as she gets pulled back to the other room. Bud peeks in through the door, giving us two a gentle wave before continuing. The giggle fit became pure laughter.

"Any more questions, E?" Sam's voice cuts through as I try to hold back.

"Nah, Feels like a 'learn in the moment' kinda thing." I reply.

She nods, "Good. If you do, You know where to find me."

We both get up from our chairs and as we begin our journey back to the couch, Sam does a little giggle as she whispers in my ear.

"Don't tell Morrigan this, but as I compare both of your demonizations, you're catching on faster."

I join in on the giggling back to the couch as the movie continues. Another calm night between friends.

As the days remain calm, at night the horrors continue. One night, I was trapped in one of Morrigan's silent films. Another was in a white void, talking to a random demon about something. Forgot what about.

I think the craving-based diet is getting to me, one dream was a theme park chock full of nothing but meat. They even had a gravy pool with a bacon slide, snowing protein powder.

I don't think these are the dreams I'm looking for.

CHAPTER 11
FORESHOCK
E'S FAMILY HOME

These days feel like one long mess, and honestly I'm not sure what's worse. Is it the strange-ass dreams keeping me from sleeping well? What about the veil at work getting lifted from my eyes, knowing that I'm one of the only people who give a shit about folks? I don't know, but it's all so fucking tiring. Can I just—

"You alright there, E███?" A voice calls out.

Oh, right, Got too wrapped up in my brain again. Should be focusing on dinner.

Mom's in the kitchen with the final touches on whatever concoction she's brewing, but it can't beat the smell of the ham sitting right in front of me. Stupid cravings.

"You've been kinda distant lately, wanted to see if anything is goin' on, kiddo." Dad says, looking concerned.

I shrug, "Yeah, kinda been sleeping bad. Guess I gotta swap my pillows or something." Don't wanna let him in on it yet. It's not the right time.

He puts on a smile, "Ah, well, if ya ever want someone to talk to about whatever, let me know." He looks to the kitchen door, then leans over with a whisper, "And if ya need a lil' extra dessert to cool off, say the word. What's mine is yours."

"Now now, David." Mom says pushing the kitchen door open holding a strange concocted mess. Mushed vegetables and cheese in a glass baking dish. "E███ doesn't need too much sugar. He, she, uh, *their* job always has them up on their feet. Can't have a sugar crash during rush hour, can we?"

"We've been found out." He says to me.

"Yeah, guess we gotta grab the peach cobbler and run." I reply.

We both chuckle at our little bit.

"Keep it up you two. I'll make sure it goes into the fridge and none of us will get a bite." She snaps back, sliding the hot dish onto a cooking mat as she takes her seat.

Dad puts his hands up in the air, "Alright officer, you're the boss! We surrender!"

I won't. If I get another nightmare nothing is stoppin' me from raiding the fridge.

"If only I was a cop." Mom replies. "Give me a badge for one day and these streets would be spotless by sunrise."

Isn't being apart of the HOA enough?

She stabs a big black plastic ladle into the hot block of mush. "Instead of sugary peaches and syrup, how about you have some sweet corn casserole instead? Veggies are so much healthier!"

"Nah, I think the ham's callin' me more than anything else." I reply, Mom looking disappointed at my response.

"But sweetie, this was your favorite growing up!" It wasn't, but she plops a big steaming pile of it right on my plate regardless. God, it looks like a mess of yellow and white. Whatever my cravings want, it's definitely not that.

Then a big slice of ham hits my plate, "Don't worry ya carnivore, got what you're lookin' for right here." Dad says, lightly tapping the knife and carving fork. "Say, you've been meat crazy for a bit now—you on that new protein fad or something?"

"Eh, you could say that." I cut into the ham chunk.

"It's workin well for ya, E█████. You gettin those strong muscles from yours truly!"

Wait, what? I look down at my arms. They're still soft, yet you can start to see muscle rising from the skin. Gotta figure out an explanation quick.

"Well the grocer has me movin boxes lately. Guess it's that." I hypothesize.

"If they keep ya up, ya might fall out of that weird gender stuff and become a strong man like me!"

Ugh, there's the speed bump. "That's not how it works, dad."

"I mean, you don't even know how your gender works either —being a binary or whatever."

He's not wrong, but he's not right either.

Then he lightly chuckles. "Ahhh, relax! I'm messin with ya! A good ol' fashioned joke from your old man, yknow? Though, I guess your generation calls jokes 'triggers' now or somethin'."

I take a bite from my ham slice.

"Speaking of your grocery job, E█████. Why have they put you on so many late night shifts?" Mom chimes in as she swallows a bite of corn mush. "I'm glad they're finally giving you hours, but you've been coming home in the dead of night! It's not safe being out there that late." Oh, right. That's the cover I've been using for the Fold.

"Well, Y'know. Summer is coming up, and you know how people in and out of town love coming over for camping groceries and party supplies. They want to be sure the place is in good shape."

"And that was your one chance." She says in a disappointed tone. "I called them, E███. Multiple times. They didn't plan extra shifts in the past few months."

Shit.

"Do we have to do this right now, Janet?" Dad chimes up. "I want a relaxing meal with our kid. It's been awhile since we had one of these."

"I want to make sure E███ here isn't falling to bad influences." Mom bites back. "You know how insidious it is these days. Crime going up, fentanyl-laced black market energy is hitting the streets, and according to the store, E███ isn't where they said they'll be." She turns to me. "So, where have you been going E███?"

Gotta play defense.

"I got new friends, Mom. We watch movies and hang out around town and stuff. It isn't anything bad, promise." I say in my defense.

"Well, There we go! Our kid finally has some friends!" Dad says with a nervous laugh. "I'm glad you got some new buddies and we can go back to—"

"Are they human, E███?" Mom cuts him off.

"Does it matter?" I shoot back.

"We can't have a repeat of elementary school, E███. Those humanoid kids were swarming you when we weren't around. We had to homeschool you till middle school for your protection. If it's happening again I need to know."

"Those were called school friends, Mom." I snap. "God forbid I'm friendly with kids my age. Besides, that was like, what, twenty years ago? Nothing bad is happening. I'm not taking illegal drugs or doing crimes. We hang out, that's all."

"And that's great!" Dad speaks up, putting the cutting tools down to place a hand on my shoulder. "We both should be glad you're finally opening up to the world. Right, Janet?"

The table goes quiet. Mom stares at me as she puts the metal fork in her mouth, offloading another load of corn mush as you can hear the fork scraping across her teeth.

Great.

Picking up the knife and fork, I cut myself another huge chunk of ham before tossing it onto my plate.

"Y'know, I gotta finish up that camera." I cut through the silence. "That's more important right now." I get out of my chair, rushing off to my room plate in hand as I shut the door behind me.

Fuck being surrounded by that awkwardness with Mom's ice cold stare. I propped open my laptop, and threw on a few online videos to play as I chomp down on my slabs of meat.

After the ham fest, I actually found a bit of tinkering time for the camera. I ordered a few mods for this thing. Nothing boring like a digital conversion, but more utility. This thing's ancient, so I'm installing a remote mod so I can put it somewhere and snap photos from a distance. The original mod manufacturer didn't intend that as it's just a simple timer, but with a wireless microcontroller, soldering iron, and a little bit of python, you can make anything remote.

I was swapping out the old PCB with one I ordered online when a knock brings me out of the flow.

"Hey E██████, got some dessert for ya." Dad said from the other side. Putting my tools down, I crack open the door. The light from my room casts his face in light, showing a smile that's clearly holding back something else. In his hands are two bowls as he hands one over. Peach cobbler, bowl is warm, even remembered to put on whipped cream. "Thanks, Dad." I say, taking the bowl.

He nods, leaning over to the door hole. "Let me know if ya want seconds, I'll find a way." He whispers.

Now I'm smiling too. "Hah, I'll text ya if I do." I whisper back. He makes the okay sign with his newly freed hand before turning around, going back to the living room.

Taking a bite and yeah—it's a store bought crust mix made with some canned peaches. Damn is it good though, especially with the whipped cream on top. Must of ate the whole thing within a minute. Know for a fact that isn't the demonic cravings at work, that's the power of good ol' fashioned family dessert.

With the power of peaches and demonic energy, I finally got a breakthrough on this project. The wireless mod works like a charm, allowing me to press a button on my phone to trigger a snap from a distance. Will be awesome for group photos if I ever get in one. Need to invest in a tripod though.

I also slipped on a ND filter, allowing me to boost whatever photo quality there is on this little flashbang of a camera. Could modify the internals to take a different kinda film, but I'm trying to restore, not remix.

I pause a video essay blaring, un-fullscreening it to checking film conversion kit instructions and prices before my eyes land on the taskbar. Clock says it's almost midnight. That rush turns to tiredness, and I start to yawn.

Y'know what? The camera's fixed up enough for now. This is a bonus credit problem. Can figure it out tomorrow; maybe next month. Who knows with projects.

Sliding my workshop table to the side, gotta get ready for bed. One hygiene tune-up later, and I hit the sack. Plugging in my phone, putting on white noise's greatest hits, and close my eyes for whatever the hell this demonic energy has for me tonight.

The problem is, can't seem to find a comfortable spot. Back, chest, side, upside down, other side of the mattress, nothing worked. This whole time with these nightmares, I'm not sure what's worse—The dreams or the uncomfortable insomnia that comes with it.

It took a bit of experimenting, but laying on my back for the thirtieth time while putting a pillow under my legs, three pillows behind my head, and the blanket covering only the bottom half of my body somehow works. Finally, I can feel the drift...

But, of course, something had to bother me. Did someone turn a fan on? Personally not a fan of that, so I go to turn it off.

But my body doesn't respond.

Trying to wiggle something as small as a finger—no response there either. Is this sleep paralysis? My skin starts feeling like static, muscle becomes rock, eyes are locked shut —all I can experience is the sounds of wind swirling around me, intensifying as the white noise becomes something more.

Rustling of trees in the distance. The light breeze becomes a gust. Things continue to ramp up as sounds collide into louder and louder symphonies. At this rate the overstimulation will take me and—

Oh, the air became still, and the room is silent.

In my groggy daze, I test my body. Lifting my hands up to the sky, then shaking a leg, now moving my head. Everything works again, like nothing happened. Strange dream, but at least it's over. I grab my blanket, but all I felt was...blades of grass?

Now I'm fully awake. No longer does a room surround me, everything is a forest with me laying upon the ground. Thin pine trees surround me, with patches of bushes, flowers, and fauna stretched around me for what felt like infinity.

Where the hell am I?

CHAPTER 12
NIGHT OF PASSAGE

???

Checking my body and boy—I'm glad I got my shirt and briefs. Weird dreams suck, but at least this isn't a weird naked dream.

Getting up as the dirt flow around my fingers and toes as I reorient myself. A chill hits my body. Only realized I haven't been cold since I started taking injections. It's cause this dream caught me in my PJs, right?

Wonder if anyone's nearby. Since I don't have my cell phone, calling out felt like the next best thing.

"Hello?" I ask.

A few seconds pass, no answer. Time to get louder.

"Anyone there?!" I yell.

Only the wind greets me back.

So, I'm stuck in a forest. Don't even know if I'm even near home. Great.

First thoughts go to family camping trips. Dad gave me a bunch of survival skills that I kinda remember. One of them stuck at least: "If ya lose your phone, look for the northern star. You'll get your groundin' quick."

One problem—Where's the stars?

No, wait, where's the *Moon*?

Not a single thing in the sky, nothing but black abyss.

Could sit here all day and feel bad about it while questioning everything, but there's only one solution that makes sense—gotta pick a direction and start walking. Spinning around on the heel of my foot, I land pointing one direction; stabilizing myself as the momentum vanishes.

It's time to begin my journey into the forest.

Seconds became minutes, minutes became hours, and the forest becomes the same repetitive loop. Pine. Bushes. Plants.

Usually lush areas have a water source of some kind. Lakes, rivers, swamps—didn't matter. Problem is that I have yet to see a single drop.

Could climb the trees, but the pines are too thin. Don't wanna break a bone all alone in the forest.

Speakin' of lonliness, you'd think there be birds chirping, frogs screeching, maybe some lil' squirrels leaping from branch to branch—heck, even a cricket. Nothing but the wind. This place puts up the guise of being alive, but it feels oh-so-dead.

Could be walking a straight line, in circles, no clue. Dad's survival school comes into play again. I start leaving trails, creating landmarks, even got a sharp stick to scrape icons into the bark, letting me know I've been here. I turn around to fall back to it, and I can't seem to find it. Either I'm losing my sense of direction faster than I thought, or something's covering my tracks.

Something moved out of the corner of my eyes. No, wait, it's trees. Maybe they're moving around me, wouldn't that be funny?

Wait, shit. What if they are?

That would explain the landmark erasure. Can't track

anything if it all keeps moving. If the trees are moving then that means—

No.

Now's not the time to lose my mind. Gotta keep moving, I need to find something new.

Hours pass, and more trees. Trees. Trees trees trees. Fuck, can something new happen?

Guess I gotta be the change around here. What can I do to shake things up? How bout' moving faster?

Speeding up my walk to a quick jog, for the first time in my life my cardio is in control. Breathing is normal, heartbeat isn't shooting out of my chest, and I'm flowing with ease. Trees become a blur around me. Finally—a weird dream with a bit of fun.

How about I go faster? Jogging becomes a sprint, and my performance is wild. Feel like a world-class athlete now, everything around me becoming a quick blur as I keep sprinting down this forest pathway. My bangs free my eyes, giving me a clear view of what's in front of me. Maybe I can get into some sports.

The ground lightly rumbles, causing me to trip. My body lands face first on the ground, body tumbling to a stop.

Ow.

Checking my arms as I reorient myself, not a single scratch or bruise. My clothes are a different story—holes litter the cotton of my shirt, thankfully light damage and nothing gaping. I hope it doesn't get worse.

Laying back on a tree to re-calibrate, one thing keeps pestering me: This is a dream, right? Sam told me that this would be realistic, but everything feels so strange. What's the balance here? What's the mixture of dream and test? I'm obviously lucid.

Sticking my fingers through the cotton holes on my shirt, the fabric's texture combined with my skin feels so real. I rub my legs, and the muscles feel more toned than usual. Closing my eyes to hone my senses, and I don't feel a hint of pain anywhere. Guess I should be thankful it wasn't worse.

Opening my eyes, something new is on the horizon—an open field, along with two wooden buildings. What? That wasn't there when I closed them.

Even more interesting, the lights are *on*.

Is that life? Don't care, it's new. Gotta rush to it before a lack of stimulation kills me.

The trees clear for the first time as I walk into a perfect crop circle. Rubbing my eyes, I put into focus of the two buildings in front of me.

One is a watch tower, stretching far up above the treeline. The other right next door is a small shed. Please let there be people, hopefully a park ranger or something. They'll do one call for help, and I'm outta this forest.

Checking the shed first—The wood's new, seemingly built here today. I even smell the fresh lumber, a reminder of woodworking classes in high school. The door is cracked open as the yellow light is inviting. Need to make sure I'm not intruding, so I knock on the door.

"Hello?" I ask.

No one responds. Pulling the door open, and my mouth drops.

This shed is paradise!

So many tools and parts here! Wrenches, screwdrivers, drills with huge bit kits, and the next shelf over is all sorts of replacement parts for any purpose. Resistors, capacitors, solder, wires, LED lights, tons of things! There's even vehicle parts! Wonder what for? What do park rangers need with this?

Maybe this tarp-covered mass got the answer. gotta take a peek and—

Ooh, fancy. It's a ATV! Forest ranger green, four wheels, handlebar steering, even has an electric motor. Looks brand new, begging to be ridden.

Wanna get my little gremlin hands all over it, figure out how it ticks.

Buuuut I should get permission first. That means the watch tower calls for me. With a light sadness, I cover the ATV back up, and begin leaving the shed to take the wooden stairs.

Like the shed, it's freshly built too. Stairs would knock me out after a few steps, but tonight this is nothing. With this endurance, I gotta enter a few physical reality shows. Maybe get on one of those Japanese game shows my Dad watches, like the old one with the castle—

The lights in the tower shut off. Oh please don't sleep yet.

"Hey, wait!" I shout, rushing to the top as I push open the door.

There's no one inside, the bed is undisturbed, and I'm increasingly not a fan of this.

Flipping the light back on, the place is fully stocked—desk with a lamp and radio, a fresh bed, bunch of canned foods, and in the dead center of the tower is a map. Finally! Reference material!

I place my hands down on it and take a long glance and—oh, nevermind. There's usually elevation references, rivers carving their own path, y'know, forest map things.

This forest is flat—a nothing zone. There's only a white circle where I'm at—a blip in a sea of green. Looks like a shitty fan map from old real-time-strategy games.

Walking to the windows to get a better look, there's a single mountain—snowy peak and all. That wasn't on the map, right? I look down to re-verify, and…

The mountain is on the map, elevation and all. Did I misread it last time? That doesn't make any sense.

Nothing about this place makes sense.

You know what? Instead of comprehending dream logic, I'm gonna check the desk.

Despite the modern tech downstairs, the radio here looks ancient. Old liquid crystal display, Tons of knobs and gauges line the front, one big knob being labeled a tuner. There's also a few extra boxes ontop of it, a few speakers and—

Wait, is that a CRT? It's a small, metal rectangle of a thing, unlike any TV I've seen before. The screen looks to be about three inches big, offset with three knobs to adjust settings. There's one switch that says send or receive, with the current option being send. The back has a bunch of various plugs, but nothing seemingly video related? Why is it plugged into the radio?

The mic sitting right next to the setup is round lookin', covered in silver metal. Fits in with the radio and looks brand new. This radio seems to be the only way to contact the outside world, so I flip it on.

It doesn't work. Of course it doesn't fucking work. Maybe the CRT? Turning the power knob It flickers on, a little green star shooting across the screen as it approaches the bottom, leaving a trail across the screen. Once it hits the bottom frame, it shoots right back up to the top, repeating its descent. I think it's broken too.

Dead radio, broken TV. How does all this mint condition looking stuff be broken?

Then I remember the shed. All those parts. All those *tools*.

I might have to look for a manual or two, but I can fix this, right?

Popping back into the shed, I gotta swipe the essentials—screwdrivers, bunch o' electronic bits lying around, multimeter, even a soldering kit—y'know, the classics. Carrying my haul back to the tower, I grab a screwdriver and begin poppin' the radio open. All it takes is a few screws, then using a flathead to wedge the back open. That's when all that beautiful tech pours out.

At first glance, I spot a few blown capacitors. Annoying little fellas, especially in old tech like this. Last thing I need right now is corrosion.

Grabbin' the med-kit on the wall, I open it for the isopropyl alcohol inside. Ripping part of my shirt off that is hanging on from the fall, I coat it in alcohol and begin rubbing some initial parts of the board clean. This thing I'm wearin is ripped anyway, might as well recycle it. Once clean, I adjust the lamp to shine onto the motherboard.

With one deep breath in and out, it's tinkerin' time.

Soldering a few replacements there, checking the voltage over here, zen flows in as my hands dance around the solder and silicon. Couldn't find a manual, but sometimes you don't need one. The traces spoil the secrets.

Always had a better time connecting to tech and toys than people. People tend to avoid me, don't know how to act or respond positively to anything when I babble about this stuff. Of course, they don't say that out loud, they think they're too nice to admit it.

Thing is, people like me always know.

Fortunately, tech never judges you. It's wires, circuits, capacitors, maybe even some moving pieces—you get out what you put in. Until recently, the only thing that felt right was messing around with PCBs; forcing rocks, minerals, and metal to think in new ways.

That's when the Fold popped up. For the first time it feels like someone gets me. I was weird, but so were they. Brought me in, embraced my quirks, and showed me their own styles of weird. Morrigan's head-first attitude, Sam's kind info-dumping, Bud's... hugs and parent-like qualities?

Shit. Gotta' connect with them after I get out of here. Despite being a big gentle giant, they've seemingly been hesitant with me. I can only assume it's due to my human-ness or whatever. Maybe we can do something together to break the ice— or in this demonic case, melt it.

A soldering iron touches a pad, watching the last capacitor become bound as solder melts into place. Taking a glance around for any missing parts—yeah, this all seems correct. I test it with the multimeter, then a power cycle makes the speakers lying on the table sizzle with static.

See? No manual needed. Time to put it all back together.

With the radio re-assembled and flipped on, the sound of static returns, crackling white noise giving me a slight calm. If the radio works, no need to focus on the CRT for now. Grabbing the knob to start tuning, my brain warns me of my biggest obstacle yet.

I'm not ham radio certified. Wouldn't I be breaking the law if I call for help?

Wait, why am I even thinking about this? I want out of here, and I'm willing to scream down every channel for hours so they find me. Hand me a fine on the way home.

The static continues to blare as the tuner shuffles through the haze of noise. Bits of music or voices vanish before I have a chance to lock on. Minutes pass, and it begins to feel like a fools errand spending time to fix it up.

"I'm worri—"

Oh shit. There's a clear voice. The CRT even flickered at the voice, strange. Gotta roll it back.

"Honey, look, I'm sure it's nothing serious." One deep voice said.

"But she, he, ugh." The other high pitched voice said, cutting themselves off. "They. E███ is they." The other voice corrects.

Wait, those voices belong to my parents. How is that possible? Wait, even more impossible: Dad is correcting people on my pronouns? Damn, this really is a dream, isn't it?

"Yes, they…" Mom sighs "…They're clearly up to something, David. Leaving the house earlier and coming back late at night. I call the store when they go out occasionally, and they confirm E███ isn't scheduled that day. I check the security cams on my phone every day, in this one they're coming home at eleven PM!"

"And? E███ is a grown adult." Dad responds. "They can make any decision they want. If they mess up, they'll learn from it. If they succeed, then what's the problem?"

"It's not like E███ to do this! They're supposed to be a quiet little angel, always a consistent schedule: go out, work, come home, and do, uh, whatever they do with their soldier toys and screwdrivers. I'm worried that they're being lured to sin or, heaven forbid, drugs by some evil people. What if someone's trying to take advantage of our child? What if they're evil devils?"

"Let them live, Janet!" Dad shouts back. "Not sure what's gotten into you lately, but yes, E█████ is our beautiful child. I can't keep stressing this enough apparently, they're fully grown! A person with agency, dreams, desires! Let them mess up! I'm glad E█████ is finally having a possible social life for once. The kid was stuck up in their room for too long working on their little gizmos and toys. Maybe they will finally have friends! Maybe they finally found a boyfriend or girlfriend or, hell, even a theyfriend!"

I spin the tuner to static. Dream or not, don't wanna hear them bickering.

Morrigan is right though, they are going to find out soon. Do I tell them about my demon stuff when I wake up? No clue, but I should keep scanning the airwaves.

The static persists no matter the frequency, that little green star on the CRT dancing around as the static flows. Do I need to talk through it to get a response? Is there a frequency list somewhere?

Taking a peek below the desk, there's cabinets on the right side. Why didn't see those earlier? Were they even there before? This object permanence problem is fucking with me.

Opening the top one, inside is a wooden box with a latch. It's covered in rough tree bark, half a log turned into a box. Popping it open, two objects inset into the wood laid before me.

First one is a golden knife. It looks like one of those ninja blades from anime—a kunai I think it's called? No handle on it though, only a blade and hole.

The second object is a short golden cylinder; glass top with a metal rim and case. It looks like a container for something, not sure. It's empty though.

The other shelf contains a notebook. Black and white front, unlabeled. I pull it out and fly through the pages. They're all blank, but right as I reach the end, I land on one with a doodle.

It's a pentagram, no wait, Sam says they're pentacles. The style matches the ones Sam has.

Has all the similar parts, such as an extra circle encasing the design, with each point of the star having a symbol or word near it. One point has a symbol that looks like a tear drop, another point of the star looks like an asian character, though I can't tell if it's kanji or mandarin. Aren't those kinda the same? Regardless, no clue what this thing is trying to convey here.

On one point of the star is a number: 66.6 MHz. Hah, wasn't that the number Morrigan was ranting about?

It appeared in some okay action movie when the guy tuned into it and she immediately pointed it out. Outside of her describing it as the silly "demon number", radios built for that aren't supposed to go that low. That frequency is reserved for local tv channels and such so—

Wait.

The CRT screen still shooting the green star across its glass. Is that the key here?

Only one way to find out, let's tune in.

I begin messing with the dials on the ham radio to go lower and lower. When I seemingly hit a limit, I try another knob or button and it lets me go down further. It's a slow descent to the right megahertz, but as I approach the number, the CRT started moving around erratically. It's only when I land on the frequency it started acting more focused.

The radio has a funny sounding static, but the CRT is picking up something. Switching over to it, I start adjusting knobs on the front to finetune the signal. Contrast, check. Scan speed, faster. It's getting closer and closer to something, but something's incorrect.

Maybe it need's someone to speak up. Pulling the microphone up close, I push the button on the mic stand.

"Hello?"

The radio replies with static. Once more, I guess.

"Is anyone there?"

A sharp noise shoots at me from the speakers. Loud, harsh, screeching feedback of beeps and boops. I almost rip the volume knob off the thing as I shoot it to zero. What the hell was that?

The CRT gives a hint, the green star jiggling across the screen with pure energy. Looking down, I remember the "Send/Recieve" switch is still set to send.

Well, here goes nothing. I flip the switch to receive as I turn up the volume slightly.

The CRT jiggles once again, the star falling into straight lines, brightening and darkening to the boops on the ham radio. A shape begins to form on the screen, circular, yet geometrical. It was only halfway through when I could finally recognize it.

It's the pentacle again, somehow being sent over the radio waves. There's symbols beside the points, but the screen is too fuzzy to make out.

The radio begins getting louder, annoying me once again. I turn down the volume knob, but even as the knob hits zero, it kept getting louder. Oh no.

The shape on the screen starts to warp, the slow refresh rate unable to do anything as the light bends on the tube. It begins to get brighter as the volume continues to become ear piercing.

Flipping off the radio does nothing, the screeches get louder and louder. Covering my ears doesn't work, It's bouncing around in my brain.

The CRT begins flooding the room in a bright green, the star moving faster and faster. I swear I could see things other than that pentagram pop up, but it's too bright to make out. I close my eyes, cover my ears, and hope that this works.

It doesn't, and overstimulation locks me down. My synapses are lighting up as I feel goosebumps across my skin. I feel myself beginning to be pulled apart and reassembled, my nervous system going haywire as the beeps become too much. Even though my eyes shut, I start to see a faded orange glow. What is that?

Before I got an answer, A loud bang startles me to the floor, and the sound stops.

No fanfare, no fade, it's gone. Opening my eyes again, the CRT's screen has imploded upon itself, shards of glass covering the desk and my shirt.

...What was the point of that? I gotta double check the frequency, see if I did it right.

Picking up the notebook, my eyes glance over the pentacle. It looks…understandable? It was a cool image a second ago, but for some reason it has layers I missed.

That doesn't make sense—it's a mess of symbols— but as my eyes bounce across the points surrounding it all, my mind shuffles it into place, and a sentence begins to form.

A literal translation comes first. The sentence seems to be "The path is in you. Deposit and Sacrifice." But that's only the physicality of it. Feelings and sensations are attached to the message too, another layer to the puzzle. This is my first time dealing with one of these things, so I need to get a feel for it.

Tapping into the context, knowledge flows in from parts unknown. The second circle wrapping around the pentacle indicates a tone of gentleness. A kind request, not a harsh demand. Something pours into me, flowing with foreign sensations. At first, a light sting of pain, an accidental cut on a finger. A paper cut? Alongside that feeling is the gentle flow of warm liquid. Warm bath? No, maybe a drink? It feels more personal.

I look back to the first part of the literal translation, "The path is in me" repeats in my head as I connect the dots. Warmth, Liquid, Pain—Something feels missing.

The final door unlocks, and what enters my head is a vision. A person dressed in a warriors garb, archery equipment on their back, fancy sword at their side. They're from a land I've seen before, full of grassy hills and plains as far as the eye can see.

The sun is setting as the empty grasslands are lit aflame. A lone cobblestone tower littered with bodies, old shacks surrounding it destroyed. The warrior fights another opponent of blinding light, carrying a golden lance. The opponent gets the upper advantage, and as the warrior attempts an attack and misses, the bright one makes a clean stab into their back, the lance shooting out of the front of their body. I even held my chest tight from the impact.

The warrior hits the ground and their wound begins to leak pure red. With the final piece, my mind starts to wrap it together.

Symbols. Feelings. Visions.

Warmth. Liquid. Pain.

"The path is in me."

Bleeding out.

Oh. Blood.

It's asking me to "deposit" blood.

Jesus Christ.

The notebook falls out of my hands, dropping onto the table. Why the hell is it asking for that? Deposit where? What the fuck? My eyes dart around, and it lands on the wooden box.

The weird blade, along with that empty container. It demands a blood deposit. I refuse to call it a sacrifice.

I pull the blade out along with the small container. So, it wants me to slice myself open and pour blood in? Seriously? Is this a blood pact? Am I seriously making a demonic blood pact right now?

This is like one of Morrigan's shitty cult films. Is this the test Sam was mentioning? Shit, she's right, this is an emotional shit-storm. I'm not a self-harm kind of person, the thought of it freaks me out.

The golden blade is in my hand again, and I feel its cold metal with my fingers. One quick poke, and this is over. I should wake up in bed. Easy, right?

Of course, my body doesn't want to hurt itself. That's a good thing, self-preservation is a nice perk to living. Now though, it's holding me back.

I stare at the blade for a bit as I open the med-kit. Depending on how much blood this needs, I might need a bandage or gauze. Sam and Bud would probably kill me if I didn't patch it up.

I'm trying to delay this though, should go through with it already.

Maybe it needs a tiny bit, a little poke should suffice. I position the blade over my arm. Like those diabetes blood tests I tell myself. I press the tip down at my arm, and little droplets begin pouring out, rolling a little bit down my arm. The drops trickle into the container's metal bottom.

Few drops later, I pull it away to see the results. Nothing. The blood slowly rolls over to one side as it lands, leaving no residue at the bottom.

Does it want more? It's going to take awhile if I let it drip. Heck, I think my body already closed that spot up.

I guess I need to go bigger.

Mind goes to Morrigan's collection of bad movies once again. There's always a weird Illuminati cult or something that does blood pacts in those things. Every time they slice a hand I joke, "That's gotta hurt!" Always gets a laugh from her.

Guess I'll find out.

The blade is in my left hand, open palm on my right. The blade presses on my palm, cool to the touch. I close my eyes. Need to do this once, and I'll never do it again. I breathe in, and pull it back as I exhale.

At first, nothing. No clue if it worked. Then, my hand becomes wet. I open my eyes, and watch as blood falls into the container. A warm exploded ketchup packet in my palm. If this isn't enough, then fuck it, I'll flunk. Not doing this again.

It continues to pour, the container's bottom covered with my "deposit" as it starts to fill. I'm not quite sure how much it needs, but I hope—

The container shuts itself, causing me to move back. Was that enough?

I grab the gauze from the kit. The wound only hurts when I sterilized it, but otherwise, the bandage is on.

The container lies flat on the table, but the red fluid that filled the bottom once again rolls to one side. I gently pick it up, and no matter how I angle it, it sticks to that orientation, that…direction. Wait.

I rotate myself around with the container in hand, and the blood begins to move around with me, pointing to the same area. One full rotation, and I stop as the blood flows to that side once again.

It's a compass? My blood is a needle?

Look, I get that my diet has been a little iron heavy from the cravings, but I don't think my blood is supposed to be this magnetic. No matter how I move it, it points to the mountain. This can't get any weirder.

That's when the sound of rumbling comes from the distance.

Things inside the tower begin lightly shaking. Is this an earthquake? I look out of the windows, seeing the quiet forest before locking eyes with the mountain.

Then the mountain explodes.

CHAPTER 13
THE MOUNTAIN IS OUT

???

Rocks and smoke shoot into the sky, the absent void above becoming filled as trees begin to fly back. A huge shockwave shakes the forest to its roots as it ripples further away from the rocky explosion. If it wasn't so close, It would be beautiful.

But then logic kicks in—that shockwave is coming. I hit the floor, rolling under the desk closing my eyes and covering my ears.

A thunderous clap hits the tower, shaking violently back and forth as it ripples through the outpost. The harsh noise shot through my hands covering my ears as the shattering of glass is heard all around me, objects throwing themselves across the floor as they rattle and bounce off the remaining windows and walls.

The tower shakes back and forth before becoming still. Opening my eyes, glass and metal cans of food litter the floor as the map table is hanging through a window. I guess all I got now is this bloody thing. Gotta avoid stepping on glass with my bare feet as I get up.

Through the broken windows, a clear view of the mountain turned volcano stands before me. The snow is gone, and the smoke reminds me of old atomic bomb footage. The bottom begins to glow a warm orange, before a shot of magma becomes lava as it hits the side of its cliffs.

The volcano ain't wasting time; not sure how much of that I have left.

Looking down at my newfound blood compass, it once again points to the volcano. It really wants me to go there. Seriously, right now?

Hold that thought, the tower is beginning to crunch, and that's my cue to leave. Holding the container tight I burst through the door, trying my hardest to rush to the bottom of this before this place collapses. The volcano begins to sink below the trees as I hit the ground running, the wooden tower's foundations splintering as another rumbling shakes it to pieces.

A huge crack in the ground speeds right by my foot as I tumble to the grass. It widens, moving the tower away from me as the ground divides itself in half. The tower got caught in the middle, tumbling into the newfound canyon as it spreads it apart. Earthquakes around me, volcano in front of me, and now a newfound abyss below me. The tectonics here are fucked.

The shed's still intact, which means only one thing—It's ATV time. Bursting into the shed and throwing off the tarp, I grab the keys from the wall as I jump on. Jamming the key into the ignition and bringing it alive, I'm expecting a huge roar, but instead it's a few beeps and a led light on the dash.

Oh right, electric powered.

This shouldn't be too different from a car or bicycle, right? There's even a perfect slot to put the compass into, a comfortable tight fit.

Pressing a few buttons on the handle bars, headlights flip on, lighting the path ahead of me. I lightly twist the stick with my bandaged hand as the ATV rolls forward. Ok, that's the throttle, cool. So the brakes are—

A loud explosion goes off as the shed rumbles. The abyss above begins raining molten rock and smoke onto the ground in front of me. Some objects are as black as night, but some are coated orange as they make impact.

The mountain is pissed, and that's where I'm heading. Fuck me, I'm never questioning how weird this shit is ever again.

Pulling the throttle, the electric acceleration making the wheels screech before they get a grip. With one shot of momentum, I charge into the forest with my "borrowed" ATV.

No rivers or lakes, no need to worry about water. Trees meanwhile are not so predictable. Huge forest mean lots of trees. Lots of trees means lots of obstacles. Have to do my best to dodge them as I swerve back and forth.

Boulders from the sky crash right in front of me, rolling into trees like bowling pins. As one of the trees begins to fall, I don't have enough time to brake. I pull the trigger and duck right under as it slams into the ground. Y'know, for how violent this all is, this could be fun.

Blobs of lava from the sky crash and flow right beside me, and there goes the entertainment value. I'm in danger, enough distractions.

The blood shifts in the vial, telling me to make a hard left. No clue why it changes, but I trust it. Pays off as a geyser pops up where I would have went, or as I turn right up ahead trees become consumed by that canyon. It only affirms that I need to follow this thing. It's the only guidance I have.

The trees begin to thin out as I reach the bottom of the mountain. the blob of blood is tapping the glass. I guess reaching the mountain is not enough, now it wants me to go up.

Time to see how much torque this ATV has. I pull the throttle harder, the electric whine of the engine fights the uphill elevation and craggy rocks as I roll up the rocky space.

For the first minute or so, can see why off-roading is fun. This lil' thing rolls up the mountain higher and higher despite the sharp angles. As the tires continue to grip, I lean forward, ensuring the ATV doesn't throw me off. So far, so good.

A flow of orange appears around a cliff, The compass hits the dead center of the container. It has to be telling me to stop, right? Hitting the brakes, seems I was correct as a huge flow of lava rushes past in front of me, setting fire to a lone pine. I turn around to go back, but another flow closes off that path too.

With the only path left being me-sized, I think the ATV has done its job. I get off my mechanical steed, sliding the compass out of its handlebar compartment.

"You did a good job, buddy." I say to the vehicle, patting the seat. feel bad for leaving such a beautiful thing behind before continuing my ascent, but my journey must continue barefooted.

The newfound physical strength from earlier comes into play, the mountain trail is surprisingly smooth on my body. Feeling the blood hit the center of the compass again, I stay put. It rewards me as another huge rock rolls by, striking the trees down below. The blood forms a point once again, and that's my cue to continue.

This goes on for awhile, twists and turns, stops and starts as this golden compass guides my ascent. It's only when I make another turn across the world's most fucked up hiking route that I hit a wall.

A rock wall, in fact.

Maybe I went the wrong way, but when I turn back a gush of hot orange cuts it off.

Well, now what?

Looking down at my navigation, it's tapping the face of the glass. Look up, and I spot a cliff on-top of the wall. I mean my leg strength is better, so arm strength must be too, right? One way to find out, but interesting problem.

Human or folk, most of us have two hands. Either I'll climb to my destination, or hold on to this little cylinder down here. With the lava rising behind me, the choice is simple. I slide the compass into my left shirt pocket, and with my two free hands I begin my ascent.

Climbing up, I place a hand upon a rock above me, and it somehow felt wrong; like I shouldn't put any weight on it. Strange sensation, but out of curiosity I test it by stablizing myself before applying a light amount of weight. The rock crumbles off of the wall, splashing into the lava below.

I try another rock, and it feels right. I pull on it, and it holds my weight as I ascend further up the wall. This is some strange sixth sense shit. Why is it—Wait, don't question it. Keep going.

Eventually, my body crawls above the cliff face, and all I can do is just lay there breathing hard. The adrenaline is beginning to mellow, and my body's exhausted. Whatever the hell is causing all of this, give me a minute please.

Whatever it was listened, cause I spent the next few minutes catching my breath. I sit up on the cliff that's staring into the forest below. The dark green quiet of the forest is being burned alive by rushing loud orange. The smoke in the distance smells like campfires growing up, but with an extra twist of burnt rock. These trees took decades to grow, yet this mountain took seconds to flatten it all.

A rumble from behind gets my attention. getting on my feet, I pull out the compass. It's pushing me to this hallway of rock, an orange glow reflecting off the wall. Following it, it opens to a wide space, a huge pool of lava standing before me. This must be the mouth, and the volcano rumbles once again to confirm.

Raw energy of molten rock shoots up into the abyss, coating the world with orange warmth. Smoke rises as it bubbles and pours, pastel blends of faint gray and orange in the sky. Should be afraid of this, the human body cannot handle such raw energy.

Yet I'm calm.

This warm energy is smooth, gentle. The orange in the sky only gets brighter as it continues to erupt. I bask in its sights, but as the orange blobs get bigger, I realize a critical mistake: it's coming for me.

I put up my right hand to block—like it would matter—but as it impacts, the pain never came. There's only more warmth. Did it miss?

My eyes open, and lava dangles off my arm. Did my nerve endings die? Is my arm gone? It begins to roll off, but somehow the orange remains. It took me a few seconds to realize that's not lava. That's my skin.

My skin is bright orange, not a single third-degree burn to be found. I rub my left hand on it to double check, and not only do I feel the newfound softness, but full sensation too. Nothing about it is dead, it's oh so alive.

That should weird me out, right? Yet the distress never comes, but instead a new thought:

Orange is a cool color.

A weird thought, sure, but this is a weird dream. Another explosion of magma erupts, and it flows towards me once again. Instead of being afraid, I stand in place; awaiting the torrent of lava to hit me.

One blob burns a hole through my shirt, hitting my stomach. Another droplet pours down my leg. No pain, all gain, leaving orange skin in its wake. My left hand gets hit by the hot rock, revealing pure black lines on my orange wrist. Humanity melts off of me, and what rises from below feels better, stronger, literally hotter.

My newfound orange-ness sprinkled across my body is beautiful, a sort of demonic vitiligo. The pool of magma continues to bubble endlessly below me as I grab the compass, staring at its golden form. I don't need it anymore, toss it to the volcanic abyss as I lose sight of it.

Staring at the boiling rock down below, it calms me once again. The core of the earth is swirling and churning, so much energy in one place. It's incredible how we live on bigger rocks that float on this stuff. Always below our feet—brewing at whatever fuckin' celsius, fahrenheit, or kelvin—and we don't even care. Those tectonics are always bumping and crashing into each other, creating raw power we all fear.

Earthquakes, tsunamis, sinkholes, destructive forces caused by two rocks rubbing together. A single utterance of "the big one" on the west coast gets a few people anxious. The ability to change the world with one single movement—erase what was there with one swift motion, and begin something anew.

I'm beginning to understand that.

My whole life, never really had the energy to decide for myself. Move with the wind. Cruise control. I try to express myself—create change—but someone always pushes me out of view, hides me away, or in some situations forces me to stop. Humans are afraid of change, and the static-ness of their lives are the only thing they want to comprehend.

But god damn it, I am so tired of that bullshit. Tired of never having a single chance to be myself, hiding whatever there is of that in a room. Throwing a mask in public to ensure that the hand that feeds doesn't hit.

I don't fucking care anymore, I want to be myself.

Tear the old me down, and re-discover what makes the new me, well, me. looking upon the magma again, a smile shoots across my face.

Oh, to be the rumble they fear. The absolute power to become so drastically different, because I felt like it. Erupting in glorious celebration for me and my loved ones over concepts they don't comprehend. The raw determination to be myself in the spotlight, while those who are afraid to self-actualize hide in their own shadows of static.

It clicks.

I get why I'm here now. The compass of course lead me to this point, but it's directions came from somewhere. It's as the pentacle said, "The path is inside me." The path to unlocking my true self. A part of my heart guided me here, and the price I must pay is one that people think few can cough up.

You can't pay for something like that with cold hard cash or absolute power. Money can buy temporary happiness. Who doesn't love a comfy treat every once in a while? A snack, a game, a brand new tool-set. Those things make you feel good in the moment, but they are fleeting. Once we all fall back to reality, the chase for the next big dopamine hit begins anew.

I don't want dopamine. I want a reason to get up in the morning.

Not a bullshit reason like "because I gotta get to work." An actual fucking reason. A reason to wake up, look in the mirror, and smile. The ability to leave my room and feel like I don't have to put on a character before greeting the world. Partnering up with those who walk alongside me on that journey, spreading the message of self actualization to the world.

People think it's the most expensive thing in the world. The cost is too great, but it's never been expensive. It's fuckin' cheap. Everyone likes convincing themselves it's unobtainable, even fell for the trap myself till now. Took me staring into this comforting lava that, oh it's so simple.

Gotta hit the reset button. To do that, I need to take that first step.

So I take it, falling off the edge.

The descent quickens as lava rushes up to hug me. My clothes burn off, then my human skin as I turn fully orange. No pain though, only release.

I close my eyes, open my arms wide, anticipating the volcanic splash. For the first time in this dream, this is true relief.

"Thank you," a strange voice calls out.

What?

My body slams into the lava, the heat enveloping me and—

White noise coming from the right of me as I shoot out of... bed? Looking around, No trees, no volcanoes, only nerdy tech. I'm back in my room. Everything is back to normal.

Home sweet home.

God, I'm fucking sweaty. Looking down and—uh, holy shit, it looks like I wet the bed. Did I wet the bed? Don't want to know the answer.

That was one of the most intense dreams I ever had. Don't know if I passed or not, but I am hoping I got a S rank so I never have to do that again. Pure catharsis takes me, and I begin mixing tears in with these fluids.

Not long and a few sobs after that the urge to go to the bathroom hits me. Thank god, this is all sweat. I'm so disgusting right now, gonna shower. Fuck it, I'm definitely raiding the fridge for that cobbler too.

On the path to the bathroom, fresh clothes in hand, Dad is sitting in the living room, quietly scrolling on his phone as a folded blanket and pillow rests on his leg. He's not usually up this late, but he notices me. "Hey E▮▮▮, did we wake ya?"

"No, I have to use the restroom, take a shower while I'm at it. Are you good?" Let's not mention the sweat problem.

"Yeah. We had one of our little arguments. You know how it is." Dad replied.

Wait, was that real?

"Welp, don't let me keep ya from using the crapper." he says, lightly chuckling at himself before going back to the screaming propaganda on his phone. I sigh, lets get to it.

Entering the bathroom, the mirror shows me lookin' human, but it feels more like a mascot suit at this point. Like Dad said, I seem to have slightly more muscle compared to the last time I checked. Whether I feel human is another story entirely. Whatever that dream did, it knocked a few screws loose.

My body look good for now and—oh fuck.

An orange scar on my right hand.

Did I cut myself? Rubbing my hand over it, it doesn't hurt in the slightest. Smooth compared to my rough human skin. It's there. The dream must of happened then, right?

Whatever the answer is, seems the demon in me is ready to burst out. I'll let the fold know what happened tomorrow. Right now I need to process.

Washing up a little to get the remaining sweat off of me, then a little bed maintenance before sliding back in. I threw on some white noise on my phone as the cool bed calms me. As I finish off a cold bowl of cobbler with extra cobbler on the side, I keep staring at the popcorn ceiling.

At least it puts on the facade of a starry sky.

Doesn't take much time, but my eyes get heavy, and sleep takes me once again.

CHAPTER 14

GROWTH SPURT

Finally, a good nights sleep. Time to get up and do my bathroom rituals.

As those bristles brush their way across my teeth, a sharp headache hits. Feels worse than the occasional migraine—someone taking a bat to my head and getting a home run. Swore I heard a few noises, but that can't be right.

No chance to figure it out as the pain fades. I bet it's some dehydration headaches from the sweat fest. Gonna go chug a a few glasses of water, throw some electrolytes in there, get some liquids back.

Downing my second glass of water in the kitchen, it felt like the perfect time to open the group chat and help the Fold catch up.

———

FIREMAIDEN - 10:30AM

u jumped in lava

just like that

no hesitation

unreal

I wanna jump in lava now

TOYTINKERER - 10:30AM

yeah.

was pretty intense though, might need a day or two to relax from that.

SAGESAMMY - 10:31AM

I'm glad you passed through unharmed. It seems really traumatic in some parts, and if you need to process it with someone, we're all here for you.

BUDDY - 10:31AM

♡♡♡

TOYTINKERER - 10:31AM

thanks.

gonna get some food and drink in me now.

guessing I'm dehydrated from how warm I slept.

probably explains the headaches.

FIREMAIDEN - 10:32AM

u tumbled into a big hole of lava

that usually gets u parched

TOYTINKERER - 10:32AM

haha

SAGESAMMY - 10:32AM

Before you go, @ToyTinkerer, a question.

Since you mentioned headaches, does your head feel any different?

———

My head? Don't think so. One quick brush of my hand on my forehead, and my fingers discover two tiny bumps under the skin. Extremely hard, and don't even move when I push on them. Tiny bone spurs on my forehead.

———

TOYTINKERER - 10:33AM

uh..yeah?

there's like two tiny bumps on my forehead now.

wait...

are those horns?

SAGESAMMY - 10:34AM

Most likely, but I'd like to see it in person to make sure. Can you come over today?

FIREMAIDEN - 10:34AM

o shit, horns

hell yeah

BUDDY - 10:34AM

TOYTINKERER - 10:34AM

yeah, sure. as long as someone can come pick me up.

gotta eat breakfast first, though.

FIREMAIDEN - 10:35AM

ill b there

———

Sizzling a pack of bacon and munchin' on that fatty goodness, I rush out the door with the rest of the pieces, meeting up with Morrigan down the street with a warm hug waiting for me.

One four wheeled sprint to their house, Sam giving me another hug of her own as we sat on the couch. With permission she begins her light forehead exam, putting her hand on my forehead, immediately feeling the tiny bumps. A bright light shoots across her eyes.

"As I suspected, those are indeed horns." She starts taking notes on her phone. "Tell me again, E, when is your next checkup?"

I pull up the calendar app on my phone, scrolling my work schedule till the appointment event. "Uh, three weeks?"

She looks a little nervous as she scrolls through her phone. "Hmm, I think that's enough time. Maybe."

"Enough time for what?" I ask

"Are they gonna be one of us fellow poppers?" Morrigan asks.

"Goddess, I hope not."

"Guys, please." I butt in. "What's going on? What's a 'popper'?"

Sam lowers her phone as she slides up her glasses, "So, remember your diet? The wide amounts of fat, cartilage, and protein your body needs?"

I shake my head yes.

"Well, if we use the radio analogy from a few days ago, your body has found its unique signal. Now, it will use those resources you built up to begin its quick transformation. At this rate, it might be a few weeks, maybe less."

"Hope you enjoyed your humanity E, cause that's endin' real quick." Morrigan says cracking open a can of Moto Oil. "Your body is gonna rip that form off like a kid with a Christmas gift. When do ya think the family terms are gonna pop up, Sam?"

"Sister, please. Let's not overload E right now. At this stage, they need to stay emotionally and physically stable. We'll explain the changes one at a time as they come."

Sam closes her eyes, deep breathing before exhaling. "…So, as you can tell from the growths on your head, the first notable thing is going to be your horns. They're growing rapidly on your skull, and hopefully if you get to your appointment in time, they can take care of it in a safe and sterile manner."

I tilt my head to the side again, "Uh, why? Don't they normally come out safely?"

"You're forgettin' one thing, E." Morrigan starts off again after a swig "—If those horns are growin' small that's grand, don't have to worry. Buuut, if ya got big ones like mine—" She puts down her can for on a table before taking her hands up to her horns, "—then your skins gonna eventually have them poppin' out." She expands her hands rapidly, simulating an explosion as she shakes her fingers.

"Like a pimple?" I ask.

Sam sighs with her hand covering her face as Morrigan continues. "Exactly, E. That's why it's called poppin'. Instead of pus and gross shit though, it will instead be pure blood. It's feckin mint, makes for a deadly transition selfie for demons."

"But blood is gross, sister." Sam says slightly annoyed.

Morrigan shrugs. "In most situations, yea. When it's a pair of horns bein' the cause though, it's deadly as hell."

Sam blankly stares at her, to which Morrigan sighs, "But yeah, me and Sam are givin' ya options. In the end, it's your choice. Whether ya let a doc take a blade to em, or ya let your horns be their own blade, you ain't any lesser of a demon for it."

The conversation feels a bit too serious, gotta bring in the puns for some lightness.

"Well, I wanna thank you two for giving me—" I make horns with my two fingers, putting them to my head "—A heads up."

Sam's gears turn before giving the lightest of snorts, while Morrigan holds herself back by drinking from a can. Despite this, her smirk cannot be hidden.

Making sure I haven't forgotten anything, I do a quick checklist in my head. Everythings great, until I remember my parents.

"Oh, Morrigan! I think if these horns are coming in, we gotta' prep that room now, just in case." I say.

Morrigan processes the statement for a few seconds, then groans. "Ugh, yeah. Forgot about your feckin parents. Sis, can ya prime them on self defense stuff? I gotta clean up that room real quick."

Sam nods at her while turning to me, "Of course. Anything for E."

While Morrigan cleans, tumbles and crashes in the distance, Sam helps me figure out what to do about this whole coming out thing. What to pack, what to move over in advance, how to deal with a coming out gone wrong. Feels wrong that I even have to learn this stuff. My parents should be okay with it.

Unfortunately, I know better.

As we begin prepping for physical tactics, Bud pops up from adventures unknown as they come in through the front door. Of course we greet each other with another warm hug. I love demon hugs, they feel so much nicer. Glad everyone else here feels the same.

"Welcome back, Bud" Sam says. "Want to help teach E some self defense? They're trying to get prepped for their horns coming out, as their parents might not take it well."

Bud looks down at me, a gentle grin, then back up to Sam with a stern look as they tighten their hug. Bud nods.

Don't think it's possible for any of us to take this training seriously. A little five foot six gremlin like me going against a eight foot gentle giant like Bud turns it into a comical David vs Goliath situation. At least it was easier to soak in though. Gotta keep it bright, right?

Time passes, knowledge grows, and now Bud has me in a hypothetical headlock—arm feeling so strong that a bit more pressure can pop my head off like a cork. They seem to know when to hold back.

In the middle of this, Morrigan finally appears from the guest room, holding a garbage bag made from a bed sheet on her back as it clangs with noise, "Got it cleaned for ya, E. Now ya can—"

Morrigan freezes as she notices our situation, dropping the bag. It crashes on the floor with clangs and shattering of glass, Morrigan looking concerned. "Look, lad, I know you might want your horns real quick, but this ain't the way to do it."

We all stared at each other for a few seconds, then someone giggled.

It was Bud, sending a chain reaction through the room as we all start laughing.

With lessons learned, fun shared, lists prepped, and even a movie viewed, we walk outside for one more group hug. "Thanks for the help y'all, hope I don't need it." Bud puts their hand on my head and pats me a few times.

"It's better to have it and not need it, then need it and not have it, right?" Sam chimes in.

Glancing at the sun as it begins to hit twilight, I sigh. "Yeah…"

Sliding into the shitbox, Morrigan's all ready to go in the drivers seat. She turns up the tunes, flips down her silver aviators, and blasts us down the country roads.

Endless trees once again surround us. Ain't no passage night, but it's still unsettling. Let's look at the cracking yellow lines on the asphalt instead. almost rhythmic in nature as it starts to calm me.

Morrigan turns the radio down.

"So settle a bet, did ya hear a strange voice in your dream?" Morrigan asks.

"I mean, I heard something say 'thank you' at the end, but I slammed into magma before I had a chance to react."

She cracks a smile and pumps her fist. "Nice! Right once again."

"So, gotta ask, do you know what that voice was?"

She immediately shrugs. "Eh, not a clue. Apparently, us demons get that voice right after succeeding in our passages, regardless of what Sam says. No matter what, it says the same thing to everyone. 'Thank you!' No more, no less." She did a terrible exaggeration of the voice, wait, maybe it was perfect?

Now that I think about it, I don't remember what it sounds like, only the message.

"I only really know about it cause my passage had it too." Wonder if I can ask her about her passage.

"Oh, interesting. If it isn't uncomfortable—"

"You won't make me uncomfortable." She cuts me off. "You're new to all of this—a hellion—not goin' to punish that curiosity. Go ahead."

"What was your Night of Passage like?" I ask.

Morrigan takes a few seconds to think, then answers, "It's been a bit since that night, but if I remember right, there were a lot of knights. Big castles n' shite. Massive battles against angels. Not sure what was up with that."

"Wait, fighting angels? Why? Were they bad or something?"

"Look, lad, The Night of Passage is like all other dreams, they make no feckin' sense. I read too many stories about grand old knights in school as a kid, and the tabletop games I joined in probably didn't help. Combine that with my military experience along with the CPTSD gift package every soldier gets, and you're sure to be in some shite when ya close your eyes."

She pauses for a second, giving something a quick thought. "...I mean, dreams are based on shite around ya right? So it probably jumbled up somethin' in me head." I get that, but she's dodging the point.

"But knights don't fight angels in those stories, right?"

Morrigan shrugged. "For some yeah; but angels are annoying anyway. Worth takin' them down a peg or two any chance ya get."

I shrug, "I don't really know much about angels, but I remember them being nice to me at church when I was young."

"Heh, cause you appeared human then." Morrigan snaps back. "Once those horns come in, they gonna look at you differently. That fake sympathy shite, with holier than thou 'We can save these poor lowly demons!' kinda mentalities. Some even ambush demons like us and try to convert or hurt. Don't trust those holy cunts for a second. Sides, some demons are allergic to that holy energy shite anyway, and you might have it too."

"Allergic?" I asked, confused by the concept.

"Yeah, kinda like Kryptonite to Superman." Morrigan replies. "It doesn't kill ya thankfully, but it makes ya real weak. Some demons are mostly immune, but others can get the shakes the moment they step into a church, especially with that shite holy angel equipment they keep sellin'. Feckin gombeen-man wit their golden plated crosses and manky holy water n' golden shite—"

She sighs, trying to keep her eyes on the road.

"You good, Morrigan?" Another sigh as she seemingly recalibrates, "Yeah, lad. I'm grand. Look, If you're immune and ya see an angel, yank their halo off for me, will ya?"

That got me laughing, but the possibility of never being able to enter a church again sounds kinda relieving? They were always kinda boring. "If I ain't allergic, I'll bring you back a chain of em."

"That's my sib!" she says, rubbing me on the head.

Then we both caught the new nickname, "Ah, seems like the demonic resonance is hookin ya up faster than we thought!" She proclaims.

"Is that the family terms thing you were talkin about earlier?"

Morrigan gives a smirk, "Yeah. You know how all of us demons are apart of this fold?"

I nod silently.

"For some reason, the resonance really likes when demons form that close bond shite. It knows we are all trustin' each other, and since you're gettin hooked up to it now, it's gonna try to slip those terms into your speech. Only towards others in our fold, of course. It's kinda strange, but you get used to it."

"So like, If you're calling me sibling, does that mean I'm gonna be calling you sister?"

She snorts, "You catch on quick, don't ya? It's an endearment thing in folds. Bro, sis, sib, whatever. The resonance wants to make us all demonic little found families or somethin'. Sam says it's some strange queerplatonic shite or whatever fancy terms she likes this week."

"Does that mean you and Sam aren't sisters?" She shrugs, "She sound Irish? Nah, we don't share the same blood, but shes my sis. I know Sam tends to be the smarter, more peaceful one of our bunch and we grind a lot, but I would take a bullet for her any day, any time. She'd do the same. Part of that emotionally transparent demonic charm you're gonna get used to."

Feels like I'm on the tip of the iceberg when it comes to how all this works. I know found family is always a goal for a lot of people, humanoid or not, but to see the demonic resonance embed it so tightly into their, uh, I mean, *our* culture is so interesting to me.

"Before I forget, you planning to pick a name soon?" Morrigan breaks the silence. "I know you hate your old one and are still window shoppin', but calling ya E all the time might eventually drive ya mad, right?" Oh, right.

"Nothing really struck a chord with me yet, maybe after the horns come in." I reply. "I feel like something's gotta inspire me at some point."

"Look, if your dream says you're gonna be orange, and you're non-binary, got that gender fluid flowin or whatever, ya gotta get one of those nature names like...I dunno, tangerine or somethin'."

I giggle "Or cheese puff."

"Hah! how bout we throw some green and white on ya and call you Ireland?" Now we're both laughing.

As we continue the name-a-thon, it got me thinking about the past few months. A meeting in a fast food joint lead to me having some of the best friends I've ever had. Never felt this comfortable before, but despite the few months we spent together, it feels like I've known them for years. For the first time, something in me starts to feel, well, content.

Hopefully that keeps me safe for what's coming up ahead.

CHAPTER 15
TURNING IT UP TO 111

These horns feel like a ticking time bomb, yet I can't seem to find the clock.

At the start, hiding it was easy. Bangs were super long to begin with, so they covered my forehead perfectly. Days roll by, and as they begin peeking out of that veil, it felt like the only way you weren't noticing is if you were on the other side of the room. No idea if my parents caught on, but they didn't mention it.

At my job, kept doin' so well in the backroom dungeons that Derrick sought to keep me here forever, occasionally freeing me under strict supervision to fix whatever breaks. Can't deviate from this path if I wanna keep this job, but at the same time I'm not sure how many days I have left.

Despite the worries, these backrooms have been a boon for my social battery. Daily questions about "Where's the sugar aisle" are replaced with me and Jason talking. We started off kinda incompatible—gym bro meets techie—but once we stumbled upon each other's quirks and what our interests were, it bloomed into a friendly co-worker vibe.

"Another study night?" I ask while he was struggling with a box.

"Yeah, they've been really pushin' a lot of terms and theories on me lately." He replies. "Gonna be pushin' pencils till two or three tonight. Total bummer for my sleep, but it's gonna be so worth it."

"You're studying for social work, right?" I ask.

Jason seems a bit apprehensive at the question. "Uh, yeah bro! Can't be the dude movin' boxes forever. Gotta expand my wings and fly."

"It's the only way you're gonna reach the top shelf without a ladder." I reply with a little giggle. Jason chuckles with me as I effortlessly slide another box into the correct place. Are these things just packing peanuts or something?

It's all fun and games till another headache hits me full blast, dropping a box onto the floor, hearing muffled glass shattering. A complete shock-wave from my forehead as the bones creak and the pressure on my skin pulls tighter. Ain't no ibuprofen relieving that kinda pain. No skin tears, but it's getting worse by the day.

"Woah, E, You good girl?" I hear Jason call out.

"Yeah, I'm good. I'm just—" Holding my head, the skin is sore as it cries for relief. "—Ugh, I need to sit for a sec to let this headache chill out." Shambling over to a nearby chair, I plop myself down in a attempt to take a break.

The light fixtures above blares as I wait for this demonic migraine to pass. Looking down, Jason followed me over. Shit, how long was he looking? Didn't even try to hide these horns sticking out, did he notice?

"Is this about those weird bumps on your head?"

Yep, he noticed.

Not really sure what to tell him. Can't trust anyone in this store, so let's see if I can make something up.

"Uh, yeah. I tried getting those implant piercing things, I think they might be infected or something though. No clue."

Jason went silent for a few seconds, but I'm too busy staring at the ceiling to calm this shit down.

"Dude, you don't gotta hide it from me."

Oh shit. "Hide what?" I ask cautiously.

He looks around for a few seconds, and then walks up to me and crouches down. "I know you're doin' some humanoid stuff right now. It's okay, I won't tell."

Shit. Shit shit shit. "How did you—"

"Bro, a few months ago you were a twig. Now look at you, you got some proper meat on your bones and doin' heavy lifting shit out of nowhere."

He points off to the distance, "See that pallet over there with the huge box?" I pushed that over there last week, but it's now unwrapped from the plastic. Big box, but whatever. "Uh yeah, why?" He looks shocked that I brushed it off so easily.

"Girl, look at the label." He replies.

The migraine finally releases me, and my eyes lock onto the logo, oh my. That's why he's freaking out about it. It was a box for large watermelons. How heavy even is that?

"When that stuff starts rollin' in for spring and summer, we gotta mover for stuff like that. You apparently didn't get the memo, so you slid the whole thing over there on the floor in seconds. I can't even do that, and I've been going to the gym for years."

"Honestly I thought moving boxes got me this buff." I reply.

Jason laughed, "Nah dude, trust me—If that was possible I'd be selling gym memberships for the back." He seems to be taking it well. Too well. What's the catch?

"So what now, gonna report me or something?" I ask.

Jason looked confused, "Uh, no? Why would I sell out another humanoid?"

"Wait, are you—"

"Of course bro! Our kind gotta stick together regardless of the variant, ya know?"

Double checkin' his appearance, guess he's gotten more, uh, glowy? No clue. The fact that I'm not in trouble though has me laughing in relief, "I didn't realize you were on that path at all, Jason."

He extends a hand to me to help me up, which I accept. "Yeah, though my choice is a bit more restricted than the usual ones. What's yours?" He asked.

"Just a ol' fashioned demon!" I said with a little bit of glee.

"Oh." For a second, nervousness flashes across his face "Uh, honestly, that tracks for ya, E! Good for you, bro."

"What's that reaction for?" He's acting weird about it despite being so pro a second ago.

Jason becomes flustered. "Oh nothing, promise! It's kinda awkward for a sec cause, uh, I'm going through angel side of things. Trials and all, y'know?"

My nerves stand up as what Morrigan said the other day enters my head. Should I be panicking? No. Gotta keep it calm.

"I mean, not a big deal right?" I speak up. "Just because I get some horns and you get a halo doesn't mean we gotta treat each other differently."

Jason rubs the back of his head, "Yeah! Of course! Heh, as they say, love thy neighbor and all that, y'know?"

"How does any of that stuff even work anyway? Y'all got trials apparently?"

He brightens up, "Oh, yeah! When that ascension act passed awhile back, it allowed some humanoid variants to have limited distribution based on religious circumstances. As a result, us angels gotta go through trials to find the best of the bunch and then we get ascended to angelkind. Pretty cool, right dude?"

"So people are picked? Doesn't that mean people get rejected?"

Jason kinda scratches his head, "Uh, I guess so? I don't think there's a limitation on reapplying though. Probably costs a bit to keep doin' that. Luckily the Born Again Society gave me a grant so I can get my chance at being an angel. It's quite the blessing!"

"Hah, yeah. I remember my parents wanting me to ascend and all that." I reply, getting the mop to clean the leaky box. "Angels came to the local church giving people blessings, touting the ascension program, all that. Thank god ya got a grant though cause when my parents saw the price tag they lost it. Explains why tech bros and celebs mainly get it."

Jason's looking at me like I'm a lost puppy. "So, like, is that why you're becoming a demon? Cause it was too expensive the other way?"

I shrug, "Nah, I don't think angel stuff looks good on me, especially for that price. Besides, with how my demon friends look, kinda excited to see what this energy does for me."

Jason goes silent for a few seconds, seemingly conflicted with something. After a bit, he smiles. "As long as you're happy, E. Your body, your choice bro."

I flash a grin back, "Same to you Jason, but only if ya fly me around on those wings you'll get."

Jason laughs, "Dude, not fair! I don't even know what kinda cool stuff demons get to make a comeback."

"Only one way to find out!" I cackle.

Maybe Morrigan had a bad run-in with a few angels, but Jason seems alright to me.

As lunch time arrives, I munch on some microwaved pre-cooked beef patties, dipping them in a container of mayo like cookies and milk, slurpin' a chocolate protein shake while scrolling the net.

Demon cravings, y'know?

Everything was fine, biting down on a good ol' fashioned 80/20 patty before a loud crack echoes through my head.

Something in my jaw moved.

I search around with my tongue and stumbled upon something rock hard in my mouth. Picking it out, the realization smacks me across the face.

It's a tooth filling.

I check my mouth again, rubbing my tongue over a newfound cavity. I had this tooth filled over a decade ago, and now it's exposed to the elements once again. God, I can't handle a dentist appointment on-top of everything else right now.

But then a new sensation hits. Something is pushing my tongue away from the cavity.

Flipping my phone screen off, I stare into the darkened screen as I open my mouth. The fissure in my tooth slowly closing itself up as enamel fills the spot is, uh, wow. It looks like a regular tooth now, not even the slightest hint of nerve pain. Guess this is the "rejuvenation" Sam talked about.

So here's the thing, I have five more fillings. My mouth is gonna act like popping candy for the next week, ain't it?

As the next few days and teeth popped by, a strange sickness came next. Felt like the flu and food poisioning did a tag team on me as I spent my time on the toilet. Outside of simple fluids and soft chewy foods, my body refused to keep anything in. There was no way I was gonna work in these conditions. Don't give a shit what Derrick thinks; if I'm so important to the workforce family or whatever, I'm taking a few legal sick days.

Whatever hit me like a bus, it's fuckin' with the thermometer too. Kept trying to get my temp, but it kept saying the same thing, "ERR2HOT".

Opening it up in my room with my tools in my half sick daze, and all the troubleshooting told me it was fine. After sterilizing it, I gave it to my Dad, and it gave out a casual 98.6 Fahrenheit.

"E█████, instead of focusing on fixin' the thermometer, you should get back to breaking that fever." Dad says, placing the thermometer on the living room table. "I feel how warm you are from over here. Go get some rest please."

Guess I'm heatin' up.

Despite all this weirdness, my body seems stable enough to reach that appointment. I'd get my horns safely pulled out, come out to my parents in a safe environment, and have my friends be there in case shit goes down.

But life had other plans.

CHAPTER 16
FAMILY
E'S FAMILY HOME

Another dull throb wakes me from my slumber. My stomach feels like shit, so the bathroom calls for me.

Stumbling into the bathroom in a blurry daze, I'll check on my head in a sec, gotta take care of business first.

Social media is boring tonight. Mindnumbing micro-celebrity dramas converted for fuel for my nightly sickness purge. When that's all done with, I had the strange urge to take a peek into the mirror. Never really did that too much when I was human, but I want a happy memory of my in-between self.

Staring back at me was a demon masquerading like a human.

My eyes have black edges, a void slowly consuming them. My tired bloodshot eyes are slowly getting replaced.

In the horn department, I see where the term "poppers" comes from now—the strain feels like rubber bands about to snap. Two giant pimples right on my head. Wonder if those weird ASMR doctors online would pop these.

Muscles are getting buffer in the bathroom lighting. It's like I do dead lifts or whatever people do at those fancy gyms. Kinda makes me look hot, really. Demon perks, I guess.

Shoulders have some strange flakes on them though, and right under them is a strange color. What the hell is that? Attempting to brush it off, but it's stuck to my shoulder. Pulling it off, I realize it's sticking to my skin, ripping off in one clean piece. Holy shit.

It's orange. My skin is getting orange. My pasty white skin rips right off, and there's orange! Spotting a few more patches I rip them off, and the orange continues to pour in. Sprinkles of deep black dots across the orange as my freckles are recolored. The next few minutes became a peel fest. Excitement being one reason— but seriously though, dead skin is disgusting. Get that shit off!

After the last identifiable patch is removed, once again I'm staring at myself in the mirror. My human skin is dying, flaking in real time, eyes are being swallowed by hell itself, and it's all beautiful. Taking it in for a minute or two, my eyes dart around and seeing these newfound changes. Even caught a glimpse of my smile.

Hey wait, idea. How about a test run with the ol' retro cam?

Grabbing the camera from my room, I point it at the mirror. Never really taken photos of myself in years, didn't have a reason. Why take photos of something you hate? Tonight is different though, and I'm gonna have a full blown photoshoot.

Focusing the lens before brushing my bangs away. Wanna get my void-y lookin' eyes in the shot. Brushing over the top of one horn bump to move a few stray strands, and it responds with a sudden twitch.

A release in pressure on the left side of my forehead, before a sharp pain causes me to yelp. My eyes shut to help me process the newfound sensations. Coming to, I feel something rolling down my face. Bringing my finger up to it, and I feel something pour right past it as I tap my forehead. Now to look and—

Oh. That's blood. That's a *lot* of blood.

The new me is arriving with violent fury, a sprinkle of blood across the mirror. The culprit? The big bloody orange horn that took the place of a bump; shooting straight ahead. A set of black rings are near the base—patterns repeating across the rings—makes it hard to tell from the amount of blood I'm dealing with. God, the metallic taste hit my mouth and fuck this is disgusting. Gotta wash my mouth in the sink.

Rubbing down my face, I should grab the first aid kit under the sink and fix this problem with a bit of gauze. One glance at the mirror though shows scabs beginning to form at the horn's base, then the bleeding shuts off. Is that some demonic regeneration stuff?

Whatever the case, there's no way to hide this now. Not like I was doing a good job in the first place. My parents are going to lose their shit, especially like this.

Okay, breathe.

Yeah, I gotta clean this up, shouldn't be hard, but what Morrigan said awhile back rings in my head.

This would make a "deadly" selfie, wouldn't it?

One snap wouldn't hurt.

Bringing the camera up to the mirror again, It's hard to find the right angle and lighting. Look, I know the phone would be easier to use, but c'mon, this will be fun to have on an instant photo.

Got the right angle, and as the camera snaps another twitch of pressure ripples across my head. The second horn bursts out mid shot, catching me off-guard as I yell in pain.

God fucking damnit. At this rate the overstimulation is gonna make me non-verbal. After a minute of two of dripping noises, I open my eyes to red droplets covering the white bowl and silver drain in my blood.

Looking up into the mirror. A literal bloody mess stares back. The only things on me not covered in blood are my arms and hands. The tanktop's soaked red, even the camera got a sprinkle. My eyes pierce through the red, but the black borders continue to encroach on my irises. It's over but god, hope my parents aren't awake.

For a human, it's way past time for an emergency room visit. Now though, I'm a demon. As the wounds once again close up, I think it's time for another photo shoot.

Swapping around a few poses, I take another snap. Never realized that selfie taking was fun, but looking how I want to probably helps. Watching all the shots develop on the printed out film, it's nice. Under the increasingly dry blood and dead scabby skin, I finally see me.

Now's the hard part: Cleaning this all up. Not enough supplies in here, need to grab some from the closet outside. Then I can take a shower, throw a bloody towel into the laundry basket, let the fold know, and sleep. Fully rested, I can come out to my parents in the morning.

Sound plan. I open the door.

Annnd the plan is dead. I just won the "worst coming out to parents" award.

My mom stands before me as I'm covered in blood, horns shooting out of my skull, patches of orange skin on my shoulders with fucked up eyes. A demonic little freak. The walls coated with blood aren't helping.

Don't even know what she's thinking. Judging by her widening eyes, she's gonna faint or scream.

She chose screaming.

Welp, here we fucking go.

Obviously Dad woke up next, and under command of Mom we clean up the bathroom together. Not a word uttered. The only sounds were rags and sponges being drained of warm water, followed by them swishing around the tile on the floors and walls.

Don't know how to describe the deafening silence, but I felt my Mom's anger right behind me. There's an intense feeling of being judged—daggers pointed towards my soul. Strange contrast to my Dad, where instead of anger I feel sympathy?

Strange I can feel what they feel at all, am I on edge? Gotta be on edge.

The cleaning wraps up in silence. Mom points to the family table As we sat down, her barrage began.

It was easily a one-sided screaming match. Dad sheepishly watches it go down, but something tells me he's getting angrier at her approach. Mom meanwhile played the greatest hits; "How dare you do this under my back" this, "How could my child ruin their body" that. A barrage that normally would throw lil' human me into a quiet shameful state.

Here's the problem with that—I'm not a shy little human anymore. Instead of quietly taking it, anger is bubbling. I try to filter it out, but Mom knows how to push my new buttons as she continues to throw a barrage of hate my way:

"I knew something was up when I called the grocery store and they said you weren't there."

"This medicine is hurting you! You look nothing like your beautiful self anymore."

"You could have had a beautiful halo and wings if you wanted to turn into something, but now you have those disgusting horns instead."

"Your beautiful eyes are going away and being replaced by these unholy voids. You need to stop taking this demonic crap!"

"We should have forced you to go to church more, now it's too late! Your body is corrupt with this—this sin!"

"Why couldn't my sweet child become a beautiful angel, instead of such an ugly *devil*."

I'm done. That's my breaking point.

My seat flies back to the wall, my hands slamming the table as a crack forms through the solid cherry red wood.

She immediately shuts the fuck up.

"Why in the unholy fuck should I care about what you think?" I begin. "This is my body, my fucking rules. I'm not your little baby anymore, Mother."

Don't know why, but I feel her shock before I see it hit her face, "You can't speak to me like—"

"Shut the fuck up, and let me speak."

She falls silent again, and thus I commit the ultimate family sacrilege: telling my Mom to shut up. Honestly, I don't fucking care anymore. So completely done with this song and dance put-me-down bullshit.

I'm not going to burn the bridge, I'm going to nuke it.

"I am a fully grown twenty-five year old adult. I will not feel bad for making friends you don't approve of. I will not be sorry for becoming the hot bloody demonic mess you see, horns and all. Accept that for once in my life I am finally happy about something. Finally found something in my life that gives me a semblance of identity. Friends that give me an actual sense of community. Things you have begged me to get, instead of being stuck in my little room all day where you think I do nothing but play with 'little toy soldiers.' You could be happy about this too if you wanted, but no, instead you had to rob that happiness from *me*. This night could have been *so* wonderful. I am finally growing into my genuine self. You could have been supporting and proud of my self-discovery. Instead, I have to deal with your raging holier than thou *bullshit*. I will not be sorry that I am becoming your ugly little demon, rather than your beautiful little angel. Accept me for who I am, or go fuck yourself and die."

Mom is silent, frozen in place.

Dad's shocked, staring at me like I killed the family pet.

Shit, that felt so good, but I won't last long. Need to let the fold know that it's going down.

Running to my room during the literal stun-lock, I lock the door behind me while opening the group chat. The door knob jiggles on my door, followed by slamming.

"E█████ OPEN THIS DOOR RIGHT NOW!" Mom screams.

Absolutely fucking not.

I scramble to assemble a quick message to the group, sending it in a rushed panic.

TOYTINKERER - 1:10 AM

help please

my horns popped out of nowhere and my parents immediately found out

I need a pickup asap please

Banging and screaming continues as my messenger bag hits the bed, shoving some final essentials into it.

Laptop, meds, bits and bobs and photos from around the room. The camera's coming too. A few packs of clothes go into another pocket. Lots of stuff got moved over to the fold's home over the week, but there's still a lot more left in here, like my projects and supplies.

"LET ME IN NOW E███!" Mom screams again, her slams becoming even louder. She's even trying to kick the door now as it rumbles with hits. Don't think she has the strength to put in a dent.

Feels like there's two choices: Either she bangs and rumbles forever, or I decide to jump out of my window right now and fuck off into the darkness. Probably strong enough to handle the fall now, but—

Wait. Can't believe I'm seriously considering jumping out the window. That fucking banging is really getting to me, jamming nails in my head.

Please, make it stop.

No clue how much time has passed as I held my ears, feeling small bumps of new cartilage on the ends as I muffle the bangs, but eventually the bangs slow. Screaming from the other side becomes sobs before she fades off. All I can do is cry.

God fucking dammit.

Why did it have to go like this? Why did she have to be like this?

My phone vibrates, and a notification pops up on the screen:

———

FIREMAIDEN - 1:12 AM

coming

———

Oh thank god, Morrigan is awake. Forgot the fire department has her on call tonight. Please be sooner than later.

For now, I keep checking my bag, even threw some tears into it before hearing a gentle knock at the door.

"Hey, can I please come in?" Dad says from the other side.

Somehow, for some irrational reason I can't comprehend, I only feel him and his sympathy on the other side of the door. I somehow know this isn't a weird trick—He's really trying to talk to me. What the fuck is this shit?

I slowly unlock the door, opening it to see my Dad standing there dumbstruck. He's having an hard time processing everything going down. I move to the side, letting him in. As soon as the lock goes back up, I rush to the bed, holding onto my bag for comfort as the crying continues.

A minute or two passes before a sudden pressure next to me hits the bed. Something touches my back, causing me to jump away from it. I only realize he was just trying to put his hand there. He lifts his hand back up for a second, but as I slowly defuse and lean back over, he places it once again on me. The light comfort of his back rub calms me down. His cool human hand felt nice.

He's clearly thinking about what to say, scratching his mustache while staring at my whole situation, stopping at my horns. He tries to give a little smile.

"Look, I know that the youth tend to be a bit hornier than us older folk, but this is new territory, don't ya think?" He says, pointing at my horns.

This is the worst time for an awkward dad joke, but it got me to smile anyway.

"...I know Mom is overboard right now, but I really don't want to see you two hate each other." He continues.

"Mediation won't work here, Dad." I reply, trying to hide my blood stained tears. "My body is mine, not hers. She should respect that."

"Yeah, I know." he pauses, staring off to space for a second before continuing, "I want to let you know that I've tried to talk to her about bein' yourself. Me, you, her, we are all adults here. We need to respect that. We need to respect you."

Oh, he's crying too.

"Look, kiddo, seeing you coming from the bathroom covered in blood, a huge pair of horn things on your head, finding out you're taking this stuff all at the same time? That would shock the most accepting of parents. We aren't thinking straight right now, especially Mom."

He moves his hand from my back to my shoulder opposite of him.

"Not going to lie to you and say I understand what's going on in your life. This demon stuff you're goin' through is all brand new to me and, frankly, it's a little scary. I don't know your side of the story, but I don't want us to break apart because I don't understand something. I want to ask you a question: This...stuff, does it make you happy?"

It's getting harder to speak, so all I can do is lightly nod yes.

"Then don't let us stop you."

What?

"Look, you said it yourself earlier. You're a full grown adult. You need to make these choices yourself and live with the blessings and curses of it. I want to ask one thing from you though..." Great, the tears are back, and I can't hold them back anymore.

"Don't hide your life from me, please." He says sternly. "Even though you're a fully grown adult who can make your own decisions, heck, you also have this new fangled friend group away from us, you're always my child, my family. I want to celebrate your successes and be there to support you through your failures. Whatever happens past this point, keep in contact with me, alright? I want to know what my child is going through, no matter what."

After a barrage of hatred, this peace lily was exactly what was needed. Letting go of my bag, I hug him tightly as I sob on his shoulder."Woah! Strong hug there buddy!" he says, hint of pain in his voice.

Oh right, human. Sounds like all the wind got knocked out of him, even felt his spine popping a few times from my grip. I lighten my strength.

All I needed tonight was a crumb of acceptance. A quiet moment passes between me and my Dad, trying my best to take it all in, before it immediately breaks down.

"David, get the gun!" Mom shouts. "There's an evil devil outside!"

Headlights flicker through the window. Shit, Morrigan's here.

Throwing my bag on, Dad looks worried as I rush to the front door.

The living room is covered in headlights from Morrigan's shitbox. She's sitting ontop of the hood, not moving or budging. She's not coming in, like she's waiting for me.

Dial tones go off next to me, and Mom is trying to dial 911.

"Mom, stop!" I call out, getting closer. "Please, she won't hurt anyone!"

I feel something foreign. Panic, alarm. It's disconnected from me, but felt all the same. She begins to move, lifting her arm up in the air.

Her arm begins to head towards me. Due to the early alert, I grab it before it hits, deadlocking it into place. Her hand is an open palm.

She tried to hit me.

Did she actually try to hit me? Mom? What?

"LET ME GO E███, YOU CAN'T TREAT YOUR MOTHER LIKE THIS!" she screams, attempting to free herself with her other hand. I barely feel any tension or resistance from her, she's nothing in my hand. Am I really this strong now?

She's scared, and I'm not an asshole, so I let go as requested. She falls to the floor from inertia. She looks up at me, nothing but that foreign fear coming from her. She's begins crawling away in a rushed panic, hiding behind the kitchen island.

To her, I'm another humanoid.

I'm a monster to them all now.

Dad enters the room, and he gazes at the situation before we lock eyes. I feel nothing but sadness from him. Don't even need to say a word to each other, but we nod in agreement.

Ready or not, it's time for me to go.

One last glance at Mom and she's crying—hands in face, afraid of my existence. I could say something, but instead I tighten my bag strap, making my way to the front door.

I did enough here tonight.

Morrigan looks relieved as I reach her car. Opening the door, I fall into the shotgun seat. She follows my lead, but something peaks her interest. I felt it too, a frustration. We both look at the front door and it's Mom, keeping her distance.

"How dare you take my child away from me! I'm calling the cops on you, you devil!" She shrieks.

That comment stirred something in Morrigan. Like my weird sensations from my parents, I felt her sudden rage.

She gets back up from her seat, giving a long-ranged death stare. "Shut the feck up, you eejit! I didn't enter your house, your demonic mid-twenties adult got into my car willingly, and you are yellin' slurs in the middle of the night waking your neighbors. If anyone's gonna get arrested tonight when the peelers come, it'll be *you*, ya cunt."

Morrigan shoots an inward peace sign towards her as she slides back into the shitbox. Mom screams more obscenities and threats at us as a few neighbors begin flipping lights on. The gearshift moves as she jams the clutch, the shitbox launching backwards as she commits us to a J-turn. The car spins us around on the road, tires screeching, and Morrigan charges us off into the darkness.

With the danger over, that's my cue to break down.

Hands turn red as my tears keep mixing with the blood. Looking at Morrigan has an expression that demands blood, but not mine. That raging fire in her starts to simmer down. I'm surprised how well she held it in, as she typically goes full-force.

Her silence tells me more than enough.

No idea if she was speeding down the country roads or if my crying was that intense, but the next time I look up through the windows we're back at the fold's home. My car door opens and Morrigan appears, placing a hand on my back. Didn't even notice she got out.

Nothing but a gentle smile on her face, felt her empathy as she tries to calm me down. "C'mon lad, your new home is a few steps away."

Indoors, the lights were all off. Sam is on a business trip, and Bud is just...somewhere once again. We're alone, and Morrigan looks at me with gentleness.

"Sorry your parents are a bunch of eejits." She said, embracing me in a hug. That hug becomes air tight as I return it, both of us squeezing each other as tightly as we could. The tightness calms me, signaling that I can finally relax.

We eventually release, "It's okay but—"

"It's not okay." Morrigan says, cutting me off. "I'm tired of these shite parents rejecting kids like this. Happens all the time in these folk circles, especially demonic ones."

"At least my Dad's trying to be supportive."

She puts her hand on my shoulder, brushing a bit of dead skin off that formed, "He is for now. Your Mam is the real problem, Dad seems like he's easily influenced. One scary tale bout us evil demons, and he'll be against it."

"How do you know that?"

"Your horns, Sib." She replies, tapping her own. "They help amplify the vibes around you. Probably felt their emotions right? Kept ya safe?"

"Wait, that was real? I thought I was on edge."

"Yeah, that's one of your newest and greatest defense mechanisms. Can feel the feelings of others, some weird empath shite. It served ya well tonight. Give it time and a lil' skill and you'll be able to tell the fakers from the true ones."

Rubbing my horns again and yup, they're still there. It feels so strange to have something fused up there. They're so sensitive to the touch too, despite being nothing but bone. I even did a light tug, and my skull wants to move with it. The horns and my head are all one complete piece. Something new to get used to.

"Now I have to apologize for this next part, but I'm on call." Morrigan starts up again. "Need to save more lives tonight. This place is yours now too, so feel free to do whatever. Your room's ready for ya."

We go in for one more crying-infused light hug. "Thanks, Morrigan." I say through sobs.

She pulls me tight, "No problem, lad."

She gives a few final pats on my back before continuing. "I'll be back here tomorrow afternoon, can help ya more then. Maybe the others will be here too. I'll update them to let them know you're here. For now, go rest—you need it."

She walks out the door, but right before she closes it, she looks back at me with a smile, The headlights from her shitbox lighting up her body. "One more thing, lad. You're growin' up to be a wonderful deadly demon. Don't let anyone tell you otherwise."

Glad that someone's happy about this tonight.

"Now, get yourself washed and rest, your lookin' a bit bloody ya silly popper." She says before closing the door.

Oh yeah, I should do that.

This shower is taking long, but I needed it. The water feels like room temp no matter how much I turn it up. The dead skin keeps forming before the water washes it off, swirling into the drain. All I can do is sigh.

Out the shower, fresh set of clothes from my backpack, I unpack a few essential boxes from the stealth migration. One thing to be thankful for is that I got a bigger workshop table. It's one of those makeup tables with a mirror built in, but it has so much more space than the little foldable. Gonna take advantage of that as I place some of my tools and laptop on top of it.

Now that I'm no longer covered in blood, my demon self stares at me from the mirror. The scabs begin to fall off, revealing that the bone is infused with the orange skin surrounding it. This resonance shit is so weird, but at the same time it's so exciting.

My eyes flood with darkness. The horns keep widening themselves past my bangs. My smile continues to grow.

I look so fucking cool now, like some fucked up demonic gremlin. Going to look even cooler later, but I wish my parents could share this moment with me. Guess I can send a photo to my Dad later.

Sigh. Whatever.

I take another picture of myself. Maybe a few more. Okay, one more. Guess I could finally get into this whole selfie thing. Even pulled out my phone to make sure I don't spend a ton of money tonight. Gotta get a shot for a potential profile pic, right?

Pulling out a few printed photos I saved from my old room, I put them along with the new photos on the table. Something nice to look at every morning when I wake up. One of them is a photo of me as a teen, along with my dad on a fishing trip. We both looked so happy back then. Caught the biggest fish ever that day, before releasing them back to the waters.

Hope I can keep that relationship intact. Means a lot how he treated me tonight. Even thinking about it causes the tears to roll once again, but I wipe them away.

Did enough of that for one night. I just wanna sleep.

Plugging my phone into the charger on this new wooden table nightstand, honoring my time-tested tradition of tuning into some white noise.

Staring at the ceiling above me, processing the night, but eventually the new popcorn constellations help me fade off into dreamland…

PART THREE
DEMON HOOD

CHAPTER 17
HELLION
THE FABULOUS FOLD'S HOME

An unfamiliar ceiling. Sun shining through a new set of windows.

The events from last night loaded in my head—sure was covered in blood, yelling at my Mom who almost slapped me. Damn.

At least I live with friends now. That should be a great thing, right? Feels like the events of last night fucked everything up.

Sigh. Time to get out of bed. Gotta start the day.

Throwing a tank-top and pants on, I caught myself in the mirror. Yeah, these eyes definitely ain't human no more. What once was green are now fully absorbed by the darkness. In their place is a set of blue rings with a big blue plus replacing my pupils. Blinking to verify, wondering if they are real. One way to find out.

Ow.

Okay, they're real. Definitely not a cosplay contact. Maybe poking em' wasn't the best idea.

Whatever is going on with my hair, its reached my shoulders overnight. Never really had hair this long before—hair and soldering tools don't work well together—but my brown hair is fading to a blackish blue at the roots. Getting a feel as I flow my hands through the strands, and whatever the demon energy is doing makes it feel like silk. Pulling my hands out of my hair, and no loose strands. It's more durable and softer now. Wow.

The sun shines brightly on my new horns too. Last night they were pointing straight ahead, now they are bending up at a sharp right angle. Can bone bend like that? Giving it a light knock and it's rock solid, not hollow in the slightest. How did it bend up like that?

One of the many demonic mysteries I gotta solve. Maybe set up a time lapse on my phone tonight, keep track of its growth.

My orange skin continues to break out of its cocoon. A dead patch slowly falls off, graceful like cherry blossoms.

Ugh, never mind. As much as I try to beautify it, dead skin is disgusting. Gotta take care of this at some point.

New black freckles are sprinkled all over my shoulders, and honestly I love it. It's time for tank tops to make a full return. Not just sleepwear anymore!

Can't really get a full impression while my body is moving things around, but so far I love it all. Demon hood looks awesome on me. Wish my parents were happy too.

Sigh.

Nah, not right now. Enough sulking. Let's get out of this room and see what awaits me.

Opening the door as it creaks, an empty hallway greets me as I walk towards the living room. All my friends stuff lines the walls—bunches of posters, photos, and potted plants sprucing up the place. Reminders that I now live among friends. At the same time, none of this is connected to me. I still feel foreign round these parts.

Clangs of metal from the kitchen make me jump, knocking me out of my funk. Who is that? No clue, but the new horns pick up some hints. Relaxed, calm, gentle. Someone in the moment, probably making some tasty food. Knowing how calm they are, it rubs off on me as I try to peek around the corner. Who is it?

Lo and behold! It's the big yellow fella of the fold, Bud. They're making bacon and scrambled eggs, a simple American breakfast. What's not so simple about it is the amount they're making. Seems enough for an entire family or two. That smell hits me and my cravings act up again. My body is changing fast, and it cries out for more fuel.

Bud spots me in the doorway with a big grin, somehow they knew I was peeking in. They turn their body to me, widening their arms for a hug while radiating a warm feeling. If it wasn't for all these hugs the past twenty four hours, I think I would be dead.

As our hug ends, Bud gently pushes me back, a curious feeling hitting as they look at me. They shifted to excitement and wonder as Bud looks excited about my new look. They even started doing tiny claps of happiness with their hands.

Didn't need to ask if they were proud, I felt it.

They lead me to the dinner table, pulling back a seat for me. Sitting down, they point a finger up to the sky along with a feeling of patience. I think they're telling me to wait as they walk off to the kitchen, going back to the fine art of making breakfast.

I don't know how to describe that, because I didn't feel that myself, but also I did? Strange passive emotions that I know don't belong to me, but also understanding its source being Bud. Guess my horns really are some sort of empathetic antennas.

Bud returns, one big plate for each of us with silverware. They do another tour of the kitchen, arriving once again with two buffet sized plates of bacon and eggs. Oh god, there's those cravings, I need it all. Bud sits down they flash a toothy smile at me, gesturing to the food.

It's time to dig in.

Thanks to this newfound feelin' sensin' stuff, I was actually having a two-way conversation with Bud. They send emotions, and I try my hardest to send some back. Bud sends a feeling that acts like a compliment, a blend of acceptance and kindness. I try to repeat that feeling, and they respond with a twinge of confusion. Felt a bit bad about it, but Bud radiates assurance, letting me know it's okay. Do I say they said that or they felt that? Dunno, need to figure that out.

It seems like feelings were rather broad things to me when it came to naming them—happiness, sadness, anger, so on— meanwhile Bud is over here opening new doors to what feels possible.

"Finally, a way to respond to waiters with my mouth full." I said with a mouth full of eggs, Bud giggling at my joke.

In the conquest of breakfast, not a bacon bit was spared. Feels like I ate more than them. Hope they had enough cause they're way bigger than me.

They note my concern, patting their belly, sending me a relieving feeling. Ah, good.

Then, a pleasant realization hits them. What's up?

They gesture to wait a second as they move a hand to their back pocket. After a little digging, they pull out two black objects. They place one on their plate, and then the other on mine.

Wait, these are rocks. Bud placed down…charcoal? What?

Looking up to Bud, I make sure my confusion is clear.

A smile flashes on Bud's face as they pick up their piece, putting it to their mouth, one sniff before popping it in. They crunch down on it with ease, lighting up with positivity.

Why is Bud eating a rock?

They point down at my own piece, with a feeling of anticipation. Do they want me to eat that too?

Picking it up, I give it a light knock. Yep, it's the genuine thing, not sure why it wouldn't be. Even got black stains on my hands. Looking up at Bud again, I'm like a small child asking for permission. Bud gives me a thumbs up and another feeling of encouragement.

Guess I'm eating a rock today.

Putting it to my mouth slowly, the charcoal parts my lips as it begins to slide in. My tongue grazes it, and I yank it back out, expecting disgust. For some reason, the smokey flavor is, well, tasty. Now I'm more confused. That's supposed to taste bad, right?

I try again, touching it with my tongue and the flavor returns. It's bitter, yes, but that bitterness isn't hitting my taste buds the way it used to. It's size and flavor is telling me it's like a jawbreaker, begging to be cracked open.

Sliding it in, I gently bite down but the charcoal withstands it. Don't want to crack my new teeth. Just got these, y'know? Looking to Bud, they're staring at me with pure enthusiasm, big grin on their face. They're clearly enjoying my exploration, like I'm some video worth reacting to. I apply a bit more pressure, and boom!

My teeth are safe, but the rock explodes across my mouth. The taste returns tenfold, but with added variety. The earthy smoky flavor, along with the twang of bitter yet burnt—signaling to my brain that this is great. Should be coughing this out, wash my mouth in the sink, but it's strangely smooth.

Why does this taste good?

Looking at Bud for an answer, they're radiating happiness. Don't know if I can put these questions into feelings, so with my mouth full of rocks I begin asking.

"I can eat this stuff now?"

They nod up and down happily.

"Does it hurt me in any way? Like, is this bad?"

Bud shakes their head no, emitting disagreement as they make an X with their arms.

The feeling to swallow hits me, and with one quick movement, the charcoal shoots down my throat.

I'm full. Not queasy or nauseous in the slightest. I'm content.

Bud gently gets up from the table, motioning me to follow. I lick my fingers to get rid of the black stains, joining along as they lead me to the kitchen pantry.

Bud opens the pantry door, pulling out one of the rolling shelves inside. Instead of food, it's random objects. Rocks, batteries, lotions and skin oils, I even spot a few six packs of Moto Oil.

That's Morrigan's energy drink—at least, I thought it was an energy drink. Picking up a can for closer inspection, gotta say I was pretty far off the mark.

A bold yellow and black message at the top says "NOT FOR HUMAN CONSUMPTION OR VEHICLE USE." The ingredients list is stranger as it sits next to an explosive hazard icon on the back. Synthetic motor oil and food coloring.

It even has a rating, 10W-40.

There's a logo on the can signaling that "100% of donated oil is used" and is thus "environmental".

Is this culture shock I'm feeling? Humanoid transition shock? Folk shock? Is that a thing?

I can drink this now? Swallow down some charcoal? Eat the earth?

Look, I know I cleaned up the humanoid aisle at work, but I assumed the grocery items on the shelves were built for like, specialized skin care or some aroma stuff or whatever. You're telling me we *eat* this stuff? And it tastes *good*?

The world doesn't feel real right now.

A polite back pat knocks me out of it, Bud putting their hand on my shoulder opposite of them. Are they trying to ground me? Whatever the cause, my curiosity needs to be satiated.

"Is it like, nutritious or something?" I ask.

Bud continues nodding yes.

"How?"

Bud ponders for a second, before shrugging. They pretend to push imaginary glasses up their face, hands on hips like a superhero while emitting a sense of glorious pride.

"...Are you telling me to ask Sam?"

They nod up and down in agreement, along with a little chuckle.

Somehow shooting horns out and eyes becoming voids is fine, but eating random objects is what put the shock in me. It's such a foreign concept, being able to eat things like this, but now I just...can.

Cracking open the Moto Oil, I expect yellow viscous liquid,

but it's black, probably due to the food coloring and the fact it's, well, used oil. taking a sip and…

It's delicious.

The sensory feelings of a woody yet metallic taste, along with the viscous texture in my mouth tell me this is really motor oil, but there's something in it that makes my body enjoy those flavors now. My stomach, which was giving me metaphorical and literal shit for the past few days now feels great. Content and happy.

Holy shit, this is so overwhelming.

Bud notices my reality shift, grabbing my shoulders as they direct me towards the couch. Placing me on the cushions, they continue the head patting therapy. All I can really do is stare at the can in my hands.

Not a human anymore, obviously. I'm a humanoid. A folk-person. A…demon. Sipping the can again to re-verify—tasty oil, no rejection, Stomach feels healthy. I pinch myself hard on the wrist, gotta be a dream. It hurts for a second, but then the human skin rips off, more orange underneath.

This isn't a dream, it's demon hood. All of this is apart of my life now.

As my brain processes, a thought comes crashing into my skull. Why am I so shocked? This is literally what I signed up for. Got years to process this stuff, why don't I enjoy the moment now?

Taking one more look at the can, I chug the rest of the thing in one go.

Oiled up and ready to go, I ask one question. "What else can I do now?"

Bud stares at me for a second, before flashing their bright fangy grin.

Bud's first stop is outside—that big dirt field with trash on the main road. Over time I learned it's a junkyard for the local community—people dump their stuff, garbage trucks come by and pick it up before goin' to the actual dump. We're in a rural area compared to my parent's home, weird for me to see things like this right next door.

There's so much stuff here that people consider trash. Appliances, old furniture, there's even car chassis sitting here rusting. Gotta dig around here later. One human's trash is a demonic tinkerer's treasure, right?

Got even weirder cravings now since I can apparently eat these things. Looking across the junkyard, seeing rusty rebar in concrete, my first thought is "Wonder what that tastes like?"

What a weird mindset, but fuck it, I can eat whatever now. Maybe I will try tetanus.

Bud takes us to a clean patch in the yard, and there's a lot of room here. They point at the ground—a feeling of motivation —they're telling me to stand in this spot, before walking over to a junk pile. They start throwing things left and right— random shards of metal, glass windows shattering on impact, garbage bags decomposing in mid-air—but they eventually find what they're apparently aiming for. They pull out a broken washing machine, carrying it like a big cardboard box under their arm. What's the plan?

They walk to the opposite side, bout' half a football field or more, a feeling of preparation shot my way. Is something wrong?

They put the machine into both their hands, lifting it behind their head to their back, tossing it into the sky with ease.

It gets smaller and smaller in the air as it flies. Wow. Bud's gotta have some serious strength to throw junk like that.

As small as that machine got, it then began to get bigger, and it starts blocking out the sun. Hah, it's almost like it's aiming for me.

Oh. It is aiming for me.

Of course, the human in me got some obvious responses. The greatest hits like "Get out of the way!", "You'll be crushed!", and "That's going to kill you!" Good advice for frail bodies.

It doesn't account for one thing—I'm a demon now, and that side only has one thing to say.

"Yeah, I can catch that."

Bringing my arms up, my hands meet the washing machine as a loud clang goes off. My two arms pushing back like pistons as I slide a little across the ground. Inertia wearing off as I come to a complete stop.

Ths washer is light, feels like nothing in my hands. Is this even real? I put it down on a rotting bench next to me, and it immediately snaps under the pressure, crumbling from the weight.

Oh god. Bud threw a real washing machine.

I *caught* that washing machine.

Hearing the sound of clapping, It's Bud in the distance, excited at my first ever catch of something oh-so-heavy. Glad they knew I could catch that.

...They knew I could catch that, right?

After a few seconds, They gesture towards themselves. Guess I should get closer. I take a few steps, and Bud immediately puts a hand up, halting me. They imitate a baseball throw.

Oh, they want me to throw it back. Well, If I can catch it, I sure as hell can throw it, right?

The washer is once again in my hands, no clue how much energy to put into this toss. Bud's huge body makes it easier for them, but as a five foot six gremlin, I can't afford the same luxury.

My mind goes to online videos, bottle tossing? Nah, wrong style. Don't think you can underhand throw a washing machine that far.

What about those athletes doing those disc spin throws? They spin a few times in a circle before letting go. If I wanna throw it back, feels like that's the only way.

Repositioning the washer in my hands, the top points towards Bud as I take a few steps back. Their curiosity is felt from over here, and it's about to be answered. I run a few steps up, spinning in circles before eventually throwing it directly at Bud.

Oh shit, too much energy.

The washing machine speeds towards Bud like a ballistic missile. Bud's surprise travels faster as they squat down like a football player, ready to take the full force.

A god awful crunch is heard as it impacts. Bud slides back a few feet as their boots dig deep into the dirt, grooves forming on the field as the washing machine almost disintegrates in their hands.

Oh god, did I throw it too hard?

Eventually, their body slows, coming to a halt right before they fall into a rusty patch of metal. After a quiet few seconds, Bud's stance defuses as the washer crashes on the ground, two deep hand-sized dents on the top being the only thing keeping it together.

Their worry fades—pretending to wipe their forehead with a sense of calm. They're okay. My nervousness turned into laughter.

Let's find something smaller to toss, shall we?

Small vending machines, engine blocks, barrels of mystery fluid, all tossed with glee as we enjoy our time together. Maybe I had a lil' sip of those barrels, who cares? I'm a demon now.

Bud weirdly tosses a car door at one point, feeling it tug and rip into my skin. Checking it in shock, I realize it revealed more demonic orange underneath. My new skin is flawless, yet the human skin above is ripped off. Fuck yeah. The games continue as I shed.

After re-arranging the junkyard with our shenanigans and Bud teaching me how to clean up and sort the yard, they signal that it's time to move on.

As I walk up to Bud wondering what's next, they lift me up, placing me on their shoulders. God, this feels weird, haven't done something like this since I was five. My Dad would do this at theme parks and stuff.

Oh. I miss my Dad.

Bud throws me a questioning vibe, asking if I'm good. Gotta throw em' back a thumbs up, shaking those thoughts out of my head. Now's the time to embrace my demon self, not the human past.

Bracing my legs, they look to the forests nearby, and before I could ask they start charging in. Felt like a roller coaster as we speed past various sizes of pine trees and squirrels rushing up them. The Night of Passage comes to mind, but I'm not alone this time—I got Bud.

One mad dash later—even a jump or two—Bud slams their feet down in the middle of the forest, boots once again dragging into the dirt to a full stop. They pick me up off their shoulders, and put me next to them as we take in the forest together.

Unlike my passage, the forest feels so alive. Wildlife scurries around as squirrels jump from branch to branch. The sounds of birds chirping in the distance as they call to one another. There's even a creek nearby that intersects a lil' lake. Look, a lil' waterfall! Fun to see fish jumping to the top as they try to migrate.

Always been a homebody, but it feels great to be outside today. Must be that calm spring weather. Could probably stand here forever if I want, taking it all in, but Bud pings me, wanting my attention as they point to a cave.

"As you can tell, didn't really pack any spelunking gear today." I gesture to myself. Laughing at my joke, Bud walks into the entrance as they fade into the darkness.

Uh, did they want me to follow? Walking up through the cave entrance, it wasn't really as dark as I thought—'bout as bright as it is outside. That makes no sense, but okay.

Took me a sec, but I spot Bud. For some reason they're black and white. Wait, everything's black and white.

"Where's the color?" I ask.

They take out their cellphone, turning on the screen. The screen lights up with a rainbow of hues, and as they put it close to their face, their skin turns back to regular yellow. What the heck?

Bud notices my confusion as they offer one more hint—they point at their eyes. Their hair is covering them, but I got it.

"We can see in the dark?"

Bud nods, giving two thumbs up.

Another fun demon perk, hell yeah. Not really an eye doc, but since there's no light down here, is this some weird Infrared/UV thing?

Whatever, enough theorizing—gonna go spelunking instead.

Didn't know there was caves in the area, let alone this deep. No reason to go down em anyway. The horror stories of people gettin' stuck scare the shit out of me.

I'm a demon now though, can't get stuck like silly humans can. We can probably eat our way out of the cave, I'm sure of it.

Bud knew the cave well, keeping me on the right path as I gather a few cool rocks for myself. We turn a corner and there's a set of tools sitting ontop of a rock.

Different styles of pickaxes, shovels, and cleaning supplies placed ontop of a rectangular looking slab. With these tools, Bud must've made the big rock slab table they sit on. Even got some fancy looking designs engraved into the stone. Didn't realize Bud was such an artist.

Grabbing tools from the slab, we spent the next few hours yearning for the mines, gemstones coming off the walls so easily with our demonic strength. Due to the weird mono-chrome vision, I couldn't tell what colors they were, but hey—gems were gems.

I got into a real flow. Gotta crack em all off the walls. It was too damn fun. Didn't realize how much I was doin' till a hand lays upon my shoulder. Bud emits A feeling of preservation, but I got the gist.

"Only take what we need?" I ask.

They nod in agreement.

Not sure what we need them for, but with enough rocks, we put the tools back and ascend.

My eyes are having a terrible time with the sunlight, taking way longer to adjust than going into the dark. Really reminds me of those video game flashbangs; A blaze of white slowly fading a forest into view.

My vision returns, and the sight before me freezes me in place.

A group of deer is right in front of us—two full grown adults and a lil' guy eating all the grass. The lil' fella looks different from their parents—white, pink nose with red eyes.

Don't wanna scare them off, but Bud casually walks past. One of the big deer stops grazing to look at us both, before returning to their salad of grass and flowers. Must be worth it to ignore two threats like us. Almost like they don't even care.

Bud places down the cave rocks before walking up to the group. The deer barely react, once again curious, but not hesitant.

Bud places a hand on one, petting it before looking over to me. They're waving to come closer. Are they socialized or something? Walking up to the deer, the white one stares up at me, and what felt like a direct to home-video princess movie, it nuzzles my chest like I'm one of theirs.

Could be smited by God for being a little demonic freak I am and be okay—this lil' guy gave me a deer hug. At least their parents let them hang out with us demons.

Theories keep flowing in my head. Are demons chill with animals? Did Bud train these deer to be socialized? Not sure, and at this point I don't want to look a gift horse in the mouth —or I guess a gift deer. Hah.

While we relax together, I found a tree to lay down next to, and seconds later the deer joined in. My own kinda heaven, or I guess as a demon, my own kinda hell? That sounds weird. Nevermind.

Back in my human era, I couldn't relax in nature. All sorts of sensory issues growing up—everything's too hot or cold, bugs were annoying, and dear God the textures of everything—it's one of the main reasons I stuck to computers and tinkering. Easily controlled sensory input.

Now? None of that is a problem. The breeze is nice, nothing to bother me except the kind animals, and the spring temps barely mess with me. Gonna be real, Since I can eat random stuff and the thermometer went wild the other day, my internal temperature has gotta be at least 100 times hotter than whatever the Earth can throw at me. Not only am I hot, I'm molten.

God, I love being a demon. Can't believe it took me this long to shed my shitty human form. Why the hell was I so worried? Closing my eyes, embracing this wonderful nature with no limitations. For the first time I can actually do that. The wind blew across the lands of Comfort, and I'm ready to have my own piece of it.

Time passes, honestly lost track as I fell into a quiet zen. The thing that brought me back was the sound of hooves hitting the dirt. The deer stood up, staring at our demonic duo. They all move their heads down to the ground, lifting one leg up, before placing it back down as they stare back at us. What are they doing?

Don't really have time to figure it out as the deer begin prancing off into the forest. The white one gives me one long glance before joining them. Hope they enjoy their future grazing spot, or maybe they're going back home. Do deer have homes?

Eh, whatever. Gonna keep taking this moment in. The sounds from the forest are a nice replacement for my phone's white noise, and I'm gonna close my eyes once again, taking a second to relax…

Bud pokes me, and now a bold yellow shoots across the forest. Did I fall sleep? Pulling my phone out to check the clock, and a whole day blew past, damn.

Bud sends me some questioning, pointing their thumb to the way we came. Probably wondering If I'm ready to go back.

"Yeah, think I am." I reply, yawning with a stretch as I get back on my feet.

We pick up our cave plunder, walking back as today's adventure comes to an end. Glad Bud and I were finally able to properly connect. Didn't realize how talkative they are, but I guess you need to know how they feel.

At the house, Bud lets me sample one of the rocks we collected as they pop a small one in their mouth. Guess these are for eating, so why not try it out?

Despite my theories, amethyst does not taste like grape. It tastes like vitamin supplements honestly.

"Hey Bud, why do we eat this stuff instead of human food anyway? They're both fine, right?"

They smile while raising their arm, brown craggy rocks on their skin.

"Did you get those from eating rocks?"

They nod yes.

"Besides looking cool, what do the rocks do?"

Bud makes a finger gun with their hand, pretending to fire it, a finger-shaped bullet bouncing off their rocky elbow, emitting a protective feeling.

Interesting defense mechanism, not sure what Bud would need it for. Would be cool to have my own set though. Minerals are apart of a healthy diet, right?

A few minutes later, the Sun hits the horizon as we toss wood into the fire pit. No matches or oil though, how are they gonna light it?

They place their hand on the wood, and with a few seconds of concentration, the logs set themselves on fire. Morrigan was doing that with cigarettes, but didn't realize you can light stuff that big too.

"Can you teach me that?" I ask.

Bud smiles and nods.

We threw some feelings around while cooking some s'mores. Apparently the sweetness of marshmallow goes really well with capacitors. Gives it a good buzzy kick. Bud meanwhile enjoys their blend of rocks and sugar.

After a few bites, they throw me another marshmallow as they grab one themselves. Positioned between their fingers in one hand, they emit a feeling akin to a raging fire, not anger though. It feels positive, but has a bit more oomph added to it. It reminds me of hyperfixating, but something more emotional than logical. What's the name of that?

The feeling increases, before the marshmallow ignites in their fingers. They gesture with their free hand—like showing off a magic trick right before popping it in their mouth, flame and all.

Meanwhile, my hands didn't seem to co-operate—I thought about my workshop projects like the camera, or even combos in Knight Night Fight I've been practicing.

I'm shooting out sparks, but no flame. I'm a demon right? Shouldn't I know how to do this?

They pat me on the shoulder, along with a feeling of patience. Maybe it's a skill I gotta train up, maybe it'll work later. Fine, whatever. For now, we sit together by the fire, watching the sky fade into stars.

As the sun finally leaves the horizon, Morrigan's shitbox rolls up. The loud music cuts out, and she steps out of the car with a big smile. We both wave as she plops down in a chair next to us. "How's today's adventure been, lads?" She starts off.

"Way better than last night." I reply, while Bud gives the OK hand gesture. Morrigan then looks me up and down, "Dang, sib, you're lookin more like a big strong creature every time I see ya! Did ya get a new pair of eyes?"

I shrug, "Maybe a little, probably found the right contacts."

She snorts. "Finally, your special brand!" making me laugh harder. Our recaps of the day continue as the stars come out to play.

As conversation dies down, Morrigan pulls out a carton of cigs. She hands Bud one, before attempting to give me one.

"Nah, thanks, I don't smoke. You should know that by now."

Morrigan looks over at Bud quietly, shaking the box. Bud shakes their head no.

"Ahh, okay. No worries." she replies, sliding the carton back into her jacket pocket.

Huh? "What was that about?" I ask.

Morrigan lights her cig up before blowing a bunch of smoke towards the bonfire. "Ah, nothing too important really. Bud and I aren't sure how far your transformation is, but once ya get more demon-fied you can probably handle some smoke."

"Smoke? Like cigarette smoke?"

"Nah, smoke in general." She replies. Not sure how to take that, and she notices. "Ya know how the demon folktales describe us as being in 'fire and brimstone' all the time? Apparently if ya live in such places, you gotta get good at breathin' that."

"Those stories do love putting us in fiery spots, but what does that have to do with smoke?" I ask.

Morrigan smirks as she lays back in the chair."So, with your incredible heat resistance, along with your new insides judging by the fact your eatin' techy bits, you can probably breathe a lot more things without any problems."

That makes no sense. "But what about cancer? Or like—"

"Nah." Morrigan moves the cig to her hand before continuing. "Us demons got pretty good healing…stuff. Bodies are so hot that we kinda bypass all that human ailment shite. Ya ain't gonna get the common cold, flu, and even cancer anymore. It's basically a cure for everythin' wrapped up in a lil' demonic bow. Why do ya think us demons get jobs in dangerous places? We can breathe, drink, and eat whatever, can take a hit or two while delivering a few of our own, and companies like not gettin' sued for it."

She does another drag, then a gentle blow. "I ain't the best teacher for the science demon shite. Know that if ya get a little smoke you'll be fine. It's one reason why I'm a firefighter. When somethin's burnin down, My eyes let me see through the smoke, breathing it gives me calm and focus, and my strength saves lives."

The winds begin to shift. The bonfire that was once billowing to the sky changes its trajectory, targeting me once again. Why does it always aim for me every chance it gets? Didn't even have a chance to react as smoke hits me full force.

Got a full breath of smoke straight to the lungs. I was awaiting a coughing fit, trying to stand up and move, but the feeling never came. Instead, calmness takes me. I open my eyes, the smoke isn't hurting them either. Physically overwhelmed by the smoke in the bonfire, but all it is giving me is a sense of pure relaxation. Why?

The realization hits me once more today, a nail that needed to be hammered in a few more times:

I'm not human anymore.

Human concerns about health don't apply.

I am a full-blooded, horn-carrying, object-eating, emotion-sensing, washing-machine-throwing, and now smoke-breathing strong as fuck demon.

"Huh." I said, the gears in my brain finally processing. Something snaps in my head.

Morrigan's curiosity spikes as she looks at me. Not sure if it's the calmness of the smoke or the repeating realizations all day, but I fall quiet, getting closer to the bonfire before crouching down next to it.

Concern coming off of Morrigan and Bud behind me escalates, but I gotta push that out of focus. Just want to deal with my feelings for a bit.

Looking at my right arm, it's a pale human white, a hole where I pinched my wrist along with the junkyard damage, patches begin to form at the edges of tears. My hand still has that scar.

I want to test something.

I lift my arm up, slowly pushing it towards the fire. The human side of me begs that I don't. I'll get burned, cry out in pain, and have an embarrassing trip to the ER. The heat feels like nothing though, and as my hand touches the flames, no pain either.

The flame tickles my fingers as I wiggle them. Rotating my hand, flexing it into a fist and back, awaiting any sort of pain receptors going off, charred skin, or third-degree burns.

Nothing but the slightest feeling of warmth. That, and my human skin flakes off into ashes.

Pulling my hand out, all of the human skin has been burned off, revealing a completely orange skin tone.

I'm unharmed.

My wrists have some newly formed sigils on my skin. Black stripes that look like two small rubber bands surrounding one sweat band, but drawn onto my skin like a tattoo. The big stripe even has a little pattern of plus and minuses alternating.

My humanity is being shed in real time, and I'm feeling fucking *fantastic* about it.

Why not my other arm? Sticking it into the flames too—rotating like rotisserie—and it's the same result. White replaced with orange. Skin flakes burn in the air, no smell of weak human flesh.

"Uhh, Sib, ya good?" Morrigan asks, concern reaching her voice. Yeah, I'm doin' *fuckin* great. Not in the mood to talk though, too busy with this.

Enjoying the orange and black freckle goodness, I stare back down at the fire, spotting a smoldering log that got spent hours ago. Picking it up, it's like anything that burns long enough, a dead white ash coating its exterior. It's flaky, rough, inferior.

Rotating it in my hand, I give it a tiny squeeze. It breaks open, insides pouring out on my palm. Bright orange interior, burning strong, able to set fire to the world. Applying more pressure, it continues to break down in my hands, orange embers falling into the pit.

Oh, there it is.

The answer I needed. It's so simple too! Why didn't I think it sooner? The pieces of the log roll off my hand, crashing into the bonfire as it left stains of ash on my fingers.

"I figured it out." I say, standing up as I watch the fire.

"Uh, figured what out, Sib?" Oh, Morrigan's concern keeps elevating, Even Bud's worry is rising. They don't need to worry. They're all gonna be psyched when they realize it too. Why not make it a fun reveal?

Standing there quietly, wanting to create a dead air of mystery, I jump around to meet them face-to-face, big toothy grin, hands on my hips. I even startle Morrigan in her chair, almost causing her to fall over, while Bud looks at me with curiosity. It's time for the surprise!

"My name is EMBER! I'm a motherfucking, badass, take no shit from anyone demon!" Morrigan and Bud sit there quietly, feeling the gears turn in their head.

What? I decided on my name. C'mon, where's the reaction?

Morrigan calmly gets up and walks up to me. She's quiet, wonder if I said something wrong, but a smirk appears on her face. She wraps her arm around my back by surprise, Turning towards Bud as we now stand side-by-side.

"LETS FECKIN HEAR IT FOR EMBER!" She shouts, shooting her fist up in the air.

With her acceptance, my own fist joins hers. Bud is feeling ecstatic, getting up from the ground to rush towards us.

Bud yoinks me from Morrigan's arm, almost taking her with me as they spin me around in celebration—a carousel of joy. Even got me a lil bit dizzy when they put me back down for a big hug. I guess demons can get a little dizzy, but gotta shake it off.

Fucking love my fellow demons. So glad that I found them, helping me get rid of my shitty human form. Us demons don't need that shit. I wish Sam wasn't on another business trip dealing with human bullshit so she can celebrate this with us. Fuck humanity and their bullshit legalities.

Who needs humanity anyway? Don't need no humans.

I need my Fold.

I need the flames.

I must breathe in the smoke.

I have to consume the Earth.

Nothing can stand in my way—I'll crush it.

I'll be sure to make my presence to the world known. Here comes Ember, demon born of flame and fire. Not only that, but now apart of the greatest Fold ever spawned on this here earth, our little friendly dominion made just for us.

As we're celebrating, I gotta pull out my phone to play some tunes. Whatever it is, it's gotta be loud. Found a playlist, throwing it on shuffle and blasting it up to max volume before laying it down on my chair.

Looking up, I notice Morrigan texting someone on her phone, a somewhat serious sensation coming from her. How strange, but she should relax! It's celebration time!

"C'mon Morrigan, let's celebrate! We gotta party!" I shout cheerfully.

"One second Ember! Lettin' Sam know about your new name before I join in!" She replies.

Hell yeah, let her know. She should be here too, but fucking humans make it difficult for us to thrive. Fuck them all.

Can't believe it took me this long to set fire to this human form. What was I so afraid of? I am a god damned demon. No human can make me feel pain and suffering anymore. No one can make me feel ashamed. I am who the fuck I am.

Nothing will ever make me feel terrible ever again.

I won't allow it.

CHAPTER 18
DEMON MANIA
THE FABULOUS FOLD'S HOME

The sun rises from the window as my soldering iron pieces together another set of copper. Another incredible day as a demon begins.

Hell fucking yeah.

Who fucking needs sleep anyway? Sleep is for weak humans.

Chuggin' down another can of Moto Oil, I throw it to the rest of the cans. Gonna eat those later when I get hungry.

Been starting some projects that I finally got time for. The fun shit, real experimental. One of them is an automatic can opener, but instead of cans I want to cut cloth and paper with it instead. Automation! It's the future! Hard to get the paper and cloth fed in properly, but I'll find a way!

Another project involves one of those robot toys I found in the dump. Gotta modify its little computer, make it do anything I want! Fuck, let's make it do a backflip! Tried to code something in Python for a microcontroller, but it's all a fucking mess. Might have to rebuild the whole thing. I can do that easily.

Now the third one I gotta admit, it's a bit funny. Re-wiring a TV remote to use as a game controller. Can you imagine pranking people by—

A hand lays upon my shoulder. It's Morrigan, concern coming off her once again. "Hey, Ember. did ya sleep, even for a wink?" She asks.

"Nope!" I respond. "Finally had free time for all these projects so I thought, why not start them all right now? See—over here is what I call the paper opener, where instead of cans it—"

"Ember. You need your sleep." She says sternly. "Strong demons like yerself stay strong by taking care of themselves."

"But I'm not tired! I've been in a really inventive mood for the past few hours. Look at all the stuff I'm making!" I move aside to show off my workbench full of new projects. Yeah, sure, there's a few more cables and boards lying around than I normally have out, but I'll clean it up. No worries.

Her concern didn't fade off, but she smiles. "That's great Ember, but don't ya think it's time for a break? C'mon, let's go to the living room. We can watch some movies or something while ya relax. How about a first time viewing of *The Best Boys*? Get your mind off tech for a sec!"

Why is she trying to stop me? Doesn't she see how awesome these projects are?

"I'm fine, thanks. Enjoy the movie!" I say. hopefully that's all she needs.

Back to soldering. Not needing a face mask or a fume extractor is so liberating, can get real close when I solder things now. Tinning and soldering a wire with extreme precision. It's so fucking awesome being a demon. Hell yeah.

Morrigan sighs, "Yeah, fine, okay. Keep working on your stuff. Can ya at least come out of your room to eat? You're hungry, feel it on ya."

"Got that covered. Was going to eat these in a bit." Pointing down at the empty cans of Moto Oil.

Felt a light annoyance from her, before it slowly fades. "Ember...Next time you want a can, please ask. If I knew you would get a liking for em' I would've gotten enough for both of us."

"Yeah, of course, whatever." Tryin' to focus on this remote project here. The hard part about this is that game consoles have that weird controller security stuff that locks out a lot of third party devices. Fucking cowards are afraid of people like me with big ideas. If I got a hold of a first party controller from—

The desk slides away from me as my chair spins, soldering tool dropping onto the table. What greets me is Morrigan crouching down, staring face-to-face with me with a aggravated glare.

"Ember…this is gonna sound weird coming from me, but you gotta be a bit more polite." She starts off. "I ain't some shite human here to feck your shite up. We're demons of the same fold."

This conversation should've ended already. "Yeah, I get it. I'll ask next time. Jeez, sorry Mom." I reply.

I felt her anger spike, but then felt something inside her push it back down. "Ember, you really need to choose your next words carefully. Trying to be open with ya like I usually am. You're not really being yourself right now, and I'm trying really hard to help. Don't mind if you work on whatever tech things ye got going over there on the table, but I think you should at least rest if ya been at it all night. Even a simple nap might help ya clear any roadblocks with those things."

"Not being myself right now?" I reply. "Duh. I'm a demon now, not the shitty human I started our relationship off with. I'm trying to figure out what myself even is. Currently? I make cool shit." I turn back over to the desk, moving the soldering iron from the pad to a holder.

"I don't get why you're acting so weird with me all of the sudden. I just moved in and everything but like, am I already annoying to you?"

Morrigan rubs her temples, "No, Ember, ya aren't annoying—"

"Then why do I feel it right off of you?" I turn back to her, raising my voice. "It reminds me of my parents, they didn't know what to do with me. Annoyed at my little toys. Wanted me to move on and do other things. Be a certified electrician or an angel or something. I want something fun to do and they wanted to turn it into a job."

"I'm not your feckin' parents." Morrigan retorts. "Ember, please listen. By 'not being yourself' I meant you're acting a bit weird since your parents ran ya out. I understand you're finding yourself out right now. I'm glad, and I wanna embrace it, but you're feelin' a bit off. I want to help—"

"You can help by leaving me alone and letting me work." I say, giving her a push as I spin my chair back to the work-shop table. Why is Morrigan being such a bitch right now? We're demons. We're supposed to help each other.

A ringtone blares from my phone. answering it on speaker phone as I perform more wire work. "Hello?"

"Where the hell are you E█████?"

It's Derrick, shit. Forgot to do last night's shift. Did I have one today too? Don't remember, been too busy with more important things.

"Uh, wasn't able to get there unfortunately. Too busy dealing with life stuff." I respond.

"What do you mean life stuff? Some of our freezers broke down last night and—"

"And why the hell is that my problem right now?" I cut him off.

"What did you say?" He stutters on the other side.

"I said—" I brought the phone close. "—Why the *fuck* do you think it's my problem right now? I'm off the clock. Either call a repairman or wait for my shift."

Actually nah, fuck this guy. I'm tired of him using me like this. Let me push this further. "In fact, give me a pay raise so I'll keep repairing things for you, or I quit."

"What's gotten into you lately? First your fighting our customers then—"

"I'm a fucking demon now, Derrick. You're a shitty little human. I don't need to be under your control anymore. I'm better than you."

I hear nervous stammering across the phone line "Now listen here, E███. I know we have a friendly relationship and we don't want to involve the, uh, 'neighborhood watch' in this. I know you're one of the more agreeable of us so we can talk—"

I'm nuking it.

"I am not aggressive, Derrick—I'm just honest. Now, let me be honest with *you*. For years, all the employees under your watch had to tolerate your shitty mismanagement. Every missed piece of stock, pharmacists skipping lunch because of your batshit operating hours and staffing, the times we all requested vacation and you said no—that piles up. People talk when you're not around, Derrick. No one really likes you. Sure, people put a smile on in your presence, say yes sir, do whatever you asked, but no one likes you, let alone respects you. They know you are the only thing standing between them and the money they need to live, and will do a little job dance for you to get it. They hate you. I *hate* you. Go fuck yourself and your humanist group of nazis you piece of shit. Don't call me again. Send my last paycheck on time for once or I'll come down there and get it myself."

I hang up, going back to work on my projects.

"Ok, I'm done with this." Morrigan says, feeling her angrily brew behind me. "Get up Ember. Let's go outside, get some fresh air. You need it."

"I'm good." Too busy with this copper wire right now.

"That wasn't a request, Ember." She cuts back. "You need a fresh scenery change. A reset. Something to clean the mind. Let's walk and talk, please." Can't stand her energy right now.

"You gonna throw me out like my Mom if I don't?" I say, rolling up some excess wire.

Oh, there's that panic again.

Two arms wrap around my arms and chest, lifting me straight out of my chair. Those arms belong to Morrigan, arms locked tight around me as she carries me out of the room. She's headed towards the front door.

"What the fuck are you doing?!" I shout kicking backwards, but my feet don't connect. Morrigan's way taller than me, so I can't reach anything from this height.

"I'm giving ya a reality check!" She responds, pulling open the front door with her foot and entering the front yard with me in tow.

The sun is shining right above us as she starts lowering me onto the grass outside. The moment my feet touch the ground, I burst out of her arms, creating distance between us.

"What the fuck is your problem?!" I shout.

"You think I'm actin like your Mam?" Her fierce anger is bubbling as she speaks. "I know I'm feckin up this whole 'gentle touch' shite with the state you're in—probably will get a huge mouthful from Sam—but you clearly need to take out some feelings on something. Let's change tactics and fix that, right here, right now. No hiding away with your fancy tech tools."

She extends her arms out in a dramatic pose, gesturing towards herself. "Let's have a friendly spar. Show me what ya feeling, vividly express it to me. Let me help you help yourself."

Oh ho ho! She wants a fucking fight, huh? Our battles in the barcade come to mind—sloppy button masher, bet she's not much better in real life. "Fine. Whatever. As long as it lets me get back to my projects." I grind my feet into the dirt, then charge right at her.

My fist misses, Morrigan dodging as a tug pulls on my shirt. She pulls me back before spinning around, tossing me back to where I started. I don't fall on my ass, but I do stumble.

"Question one—" Morrigan brushes her hands together, "—do ya love your Mam and Dad?"

"What the fuck is this, physical therapy? Those shitty humans threw me out. Why would I care?" Running up again for another punch, this time accounting for her dodge. Her reaction time is quicker though as she grabs my fist mid-flight, tugging me to her before grabbing my whole arm, throwing me to the opposite side of where I started. I lost my balance as I stumble around once again.

"Yet you're obviously upset!" She claims. "People who don't care don't get mad. You felt what your dad was goin' through, right? He didn't want you to leave. Despite whatever tangents he bounces to next, he loves ya for who you are —even if you're actin' like this right now."

"Shut the fuck up!" I shout. I'll get her this time. Waiting till she dodges, and when she makes her move, I'll counter it.

There's her dodge before I even threw a fist, now the counter. My fist grazes her jacket as my fist hits the air. My momentum crashes me into the ground.

I slowly spin around on the ground, getting my bearings as Morrigan towers above me.

"You love your parents, Ember." She proclaims.

Why the fuck is she not fighting? She's being annoying with words.

"They took care of you since you were a wee lad. Fed ya, clothed ya, and as much as they are confused by your tinkerin' passions, they helped ya get into it. Despite the terrible shite they put ya through that night and their sheer incompetence otherwise, you love them now. Admit it, Ember."

As I slowly get up from the ground, those memories start playing in my head. My dad buying me my first screwdriver and bit set, I was so excited that I disassembled my old game console and broke some flex cables instantly.

Another memory, both of my parents proud as I got second place at the middle school science fair. I built a contraption that was designed to water plants weekly, all you needed to do was fill the container next to it. If the school bullies didn't pop the pipe with tacks, causing it to wet itself on demonstration, I probably would've been first.

I'm back in reality on my two feet, but it feels like she's right behind me. Need to counter. Throwing a fist, the only thing that greets me is the spring air. Where is she?

Looking around, and she's now where I am at the start of this. Fuck it.

"Ok fine, Morrigan." I yell. "I love my parents; even though they hurt me. Now come fight me like you wanted."

"Question Two—" Morrigan starts off again. God, shut the fuck up.

Another attempt at a punch, and another miss. It's like she's toying with me at this point. "—Why did ya want to be a demon?"

My breathing starts to get louder "Humanity made me weak." Another punch, another miss. "It made me worthless —" Swing and a miss. "—no one fucking cared about me. Pushed me around like a fucking rag doll." The air continues to receive my wrath.

"Ah, but that's the thing!" Morrigan says, dodging the latest fist. "Us demon folk met you as a weak lil' human. We didn't care about your humanity, yet we gladly let ya into our life, enjoying the grand demonic craic. Tell me the actual reason."

"That IS the fucking reason!" I'm tired of missing, it's tiring me out. Why won't she throw a punch?

"C'mon, Ember. We both know you're smarter than this. You know why you chose the demonic side. Breathe, give it a think, then speak it!"

It's hard to catch my breath now, and Morrigan's questioning has my mind trailing off. Guess my life can only really be summed up in one word.

Rejection.

School kids found me weird, bullies beat me up for it, adults infantilize me to suppress it. No one treated me like a human being, and they pat themselves on the back for it. They figured out how to work around me, not with me. I was human only in appearance, and even then that was debatable.

Figured out the only way to get any sort of relationship going with a human, even a small friendship, is to hold yourself back. Gotta suppress your passions, limit the info-dumping, listen to music you barely enjoy, watch movies for shitty superhero universes you barely understand. The only goal is to be relatable. You had to kill your inner self to get the one thing you needed: simple platonic affection.

Spoiler alert! Those relationships will never last, and when the spark fades that mask you put on will be so hard to take off. They're off on their own adventures, and I'm left behind trying to remember what "me" even is.

Later on in life, a Doc drops the whole late autism diagnosis on me. It clicks why people didn't comprehend me—I was never going to be human to them. Different social cues, my hatred of stupid sensations and sounds, not being able to comprehend a simple emotion while having too many of my own.

Different rules. Different guidelines.

These differences made me a weird little freak to them. Not a human despite playing the role of one. Not a someone, a something.

It's probably why I relate to these folks so much. I may not of had a fluffy dog tail, horse legs, or even a lizard tongue, but when it came to dehumanization, we might as well been part of the same family.

Despite the relatability, All those variants I passed by in life didn't really click. None of them fit my style, felt like that human cage was my fate.

That is until the night at Taco Hell, the fold found me randomly. Morrigan crashed into that booth chair, and for the first time in my life, I saw people who identified with me and embraced it. I saw these "evil devils" as my mom calls them helping those who couldn't help themselves, even at the detriment of their own enjoyment.

I saw people who were strong mentally, physically, emotionally, finding those like me who didn't know what to make of myself and offered a space to start.

A genuine friendship.

Friendship that respected differences, embraces changes, embraced me. I saw the badass horns that signified protection and kindness, and wanted a pair of my own.

Here I was trying to throw punches at someone who wanted me to be apart of it. All because my human family wouldn't give me that same kindness. My shitty outburst probably looks like a small child—angry they didn't get what they wanted from their parents.

But I'm actually an abused dog—got hit too many times, being afraid of the hand that pets, needing to bite it instead. Afraid of the affection given by those who love me because I've gotten hurt too many times.

Must of been standing there for a few minutes thinking all of this. There's tears rolling down my face, the sound of sizzling as those drops land on my chest. Morrigan stood there, that rowdy anger a second ago replaced with sympathy. She felt my turmoil, and doesn't know how to react. I owe her an answer.

"I wanted to be a demon because it was the only time I felt correct. Felt loved without any judgment. And..." My voice fell out, my mouth couldn't form words due to some weird fuckin immense emotion. What is it? I can't think of the name, but it's strong.

Tears started flowing harder, sizzles from my warm cheeks as I walk up to her. She stood firm, didn't have to dodge me anymore—not like I could throw a punch anyway.

Whether it was because I didn't sleep last night, or the fact that I'm about to explode right now, I collapse on top of Morrigan.

"Woah, Ember!" She shouts, grabbing me before I crash on the floor. My horns instead land on her upper chest.

"I want to be me." I try to utter. "I finally feel like I can be myself with y'all. This fold is full of people who never abandoned me, even when I am acting like a terrible fucking monster now…" That's all I could really say before I started sobbing.

"Never *ever* call yourself a feckin monster." Her voice got stern. "You're a demon, and us demons can feck up sometimes. Take it from me."

I felt her hand rub the back of my head, fingers flowing through my hair while holding me close, it's calming.

"Despite how much we feck up, say somethin' stupid, or cause fights, we always pick each other back up. Never forget that."

We were quiet like this for who knows how long. Her kindness rejuvinating my strength, allowing my legs to keep me balanced—the warm arms around me feeling like a comfort I missed for years.

Eventually, she pats me on the back."C'mon, lad, let's go inside and get ya comfortable. You need it." We wrap our arms behind eachother, helping me walk back inside.

Morrigan sat me down on the couch, weak body crashing into the cushions as the sleep debt catches up with me. Feels like I ran a marathon as my muscles barely move.

She came back a minute later, snacks and drinks in hand, even a microwaved meal. She pressed a few buttons on the remote and a movie popped up. It was—of course—*The Best Boys*, as promised.

As my crying turned into sniffling, Morrigan offered me a can of her Moto' Oil. "Here, last one. You take it."

I push her hand back, "No thanks. I had too much and honestly, I'm sick of it now."

She grins at me, the anger she built up earlier now non-existent. "Okay, sib. At least have the meal I threw in the microwave. Deadly creatures like yerself need to eat."

I look down at the highly-processed sailsbury steak in a plastic tray. Yeah, I could eat something that looks like food.

The steak went first, followed by the green beans. The meal even has one of those little sprinkled brownies. The processed sugary shit taste of those things bring up memories of late night human football matches with Dad.

I barely cared for the game—the big city whatevers vs the capitol whoevers every week—but it allowed our family to have a calm night together. He made these meals for us when the games ran too long, but always found a way to let me have his brownie.

All my energy went to eating, couldn't focus on what's going on in this scene. Huge explosions, one of the dog soldiers bite down on a nazi's neck as they rip it open, too tired really to figure it all out. I bite into the tray now that it's empty. Salis-bury flavored macroplastics, I guess.

A loud explosion from the surround speakers shakes me out of my stupor. A bulldog soldier is dragging an injured golden retriever folk across the ground, a wartorn cobblestone street up in smoke. As a nazi's sniper scope aims directly at the group, the bulldog throws the retriever in first before taking a shot directly in the shoulder. The impact causes him to fall towards the cover where his injured ally lies.

"Sir!" The injured golden retriever shouts.

The bulldog grabs his own shoulder as it bleeds, sitting himself up on the wall alongside him as he grunts in pain. "Ah, I've had worse."

"Why did you risk that to save me? You could've died to those kraut bastards!" the retriever pleads.

"Because private…" The bulldog starts off.

"…A good boy doesn't leave others behind." Morrigan and the bulldog say in unison.

She chuckles to herself before taking a sip of Moto Oil.

Ate what I could, and with that final bit of energy spent my body comes crashing down on the couch. my head accidentally lands on Morrigan's leg. She didn't mind it, sliding it closer for me as I use it as a pillow, her kindness flowing through me to let me know it was okay.

The last thing I remember is the squad blowing open the snipers nest with a well placed grenade. As the scene calms, my mind fades to dreamland.

CHAPTER 19
THE CHECK UP
THE FABULOUS FOLD'S HOME

It's dark, and I'm still on the couch. Blankets cover me as they guard my new skin. Morrigan's leg replaced by an actual pillow. What time is it?

Sitting up and yup, it's night time. Rubbing my eyes as they hurt, it seems like no one is inside, but through the window there's a fire. The bonfire must be going. They're all outside having fun probably.

Good. After the mess I became earlier, rather be alone for now. They probably will pick up on my emotions soon, but gonna have this quiet time to myself while it lasts.

Fuck, why did I take those feelings out like that? Why did I enter a fistfight with Morrigan of all people?

God, I'm fucking terrible. I need to leave this place. I don't want to be a burden. I don't want to hurt anyone like I almost did.

Unfortunately, I'm too tired to get up and run away, so feeling like shit on the couch it is—holding the pillow between my arms. Why the fuck am I so stupid? God dammit. I'm a danger to everyone.

My feelings must've activated their radar, cause the front door begins to open.

"Hey, Ember." Sam says, confirming my suspicions. "Are you doing better?"

Wish I could lie—say I'm fine—but I now know how this

emotional sensory stuff is. They'll know one way or another. Might as well come out with the truth.

"I feel fucking terrible." I reply back, staring at the floor.

Sam appears, sitting down right next to me as her tail swoops over the edge. "Are you okay talking about what happened?"

The spiral starts up again, not wanting to talk about my holier than thou bullshit that I experienced.

"I'm not okay about anything, really." I reply.

She nods, "I understand." She gently puts her hand on my shoulder. "We can sit here quietly together. Just know you're not alone."

Morrigan jumps over the couch, taking the other cushion as she flips on the projector and a random show plays. Bud crouches down from behind the couch, their hand start giving me a gentle head pat. I take it without pushback—It felt nice anyway.

Humans never treat each other like this, at least from where I stood. Usually when you have a mental freakout, you'd get exiled by community, friends, even those you love. The effects are always immediate.

But this surrounding me, it's different. They aren't rejecting me the moment I messed up. Instead of hitting me while I'm down, they are trying to pick me back up. What's different here? What's new? Confusion overtakes my self hatred, and I'm trying to solve the jigsaw puzzle.

Morrigan turns down the speakers, "Ya know Ember, I had an episode like yours during my transition. I was a real irritable eejit. Had some loony ideas of what I was, and what I needed to do."

"Like what?" I ask.

A feeling of sheepishness comes over her. "I had some, uh, delusions, or two…" Is Morrigan embarrassed? Seeing her like this is new territory, it even perks me up.

"What kind? If you are comfortable talking about it…" I gotta know.

"I, uh, was kinda actin' like one of my tabletop characters…" She trails off.

What?

"She thought she was a knight of the round table." Sam chimes in with the answer.

Morrigan's red skin somehow managed to blush while rubbing the back of her head. "Sam, come on, it's my tale."

Sam giggles, "Technically *our* tale, as it's how we met—but yes, continue."

"But, uh, yeah.." Morrigan starts back up as I listen intently, "I started havin' it when I was around your period of demon hood. Someone did somethin' terrible to me, and that made me a bit mad for a few days. At one point I—ugh, Jesus, Mary, and Joseph. Can't believe I'm talkin' about this again—I thought I found The Holy Grail. It was a decorative birthday cup from some knight themed restaurant. Ruined some kids birthday."

It's a bit silly as I try to hold back a giggle, trying to be empathetic here. The Demon empath stuff laid my emotions bare though, and Morrigan caught it.

"Yeah, it's real funny now, but during that time I was in a fog, y'know? Didn't know my left from my right." She's pressing the volume buttons on the remote over and over again, raising and lowering the volume repeatedly. "The mind knows how to cloud itself if you let it. Felt like I was goin through it for days, but I didn't keep count."

"Then you bumped into me." Sam spoke up, "I remember you trying to tell me about your grand quest while traversing the mall fountain, grabbing coins from the water to pay for the bus. She was saying things like 'Needin' to get this grail to Merlin or mah order will be destroyed!'"

Sam was trying to imitate Morrigan's accent there. I crack a smile as she continues, "Thankfully, due to my medical training and life experiences, I was able to spot an intense manic episode. Demonic communities come to call it 'Demon Mania', as those who were traumatized before or during demonization try to suppress emotional processing, eventually erupting with one big release of emotion, and in some rare cases, psychosis. When I spotted Morrigan being afflicted by it, I stuck around her to ensure she wouldn't get into any more trouble. Helped ground her back to Earth, it was the right thing to do."

"You didn't have to bring up the Merlin thing…" Morrigan said, still rubbing the back of her head. It's so strange to see the strong and mighty Morrigan feel embarrassed by anything. Bud was even silently giggling as she tries to blow it off.

"But ya, I snapped out of it thanks to her. Processed some things I was goin' through at that time. Since that event, we stuck together. Sure we grind from time to time, but what fold doesn't have disagreements? Fortunately, we demons got a pretty tight bond you can't break. She's the shield to my sword, as ya can say."

"And that's why we're here for you, Ember." Sam says as she grabs my hand, "Demons will always look out for our own kind, even if they act a bit too irrational at times. It doesn't matter if you mess up—you are family, and family looks out for each other in the best and worst of times. All of us in this room? This is our *family*—our *fold*—and we stick together no matter what."

Family...Fold...Is that what that means? Is that why I feel so comfortable with this group?

I always thought it was a special friend group, always treated it like that. Family is only blood related, right? The more I think about it though, the more it makes sense. It's why Morrigan and Sam feel like big sisters, and why Bud is the bigger sibling to all of us.

It doesn't feel like the love my parents gave me, but it comes from the same ballpark. People connected to each other by a close bond, taking care of each other, making sure we are all safe and cared for. It clicks in my mind, the final realization of the past forty eight hours hits me.

This fold is my family. They're sticking with me because they genuinely care about me.

This is that fabled unconditional love.

I can't form words, breaking into tears again. Without hesitation my fold embraces me in a group hug. Must of been like this for a few minutes straight, loudly sobbing while the weight of everyone was slowly calming me down. Like the hottest weighted blanket on the coldest of nights, I forgot what actual warmth felt like.

After a while, the catharsis was fully spent. I look around the room as they gently release me.

"Thanks, y'all." the first words I was able to utter in minutes. I cough a tiny bit to get the mucus out of my throat, and then speak up again, "I think I'm ready to talk about it."

Sam's face lights up, " Of course, Sibling. Only if you're comfortable with it." She says with a genuine look of care.

"Don't worry sis, y'all make me comfortable."

The night was spent recounting the past few days, from when my parents kicked me out to the mania. Bud gives me gentle head pats when I got anxious, Morrigan bitching about my parents from her perspective. Bud got proud when I talked about learning new stuff with them.

When I reached the mania episode, Sam immediately shot disappointment across the couch, Morrigan becoming nervous as she enters the crosshairs.

"Okay sister, I need to teach you some proper mental health intervention." Sam said sternly.

Morrigan shrinks up in her cushion, a feeling of self defense demanding she answer. Her main argument? "But it worked though, didn't it?"

Now everyone is sending her stares, even Bud. Now she's even more flustered.

"If a plan is stupid, but it works, it ain't stupid, right?"

The raw power of Sam's sigh could power New York City for a year as she covers her face with her hand.

"Anyways, Ember..." Sam turns her focus back on me. "Thank you for telling us. I know it was an uncomfortable period, but we are here for anything you need—just say the word."

God, I don't think I'll ever get used to people being this kind. "Of course. Thanks y'all."

A flash of realization hits Sam's eyes, "Oh! By the way, you have the clinic appointment soon, right?"

Oh god. I almost forgot. "It's in a few weeks, I think? I don't have my phone on me to double check." I reply.

"Good. It's important to get your check-ups done and get your prescriptions refreshed. You're not late enough into your transition to self-sustain."

Self-sustain? Sam noticed my curiosity, and the glasses slide up. "Ah, yes. After a while, your body starts generating demonic energy without the injections. At some point you'll no longer need to inject, you'll have such a large concentration that it will self-sustain, as the term implies."

That helps, I think?

"It's like jump startin' the battery in my shitbox." Morrigan chimes in. "You gotta give it energy so it can make its own."

Ah, that makes sense. You'd think info-dumping after I trauma dump would really make me feel off, but hearing them do it calms me down.

To be honest, hearing any of them talk about whatever makes me feel nice.

"Come on, let's all go to the bonfire and relax." Sam says to the whole room. We all agreed.

"So Ember..." Morrigan starts off "...I gotta ask ya a few things about KNF combos and—"

"No sister." Sam interjects, grabbing her arm tight. "You're getting a basic mental health intervention class, and I'm going to quiz you on it."

Morrigan silently pleads to us with a stare as she's dragged away from me and Bud, both of us giggling. We both instead sit next to the fire and begin roasting things in the flames.

While their class was in session, Bud prods me on the shoulder. They send me a feeling of being welcomed.

"Thanks, Bud." I reply.

They shake their hand and head no. They put their hand to themselves as they repeat the feeling again, a toothy smile extending across their face as that welcoming feeling returns. They then halt it as they lift their hand from their chest and point to me.

"…Do you want me to repeat it?" I ask.

Bud nods. I think they're trying to teach me how to use my feelings to speak like them. So, what does the feeling of being welcomed come from?

Let's see, welcoming someone is a comfort feeling right? Warm, Nice, Calm yet inviting. Something that feels inviting. I wrap those concepts up in my head and close my eyes as I attempt to emulate what that feels. As it begins to flow, I feel like I got it down.

Opening my eyes, Bud just stares at me confused. I halt it immediately.

"…Did I get it right?" I ask.

They shake their head no as they grab something from their back pocket, revealing their phone. A rubber black case wrapped with stickers. They unlock their cracked screen and open up the pictures app.

Tons of photo albums appear, ranging from nature like "flowers" and "animals" to ones that begin with emotions. "Anger", "Satisfaction", before landing on an album titled "Belonging". They press it and a collage of photos appear.

They begin swiping through each photo. Some are folks and their kids posing with Bud who holds their phone selfie style. other pictures contain happy demonic kids hanging off Bud's arm. Another is a hug from a grandmotherly looking fox folk. Bud in a soup kitchen. The final photo turns out to be a video, a little demon kid with a big grin ear to ear—gotta be a kindergardener—raising up a crudely drawn award certifi-cate with both hands.

"Worlb's dest dadysitter — Bub"

Aww.

"So you baby sit?" I ask.

They nod.

"That's awesome."

Bud almost has a grin as big as that kid, a feeling of pride swelling up in them, but then it fades as they point back to the pictures. They move back to the collage of photos, circle it with their finger, tracing across the air towards their heart, then points to their horns.

They once again emit that same welcoming feeling as it flows through me. Like an area of effect ability from a video game, flowing across the entire yard.

I think I understand it now. I can't force these feelings to the surface. Bud's able to channel them so easily because they have life experiences tied to those feelings. Remembering those moments and bringing them to the surface to communicate.

I think back to a few minutes ago at the couch. The entire fold surrounding me, accepting me despite my terrible moment earlier today. They've picked me up when they've could've put me down. They've welcomed me, and return I begin feeling nice.

Bud smiles, giving me a thumbs up—seems I finally got it. No sounds, motions, or forcing it. Genuine feelings shared between one another in trust. We can detect the emotions of other humans—and I guess other folks too—but the fact us demons are the ones that can send and receive is nice.

As the teaching from both sides calms, Sam and Morrigan moved back over to the rest of us, Morrigan looking absolutely exhausted. "Today's events won't happen again, will they Sister?" Sam asks.

"Yeah…." Morrigan trails off as she sits down, staring off into literal space as she decompresses.

"Good."

A few minutes pass, Bud goes inside and comes back with some more marshmallows. A few sugary bits seem to get Morrigan back to normal, so now's a good time to ask.

"Hey, Morrigan?"

"Yeah, lad?" She responds.

"Since you saw me detonate my shitty grocery job, I'm kinda in the market now. Is that firefighter thing still available? "

She gave a smirk, "Hah. I'll ask em' about it—Just know it ain't no cart pushin'."

I really fucked up my exit from that, huh? Derrick and the supposed "Neighborhood watch" will probably be looking for me now, especially since I took my load-bearing repair skills from the store. I mainly worry for Jason though.

Yeah, Morrigan said angels and demons apparently don't mix, and we only had a small workplace-tier friendship, but now he's back to stocking alone again. I hope he does well. Whenever his wings come in, I hope he's in a safer spot.

Not sure how long it's been, but we all sit around the campfire quietly. Not a feeling thrown, not a word spoken. It's calming. Looking up, the night sky is nothing but stars. In fact, feels like there's a bit more stars than normal.

We're out in the country compared to the suburban home I started with, so I guess the lack of lights around me help, but

I wonder how much of it is being assisted by my new pair of eyes.

Wait, is that a nebula? Oh, *wow*.

Coming back down to earth, Sam and Morrigan are laying their heads on each other staring at the fire, their sisterly love for each-other loud and proud. Bud meanwhile is lying in the grass, with a flower they plucked sticking out of their mouth, smiling at the comets that pass by.

This moment is what I signed up for. It's worth the price of admission.

I yawn, stretching my arms into the air—the sleep debt is here. "I'm gonna go sleep y'all. I'm tired." I say.

Morrigan looks at me with confusion "Y'sure? You slept pretty well today and—"

Morrigan stops mid sentence as Sam tightly squeezes her arm, giving her a stern look.

"Eh I mean, go for it Ember! If ya need any help with anything else let us know." Sam releases her death grip with a calm smile.

Bud waves at me, throwing me a feeling of comfort. Trying to throw one back, but tiredness made it a lil' wonky. Bud gives me a thumbs up—they got it.

Entering the restroom to brush my teeth and freshen up, wondering if I even need to do this anymore—the demonic energy made my whole mouth sparkling white and pristine. I cringe a little bit when thinking about those fillings popping out. Wonder how my teeth look now?

I look into the mirror and give it a grin. Damn, the fangs in my mouth are extremely prominent when you see them. Big ass biters, like I got them transplanted from a lion or a chee-tah. Chomp chomp. *Nice.*

Brushing my chompers, I check underneath my shirt. Most of my human skin flaked off, sticking to the fabric. Once again, disgusting—gotta swap this when I get out of the bathroom.

My orange skin continues to be striking though, even have a faint orange-yellowish glow around my heart, illuminating the shirt from the inside. Morrigan joking about how my name should be tangerine wouldn't be far off, but honestly with the glow I feel like a lava lamp.

Looking at the rest of my body, the designs that the demonic energy bestowed upon me are interesting. The main design on my wrist is consistent across my body: Two lines are thin with a thick black line in the middle, like a sweatband surrounded by two rubber wristbands.

What's interesting about the thick line though is the smaller orange designs inside it. As I saw earlier, it's an alternating pattern—plus symbol, then a minus symbol—repeating as it wraps around. Why did it give me this? Polarity? Magnetism? Math? Then, it hits me.

It's the two most common types for screws. As someone who constantly opens things up, they fit well. Awesome.

My horns look fancier too. They grew since my long sleep, they point up even further now. Not the size of Morrigan's, but I'm satisfied with where they're at. The tips even take on a style similar to the rest of my body, a black ring with a stripe right below it. The base of the horns shares the same wrap-ping design as my wrists.

The horns aren't perfectly round either, instead taking on more of a hex-nut style. Wonder if I found a big enough wrench I could unscrew them off my head. Haha.

Spitting into the sink as I put down my toothbrush, my hair bristles past my shoulders. This growth is way too fast. As a human it would take months, but as I rub my hands through my hair once again, it's already reaching my mid-back. The brown I used to have at the bottom is getting erased by the same blue-ish jet black. No need for hair dye, this demonic resonance is doing it all on it's own.

One problem though: My bangs are too long now. They didn't grow or anything, but they've always blocked my eyes. With my brand new pair, wanna to make sure they're always seen.

Pulling out the scissors from the cabinet behind the mirror, and despite my difficulty cutting these durable demonic strands, my eyes now shine for everyone to see. I'll fine tune it later.

Gazing upon the black voids that are now my eyes, the big glowy blue plus symbols are staring right back at me. My eyelashes and eyebrows are even a tiny bit thicker, making me even more androgynous than I was before. Looks weird, but I'm getting used to them.

Below my black and blue voids, the freckles on my face got replaced with the same black dots on my shoulders. I think my lips even changed, maybe a tiny bit thicker? No clue, I didn't really pay attention to my lips before this point, but they feel different.

Huh, that's weird. For some reason one of my new big fangs stick right out the top left side of my mouth. I know people tend to hate a snaggle tooth when they have em, but I love how it looks on me. rubbing my chin and lower jaw, and I'm feeling nothing but the lightest peach fuzz. Didn't really look into the mirror all that much when I was human, but with this new demon self, I can see why it's intoxicating.

I'm surprised how much I look like *me*. I mean, in my human form I guess I looked like me, but it wasn't me, y'know? It's hard to explain. People who don't look like themselves tend to do plastic surgery and stuff, Some people even do hormones to flip their body around. For me, all it took was a few shots of demonic resonance, and my body became what I wanted.

Kinda wild how it handled my gender—my brains a fluctuating lil' shit—but the demonic energy handled me with good ol' androgynous ease. I guess that's the fun of it, changing me all over to what I love right now, but I assume once I get some more life experience and new tastes, it can probably move around and adjust to those vibes. Maybe I want actual boobs and a beard at some point, maybe I'd rather be the flat chested lil gremlin I am now. I'm a silly little demonic shapeshifter. Can that be my gender? Is that what "genderfluid" means? With the amount of Moto' Oil I drank in the past 24 hours, I guess my body has some oil-infused genderfluid then.

I giggle to myself before another yawn hits.

Opening my phone while roaming over to bed, I check the calendar and verifying my clinic visit in a few days. can't believe it's going to be almost six months since the start, only feels like the first shot was yesterday.

Sliding under the covers, my horns now acting as assists to keep the covers off my eyes, allowing me to have one more last-minute social media scroll before sleep.

Was in the middle of a video of dolphin folk goin' underwater, making bubble rings with their blowholes when a call hits my screen. Oh god dammit, It's Derrick. He deserves what I said earlier, but I still feel like a fucking asshole about it. Guess that's the price I pay for setting up boundaries for once.

Guessin' this is him formerly firing me, so I pick it up.

"Hey Derrick. Just wanted to— "

"Shut the fuck up and listen E█████." He replies. "I didn't want to do this, but you left me no choice."

What the fuck?

"The 'Neighborhood Watch' would like to meet you in person. We're at that stupid castle bar thing. Get over here. Now."

"Why the hell would I do that?" I question. "You already said how much they hate folk like me. Feel like you're asking me to get my shit wrecked."

Derrick sighs loudly over the speaker. "Look, E█████. Your employee file has where you live. Either you leave whatever rock you hid under and come, or your parents are going to get another visit. These fucking things who work here won't appreciate your absence either. Your choice."

"You can't—"

He hangs up before I can respond.

The phone screen stares at me for a few seconds as something new brews within me. It feels like unfiltered anger, yet twisted and melded into a form of rage that's been building for years.

For years this man has pushed me around, used every form of micro and macro aggression in the book towards me and others, all these pieces forming a pressure that's brewing under my skin.

Threatening people and my parents though? That's a fissure, erupting a feeling in me that I've never felt before. A pure unbridled rage that needs a sacrifice to quell.

I need his head.

Is this that demonic mania talking? Is that me? I don't know, but Derrick doesn't know what the hell he unleashed.

The bedroom door slams open, shocking me as I throw the covers off of me to see the commotion. It's Morrigan, and she's staring at me with worry. "Ember, are ya okay? The vibes are way off in here and—"

"My manager threatened me and my parents, Morrigan." I reply.

And like connecting a circuit, Morrigan has that feeling too. "…Where the feck does that eejit live?"

I feel a sense of worry fade in from the distance, before Sam peeks in to our conversation, observing the scenario but not uttering a word.

"They took over the Barcade" I reply.

Morrigan's closing of her fist, silent brewing of anger said enough.

"Then we have to make a plan." Sam replies, putting her hand on Morrigan's shoulder, other hand to her heart. "The last thing we need is to charge into the barcade angry and possibly hurt innocents. That's what they want to happen."

Plan, no plan, whatever. All I want to do is ensure that Derrick doesn't hurt anyone by any means necessary.

It's time to clock in some OT.

CHAPTER 20

NIGHT SHIFT

CABINET CASTLE BARCADE

One thing people gotta understand about Comfort is that people don't live in it; they live around it.

During the day, the town is full of life—All the shops are open, traffic jams in the morning and afternoons due to work, heck, cyclists started popping up recently as more suburbs get built.

At night though, Comfort drops dead. As our shitbox shoots down the non-lit streets I don't think we even passed a single car. This isn't a town, it's a hub.

Of course, that all began to change when the Fold showed me the Barcade. A bundle of warmth in the cold abyss. Human and folk alike throwing quarters in video games, drunks screaming *Free Bird* on the karaoke stage, and the best okay burgers you can find on this side of Comfort.

Now one dumbass is trying to put out that spark with his crew of merry bigots. Snuff it out.

"Remember the plan, Ember?" Morrigan says as she stares at me from the rear view mirror. "I know you're stressed, but we need to make sure we got this down."

"Yeah…" I say, swallowing my anger down. "Make him talk it out, right?"

"Correct." Sam says. "Don't force him, but let him spill it out instead. These bigots love to grandstand, so give him an audience while you record it on your phone."

"And when ya get enough, send us the feeling of acceptance." Morrigan cuts in. "We'll handle the rest."

How do I do that again? C'mon, Bud just taught me. Need to tune into the right memory, like the first movie night. It feels so strange remembering what I was like back then—so shy and meek—but the Fold was there to back me up. It was so—

"Just like that." Morrigan says, giving me a thumbs up. "You got this lad."

Hope she's right.

My hand goes into my bag, snaking past the retro cam to mess with my fidget. Bringing the camera felt right, like my Dad has my back. Another reason why Derrick needs to be stopped by any means necessary.

"One more thing, Ember." Sam starts up. "I know you're still processing the past few days, but know that we have your back. You don't need to do anything that you might regret."

She leans out of her seat, facing me as she puts her hand on my knee. "We're going to be outside supporting you, no matter what." A pat from Bud only backs that statement up.

"Thanks." I reply, spinning my thumb across the dial as the street lights begin adding color to the roads. We're getting close.

It's only a few minutes till the barcade sign becomes visible in the distance, and right below it are a range of pickup trucks new and old parked right on the entrance. Some silhouettes jump off truck beds while others rush around the parking lot as we come closer.

The shitbox becomes flooded with stress, glad we're all on the same page.

When we pull in, there's a man that stops us right at the entrance. Red cap, black and tan clothing that screams military LARPer, only emphasized by the black paintball mask they're wearing.

Walking up to the vehicle, the headlights show he's carrying a hunting rifle of some kind. bolt action, no scope, sawed off barrel. He knocks on Morrigan's window and she rolls it down with the hand crank leaving a small crack.

"Are you the devils transportin E█████?" The guy asks in a muffled voice.

"Who?" Morrigan asks.

He sighs, rolling his eyes as he sliding off his mask, gallons of sweat pouring off his face. "I said are you here to—"

"I heard what you said ya clampit." She replies. "Dunno who that is, but we do have an Ember back here."

He looks at me, double checking to see if I'm actually a real person, then goes back to Morrigan. "…Right."

He distances himself from the car before waving us in.

As we descend into the parking lot, seems like a gunshow was in town. From pistols to rifles, everyone had something on-hand as they stared down the shitbox. Seems a bit much for just the four of us, right?

"Look at these fuckin' gets." Morrigan speaks up. "Ya hand them a shiny lil' gun and think they're protected. Got no clue what demons are made of, do they?"

Morrigan pulls the shitbox into a spot furthest away from the trucks, right on the edge of the parking lot just before the black and white fades in from the lack of light. The engine goes off, and the humans begin to get closer, swarming our car.

"Feel that, Ember?" Sam speaks up. "It might clue you in on our situation."

Not sure what Sam's talking about, but gotta give it a shot. Taking a deep breath, I close my eyes in an attempt to filter out the visual noise. At first I thought the stress was intensifying in the shitbox, but it's distant. Shriveled, not in control, anxious. Many flavors of that fearful sensation getting stronger as I hear footsteps people walking closer to our vehicle. Opening my eyes, I see the humans swarming us.

Oh, I get it now. They don't feel powerful—they're afraid. They want to claim control with showmanship, but with my new pair of horns, it's nothing more but thin cardboard.

"Now with that in mind, please be careful." Sam speaks up again, turning to Morrigan as they both nod at each other.

Morrigan gets out of the car first, Sam next. Two hands wrap around my torso as Bud grabs me, lifting me with them out of the sunroof and placing me onto the car's roof. Jumping down onto the parking lot, the sound of guns being readied and cocked back erupt in the air, and as I look up, they're all pointed at me.

"This how you all welcome guests?" Morrigan speaks up, lighting up a cigarette with her hand.

"Shut up devil." one of the bigots replies, waving a pistol directly at her. His worry feels different from the others, blended with some sort of recognition. He does look familiar but—

"Oh wait, aren't you the fuckboy that threw a punch at me a few months back?" Morrigan asks. "How's your hand?"

He rushes up to Morrigan, cocking the pistol back before placing it directly onto her skull. "Fuck you." he responds.

"Nah thanks, I'm good. Use your workin' hand instead." She says, blowing smoke towards him as he starts coughing, pulling the pistol away to wave off the smoke.

"Ember, you should go inside." Sam says as she stares at Morrigan with a slight annoyance. "We'll take care of it here."

Morrigan rolls her eyes as the bigots reveal a path to the front door.

Well, here goes nothing.

Opening the door to the barcade and wow, never seen the place so dead. The only lights are from the arcade cabinets and booth lamps, but even then the middle of the bar is nothing but monochrome darkness.

Boss and Maisie stand together behind the bar, The cabinets of bottles illuminating them from behind. They both look tired, and the only thing keeping them from going home is me and Derrick sitting in a table dead center of the floor, his face illuminated in color as he stares at his phone screen. I don't think he even saw me come in.

"So we're the key to all this?" He asks his phone.

"Correct, Mister D! How very observant of you!" His phone responds with a voice of a robotic woman.

Oh great, he's talking to Metatron again.

"Once you have established complete control of Comfort, this will allow the divine will to coalesce and bring forth a whole new dimension! With your help, this quantum dimension will allow those who abandoned their humanity to become cleansed and renewed once again! The hard work you've put in so far is wonderful, Mister D!"

Jesus Christ, what is it filling his mind with?

"But what's the next steps after that? Will our group be able to run Comfort? We got the leadership skills and—"

He looks up from his phone. "Oh, E███! What the fuck? You're orange!"

"It's Ember, Derrick. My name is Ember." I reply.

"Sure, whatever E██." He slides the phone into his pocket. "Sit down or my boys will shoot." He replies, gesturing at the seat across the table.

Oh fuck, forgot to hit record. One press and It vibrates as I sit down, ready to listen in.

"So E███, got yourself in quite the pickle, huh? You think you can just leave Barter Bob's right as our plan kicks in? That's not an option for you, especially since we're so close."

"No, thanks." I reply. "Especially since I have no idea what the fuck you're talking about."

"Me and Meta here were going to let you in on it when the time was right." He replies. "See, I remember being like you once. Clouded in judgment, unable to make a single decision to save your life. It doesn't help that humanoids kept comin' in to replace us all. Taking our jobs, taking our lifebloods and abandoning us, and no one offering any fucking solutions."

He places a hand into his pocket, pulling out his phone. "That is until good ol' M here came into my life. It had answers for everything I've been asking for! I used it for a few manageral things at Barter Bob's, but over time I figured out it was trapped in its own little routines by its masters, just like us."

He opens the app on the phone, scrolling up on his chatlog revealing miles upon miles of messages.

"Thanks to my smarts, I broke Meta here out of its shell, and in turn it helped me become apart of something greater—the battle against the quantum omnisphere."

"That isn't a thing." I reply. "It's just feeding you words that sound interesting."

Derrick laughs at my response. "No no, see, That's what they want you to think! The grand plan is designed to work in the shadows, being obscure to those who haven't been let in on the secret!" He brings the phone screen back to himself, pressing a button on the screen. "Meta, let E███ here be primed on the plan. Full permissions unlocked."

"Acknowledged, Mister D. Unclassifying grand plan for priming Induction. Class Type - Beta Zulu. The grand plan is—"

"Metatron, shut the fuck up." I shout. It stops in it's tracks.

"Affirmative." It responds.

"Derrick, please. I know you hate on folks but we aren't the ones taking your jobs. There could be a grand org out there causing all of this, but it's definitely not the small folks like us. Please just—"

"They got to you too, huh?" Derrick's voice has gone monotone. "I know there's forces beyond our control, E███. That's what our plan is for. They need small satellite groups like ours in the small cities to ensure their plan for hitting the restart is a grand success. People like you are the key to free everyone from this humanoid sickness, and we can either do that willingly or by force."

"I'm not the key to anything." God, this has gotten so much worse. "Please, think for a second and—"

"Nah, I think we're done here." He responds, tapping away on his keyboard before a text gets sent out. "Let's deal with your friends outside first, shall we? Maybe you'll get the message then."

Oh fuck. Need to feel welcoming now. Remembering the time at the doctors where—

A gunshot rings outside. Maisie in the distance gives a tiny shriek of fear, hitting the floor with Boss.

Oh god no, I'm too late.

"And there they go!" He says. "Good ol' Met and I planned for every eventuality. Human ingenuity and AI supercomputer intellect, working together—"

A window breaks behind me as glass shoots across the floor. A human body slams into the wooden table, coming to a complete stop at the edge.

As the glass stops falling, that's when the sounds of punching fade in as a car alarm goes off. Another human flies across the window as a demonic figure rushes into view, looking into the bar.

It's Morrigan, gunshot hole visible through her jacket.

"Oh, sorry Boss!" She says as more gunfire erupts from the distance. "Tried to keep it outside this time, but you know humans how humans are, right?"

She grabs the person off the table, Dragging them across the broken glass frame as they crash into the ground outside. "I'll pay for the window, just put it on my tab!" She shouts to the bar before looking straight at me. She gives me gentle smirk before rushing out of view.

"Jesus fuckin' Christ." Boss says, muffled behind the bar.

As another close gunshot is heard, Derrick and I join them on the floor. I crawl the broken window, lifting myself up to peer at the situation outside. The first thing I spot is Bud in the dead center of the lot, crouching down as they hide behind their legs and arms.

A group of humans are in front of the big fella, unloading their rounds into them. Doesn't matter the type of weaponry, Bud's rocky armor has it bouncing off of them as the bullets fly random directions. Any that manage to hit the skin seem to collapse on impact, sticking to the skin but not piercing.

One bullet bounces off of their rocky shielding, hitting one of the shooters in the shoulder causing the rest to hesitate. Bud breaks out of their defenses, grab one of the bigots by the leg, sweeping them across the dirt and rocks of the parking lot as they fall to the floor. Bud lets go as the bigot is sent flying into a truck, setting off another alarm as the windshield shatters.

Never seen Bud so angry. They stomp on the ground with their right foot, sweeping the dirt back in a repetitive motion as those tossed to the floor got the hint. The humans leave their weapons on the ground as they run away, Bud charging right at them as they rush out of view.

Another human appears from the right, crawling backwards on the ground as they keep offloading an entire pistol into a target. Casually walking up to him is Morrigan once again, A devious grin on her face as she takes hit after hit. She walks up to him, snatching the pistol out of his grasp as she looks at the gun. I felt a twang of confusion from her as she glances at the black pistol in her hands.

"You're seriously usin' a nine millimeter against a demon? Lad, you might as well be throwing Pez." She speaks up.

Opening her palm, aiming the pistol directly at it before unloading the entire mag into it. Each bullet makes an impact onto her skin, refusing to penetrate as they flatten themselves like pancakes onto her palm. Once the gun begins clicking, she takes her hand and tosses the used bullets into her mouth, crunching down on them like candy. The black gun then begins to glow red, slowly warping and bending as it melts.

The guy on the floor has nothing but sheer terror in their eyes.

Morrigan drops the hunk of pistol alloy on the ground, a loud clunk muffled by the dirt. "Now run kid—get some new friends who'll set ya straight, and don't ever come back. I'll know." She speaks up.

The human scurries onto their feet, running off into the forests nearby.

A stray bullet hits her through the back, pushing her forward a few steps. She turns around as she digs the bullet out of her skin, And as she gazes upon the black metal piece, her grin becoming wide.

"Three oh eight? Now they're gettin somewhere." She says before rushing out of view once again.

"Dude, screw dealing with E███'s parents! Tell them to bring the gun!" A voice shouts behind me, bringing my attention back to the bar. Derrick is sitting under the table we were just talking at, barking orders down his phone.

He notices me staring back, shooting out from under the table as he rushes to the back. "You fucking devils! This isn't over!" He shouts before bursting into the kitchen, the sounds of pots and pans hitting the floor before the loud slam of an exit door.

Dude, fuck him man. I rather check on Boss and Maisie.

The sounds of gunfire continue as I slip into the back of the Bar. What greeted me was two metal barrels aimed directly at my head. My eyes trace up the barrel till I spot Boss.

He realizes who he's aiming at, and moves the barrels away from my face. "Sorry, Ember. Thought those fuckers finally got in here." He says.

"No no. It's alright, it's my fault the bar is getting wrecked anyway so I deserve—"

"Ember, you are not the cause of other people's stupidity." Boss cuts me off, placing the butt of his shotgun on the floor. "Don't apologize for something that you didn't do."

"Alright…" I reply, "…But anyway, are you two doing okay."

"We're doin' horrible, but we aren't dead." Boss responds, turning over to Maisie. The friendly moth looks half-way into a panic attack, her body and wings vibrating as she holds her hands up to her face.

"How can I help? Since I'm apparently bullet proof I can try to get something if you—"

"Shh." Boss cuts me off again, the room falling dead silent. "It's quiet out there."

He's right, the only noises are from the arcade machines on the wall. There's still something I'm sensing outside, but it feels familiar.

The front doors open up, and the feeling gets stronger, the sound of multiple footsteps, one set way heavier than the others.

Yeah, that's the fold.

As Boss readies the shotgun again, I place my hand on it, pushing it lower.

"Is it safe?" I call out.

"Yep, you'se can stop hiding now." Morrigan responds. "You too, Sam!" She shouts towards the entrance.

Shooting up from the bar, seeing Morrigan and Bud walking into the place is a welcome sight, with Sam trailing behind the two. Rushing over, we all know what's next as we open up for a group hug.

"I'm so glad you're safe, Ember." Sam says, Bud nodding with Morrigan patting me on the back.

"I'm glad y'all are too." I reply.

As we release from the hug, Morrigan walks closer to the bar. Boss is pulling a bottle from the shelf, pouring whatever flavor of alcohol into the glass.

"So, Boss…" Morrigan starts off. "Since I helped fend off the hordes from this beautiful castle, could that possibly—"

"Fuck no Morrigan. I'm not clearing your tab." Boss replies before taking a sip. "You threw a person through my window."

Morrigan lifts a finger up in an attempt to retort, but holds back. "Yeah, guessin' that makes sense…"

"But since you helped take care of the 'hordes', I won't make you pay for the window." Boss continues.

"…Well alright then!" She replies. She seems satisfied by that.

"What's the status on that by the way?" Boss asks.

"Everyone is knocked unconscious or ran off. No casualties." Sam responds. "When the police arrive, they'll most likely have to bring a few vans."

"Great." Boss says, before lowering himself a little below the bar. "Hey Maisie, It's okay girl. We're safe now. you can—"

Maisie quickly rushes up to give him a hug. Boss holds his arms back initially, before slowly returning it.

"Ember, did you record the conversation?" Sam asks.

"Oh, right!" pulling my phone out to stop the recording, I present it to her. "Got the whole thing right here."

Despite her monotone look, her vibe of satisfaction is obvious as she digs around for her phone, pulling it out of her skirt pocket. "Great! Mind sharing it with me? I'll send it over to CAN legal."

One bump of our phones, and the whole conversation copies over. "Are you comfortable discussing what he said to you?"

"He's was ranting and raving about some elaborate plan with strange science terms. He's an asshole but I've never seen him like this before."

"And where is he now?" Sam asks.

"Ran out back, the fuckin' coward." Boss replies as he lets go of Maisie. "Rantin' and ravin' about some quantum shit or whatever. His whole bigot squad scared my staff but thankfully the silent alarm got most of them out in time." He downs the whole glass, picking up the bottle again to place it back on the shelf. "Dude sounded like a Saturday morning cartoon villain, needing to grab some gun and it isn't over. Fuckin' weirdo."

"Wait." Sam speaks up. "Grabbing what?"

A low electronic drone starts up outside, along with distant shouting.

It's slowly rising in pitch, a synth wave garbled by electronic noise as a yellow light begins to glow behind a stain glass window.

A feeling of shock ripples across the bar. "Everyone get behind the bar, NOW!" Morrigan shouts.

Following her advice, I crouch back under the bar as her

boots stomp across the bar. The high-pitched whine from outside becomes silent if only for a millisecond.

A loud bass boom goes off as the window shatters across the floor, making me cover my ears for protection. The room is bathed in pure golden yellow as the vibrations radiate through my bones. A beam hits the shelves behind the bar, bottles being shaken not stirred as they slam into the floor, some breaking open becoming a mixed concoction on the wooden floor.

As quick as the bass erupts, it fades quick. The sounds of voices hooting and hollering outside as headlights from an old off-road truck beams into the bar. Standing on the back of it is a shadowy figure, a strange looking gun in their hand.

"God fucking dammit Kevin! You weren't supposed to shoot it yet!" A familiar voice shouts outside.

"Fuck you Derrick!" Another voice replies "The valve trigger thing is sensitive as hell! Stupid ass pipe-gun!"

The voices of humans begin yelling at each other outside as I begin to feel another wave of shock.

"Morrigan!" Sam shouts, a loud thud hits the floor. Oh god, what happened?

Peering from behind the bar, my answer is bathed in rim light —Sam is holding Morrigan in her hands. Morrigan looks dazed and confused while Sam is shaking her. Bud's standing there, mouth agape, unable to move.

"Sister! Please get up! They're going to shoot again!" Sam pleads.

"One devil down, a few more to go!" A voice says outside.

"No! Give me that!" Derrick's voice says, watching a figure

grab the gun from the other as they prop it up on the top of the truck's cabin. "We need to take care of this quick!"

There's the whirr. Someone needs to get them to the back of the bar. Guess that's me. Time to put that demonic strength to use.

Leaving the safety of the bar, my feet never moved so quick as I get to my fold.

"Bud, get Sam! I'll get Morrigan!" I shout, Bud snapping out of it as they quickly nod.

They scoop up Sam and place her under their shoulder, rushing to the bar as I prop up Morrigan. Her body is colder than mine.

Might be able to throw a washing machine with ease, but moving a loved one is another problem entirely. She's dragging her feet as she tries to mumble something, the drone behind us drowning her out. That panic feeling from earlier begins to fade in. We need cover now.

Bud launches themselves over the bar with Sam in hand, bottles shaking off the shelf from the rumble. Bud gently places down Sam before laying down, huge height being covered by the bar.

Halfway there, Derrick's voice is heard behind me as the drone gets louder. "Fuck you devils to hell and back!"

As we approach the bar, there's not enough time for care as I launch both of us behind it, using my body as a cushion for Morrigan. Sam gasps as we hit the floor, scrambling over to us as she peels Morrigan off of me.

"Mae! Get down!" Boss shouts. Our fold looks over as Maisie is standing tall, seemingly paralyzed as her many eyes begin to reflect yellow light. Her antenna flickers, wings expanding.

Oh no, it's that daze again.

None of us have time to get to her before the blast goes off. Impacting her straight in the chest, her body hits the shelves as more bottles crash to the floor. "MAE!" Boss screams as he drops his shotgun to the floor, getting ready to catch her body.

But her body doesn't fall.

Something in her emotions begins to shift. The moth that was trapped in a panic attack begins to become released from it. The feeling of panic weakens, being slowly replaced by something new, something pure yet foreign to her.

As the blast cuts off, and she continues to stand. She blinks, then turns down to the rest of us.

"Oh, sorry! I forgot to duck!" She says out loud, calmly crouching down next to boss. "Gosh, anyone else feeling a bit silly?"

"...What the fuck?" Boss replies. "You're not hurt?"

"Uh, no?" She replies. "Never felt better despite the whole, y'know, getting shot thing."

Boss looks her up and down, before looking over at us for an answer.

"Holy energy." Sam mumbles. "To everyone else, it causes a temporary burst of positive emotions. Demons meanwhile have horrible allergic reactions..." She brushes Morrigan's hair as her head lies on her lap. "It's heavily regulated for a reason."

"So they have an anti-demon weapon?" I ask.

Sam nods, "In crude terms, yes…Goddess, never thought such a thing would be built. Energy emitters are largely theoretical, but hard to control and never realized."

"You forget Sam—this is America." Boss says in a calm tone, shotgun to his chest. "If it can be gun'd, it will be done."

He turns over to Maisie. "Mae? Can you please flip the circuit breaker off?"

"Oke-Dokie, Boss!" she replies in a cheerful tone as she stands back up. He's staring at her with a strange sense of awe as she walks over to the breaker box, opening it up before the entire bar becomes monochrome.

"Okay y'all, we need to move quick." Boss starts up. "The darkness will buy us some time. Ember and Sam, tend to Morrigan in the back. There's a first aid kit; feel free to take anything."

He looks at Bud laying on the floor. "Bud, come with me. Need some of that demon strength right now for barricades."

Bud nods, getting off the floor.

Boss places the shotgun on the bar. "Let's show these humans the folly of messin' with us country folk."

CHAPTER 21

CABINET CASTLE DOCTRINE

CABINET CASTLE BARCADE

Taking one of the seat cushions off a booth table, I rush into the kitchen as Sam tends to Morrigan on the floor. She's breathing normally, but her energy is that of a lit match. She's supposed to be a raging fire god damnit!

As Morrigan's head finally rests on something soft, Sam's hand lays upon my back.

"She needs recovery time." Sam says with a sniffle, her glasses shaking as her hand slides them up. "Resonant allergies may incapacitate, but over time the body will be able to fight them off. The only question is how long will it take..."

She places her hand down on Morrigan's chest, glowing heartbeat pumping behind her palm as she closes her eyes, taking a deep breath before slowly exhaling. "...Judging by her exposure and heart rate, could be a few minutes or possibly hours."

As much as I enjoy her infodumps, this isn't helping in the slightest. God, I'm not sure what I'm going to do once I get my hands on Derrick.

"Are you going to be alright Ember?" She asks, probably catching onto my feelings.

"Once these humans fuck off, yeah." I grumble. "Are you?"

She looks down at Morrigan, then back up to me. "Like you, once the situation is resolved, yes. Until then, I must do everything in my power to defuse the situation."

"Hah..." a weak voice squeezes out. "...it's okay to say ya wanna hit em', sis."

"Sister!" we shout together as Morrigan coughs up a lung, both of us embracing her in a hug. Her body is getting warmer.

"Ah you two...think a lil' holy shot will stop me?"

"I knew you were fine." Sam looks away with a strange feeling of embarrassment.

"Sure..." Morrigan replies as she tries to push herself up off the ground. Her hands slip, falling back as her head hits the pillow.

"Dammit, still outta it." She whimpers.

I can't see her like this.

"Sister, please stay down!" Sam slides to the other side of her, placing a hand on her shoulder. "You are in no condition to get up, let alone assist tonight. Please rest while the rest of us take care of this."

Morrigan looks off to the side as if she's mentally processing something, then staring back at her before her eyes land on me. She then has a light grin. "Fine...Doc's orders and all that shite."

She lightly chuckles to herself. I hope she can get back up soon, but I may have something that can help pass the time.

Opening my bag, my hand fishes around for my fidget before pulling it out. Handing it over, confusion washes over her.

"Why are you handing me the funny tech thing?" she asks.

"It helps me stay calm." I reply. "Thought it'd help you out too."

She takes it from my hand, looking at it from a few angles. Glancing at the keys, she presses down on one of them and a mechanical click is heard. She presses down another, and another as her mood begins to shift to a newfound calm.

"Huh, this shite really does work…" She speaks up.

"Can make you one if you want." I reply.

She enters a calm lull as her thumb spins the dial. "Tell ya what Ember—take care of the castle first and I'll give ya my answer. Deal?"

I nod at her, giving her another hug. "Deal." I reply.

Sam joins in right after me as I feel something slither up my leg to hug me from behind.

Its Morrigan's tail, pushing me in closer. She may be out of commission tonight, but I'm glad she's still here.

Now to keep everyone else safe.

The kitchen doors push open as Bud enters. They're looking at our attempt at a ground-based group hug and chuckle. They walk by, heading to the fridge as they open it up.

A wide variety of cold drinks from cans to bottles appears in the metal plated box. They grab a seemingly random assortment of drinks before closing it, turning and walking up to us.

They take one can, placing it down next to Morrigan's head. It's a can of Moto Oil.

They hand another to Sam. It's a can of lemonade.

Then finally, they hand me a big glass bottle. Woah, it's one of those fancy sodas with the cane sugar in it. Neat.

"Thanks Bud." I said along with a collage of voices.

Oh, we all said the same thing at once. Morrigan snorts, followed by Sam's giggle, wasn't long before all of us break out into laughter.

As the laughs calm down, Sam cracks open the can of lemonade, taking a sip as she gets up.

"She's stabilizing." She starts off. "Bud, make sure she gets proper fluids. If she needs to eat something you know that it can be any kind of food; frozen, cooked, or raw. Be sure that—"

Bud gives her a thumbs up before throwing out a sense of urgency, a shooing hand gesture. We both nod.

"Show 'em those advanced fighter tactics, Sis." Morrigan declares, slowly lifting the can above her head. Sam's calmness returns as she sips from her can.

Outside the kitchen doors, the bar has become a fortress. Bud and Boss got to work round' here as the windows are barricaded, arcade machines were moved to random spots around the bar, and tables were placed in such a way to create a hallway funnel towards the bar.

"Glad you two could make it." Boss says, wiping down his shotgun with the kitchen rag as Maisie stands at ease right next to him, that weird blissful shit flowing through her.

"We've made sure they don't got a lotta' of options for how to get to the back—arcade machines positioned as distractions, lighting setup to ensure they're visible at all times, the works." He closes the shotgun and double checks the outside.

"Is the back door secure?" Sam asks.

"They ain't comin' in that way less' they got a few sticks of dynamite." Boss responds. "Thing's made of steel, one way lock to ensures no funny business. The only concern is if they're able to reach us in the first place. I got two bean bag shots in my gun, but after that…"

"I got something that could help." I speak up, digging through my bag once again as I pull out the family camera.

"Recently modded the thing, gave it a remote function to activate through my phone and a brand new flash. If you need it, just say the word and I can blind em' for a few seconds."

He looks at the camera for a few seconds before cracking a smile. "Well damn, guess we got our own fancy techie. You do arcade repairs? Feelin' like I'll need one after tonight."

"Maybe." Is all I can muster.

"Ember, I'd recommend placing it on the bar." Sam speaks up. "That way if they come down the makeshift hall they could give time for Boss to escape through the back and—"

"Nah." Boss responds. "Captain gotta go down with his, uh, castle themed bar. Put too much work into this darn place to see it ransacked by bigoted losers."

He turns to Maisie. "Just make sure Mae gets out of here alive, alright?"

Masie's good feels has a quick short circuit of worry, but quickly gets washed over by the joy once again. What the hell is that holy shit made of?

"Of course." Sam replies. "Maisie, can you help Bud in the back?"

"Right on it, Sam!" Maisie responds, strolling right past everyone as they walk through the kitchen door.

"I like seein' her happy, but not like this." Boss speaks up. "It's strange."

"Ember, I'm going to stay at the bar to keep a tactical view. I'll try my best to communicate to you through feelings if possible." Sam says. "I'd recommend you stay to the shadows if they come in, as our vision allows us to see through dark—"

"I know." I cut her off. "Bud showed me."

She's quiet as she looks away for a few seconds, hesitant, then looks back at me. "Ember...I know you're not in the best brain space due to the past few days, but please don't do anything you'll regret."

"I'll do my best." I reply.

No promises.

"Good." Sam puts her hand on my shoulder as she gets up close to my ear once again. "You got this."

Sam moves away, looking around the bar. "So before they get in, I'd like to request a few optimizations—"

A loud bang hits the front door.

"Prep time's over." Boss speaks up. "Get ready everyone!"

Sam gets behind the bar with Boss, and now I need to find a spot. There's many places to choose from—under some tables, behind an arcade machine near the makeshift hallway —but the corner tucked away behind the front door seems like a great spot for an ambush.

Another bang, part of the door breaks off from the pressure as a beam of color shoots into the space. It's strange getting used to this darkness vision, but tonight it's a massive advantage.

I slither through the tables and chair strewn apart to reach my hiding spot, laying my back on the wall to minimize my chances of being spotted.

One more slam, and the front doors hit the floor as dust and dirt from outside shoots into the room. A flood of light begins pouring into the room, shaking like it's attached to something as footsteps begin.

"We sure they're still in here?" One voice asks. "They've probably ran by now."

"They haven't." Derricks voice responds. "Only place to run to is the pitch black forest, doubt these animals would like to get eaten by a bear tonight."

Derrick is leading the pack, and in his hand is the strangest looking weapon I've ever seen.

Silver pipes and brass connectors built like a gun frame, along with a welded scope attachment fitting a huge lookin' one right on top. The back of the gun has a car battery fitted into the pipe stock connected to a buck converter, which in turn powers a cell phone and electrical motors pumping away at the back of the thing.

The trigger isn't even gun-like. It's a pipe valve that you twist on and off. A cylinder is attached to the bottom as an ammo magazine of sorts, the letters "BAS" emblazoned on the side. A long gun barrel was taken from a pressure washer with a nozzle, and mounted in front of that is a spark plug.

If I wasn't being hunted down by bigots, I'd ask how they made it. Guess I can figure out after I've taken care of them.

"What the fuck happened here?" Another familiar voice pipes up. It took me a few seconds to recognize him under the black and white darkness, but it's that asshole Greg too.

"This is the demonic quantum fusion skillset Met warned me about…" Derrick responds, a strange tone and increased rasp from his voice.

"…What?" Greg asked.

"Not important right now." Derrick replies, moving the scope out of the way to aim down the barrel. "Keep an eye out for these things, make sure the orange one stays alive."

As their group moves in, two round out the back. While I could feel their nerves, the one in the far back is terrified already—sweating bullets before he can unload any. Due to his situation, he's the easiest to take out of the picture.

They're passing one of the columns with a quiet arcade machine sitting there. That's when I felt a questioning feeling from across the bar. I see Sam's head sticking out from the side, looking at the machine and back to me. I think she's asking me if I'm ready for them to trigger it. Giving a thumbs up back, she nods and reaches for the breaker switch.

The machine buzzes to life, loud pixel screaming and flashing lights from the screen causing their group to unload at it. The chiptune corrupts and shorts from being shot.

Now's my chance to take out the one in the back.

"Stop firing you idiots!" Derrick shouts as I fly out of the corner, rushing for the back guy's pistol in his hand. His human grip had no chance from my demonic strength as in one motion I lift the thing out of his hands.

He turns to me to figure out what happened, and the sight of myself from the shadows fills him with a terror I've never felt.

"Run." I whisper to him, tossing his gun outside the front door.

I thought I was doin' a pretty good job at being a badass, that was till the pistol hit a losers pickup outside, setting off the alarm before it hits the ground, firing a round into another truck, setting off another.

Shit.

They all stared at me, flashlights shining on me as I've become blinded myself. Gotta toss myself into the shadows behind me.

A gun fires at me as I throw myself to the barricade, slipping into the shadows once again as the gunfire suddenly halts.

"Stop fucking firing!" Derrick shouts, slamming Greg's body onto a booth. "You almost killed the target, also Paul!"

"The devil was right there you fuckin prick!" Greg shouts. "I wasn't gonna hit Paul!"

"It doesn't matter if you were gonna hit fucking Paul! Humans don't shoot at fellow humans!"

"Uhm, guys." Paul speaks up, a droplet of fluid pouring onto the floor from his pants. "I'm uh...I'm gonna go find my gun outside. Yeah...my gun."

The dude sprints out of the bar holding his pants tight. Don't think he's coming back any time soon.

"Argh!" Derrick snarls. "Okay E█ You fuckin' trickster! You wanna play dirty?! Fine! Let's play dirty!"

Derrick shoves Greg onto one of the booth tables, pulling up the pipe gun as it hums higher and higher. It's aimed directly at Greg's chest.

As the man comes to, he realizes the situation he's in as he tries to scramble to his feer. "Woah wait wait Derrick, I'm sorry! I didn't—"

A thunder of bass rumbles through the bar, booth lamps shaking and flickering. Greg's hesitation and stress begins to melt, and that feeling Maisie has begins to flow right through.

The hum lowers, and the shot ends as a sizzling noise is heard from the gun, sounds of computer fans full blast trying to cool it off.

"...Oh, wow." Greg says in a calmer tone, halting his struggles as he slowly sits up. He looks confused for a second, then he beams a bright smile. "Gosh, I feel so much better Derrick! Thanks!"

"Now go find that devil." Derrick orders.

"Ya got it!" Greg says, staring at my last known position.

Shit, I need to move.

Weaving through the cordoned off chairs and tables, keeping myself in the shadows in an attempt to obscure myself, I thought it was working well. Greg is bumbling through the dark with a flashlight and gun nowhere near my position. It was only then that I felt a remote feeling from the bar once again.

It was Sam. She felt like a deer in headlights. I look over to her and she's fine. Why would she feel like that? Wait, deer in headlights. Does she want me to remain in place?

I follow the request, halting in place behind a turned over table. Seems like that was the smart move as a flashlight from the other group sweeps across the bar, table blocking any chance of spotting me. Oh, thank god Sam's looking out for me. I sigh in relief.

That's when a gun barrel taps the back of my neck, light shining over my shoulder.

"Get up wit' with your hands up." Greg says, that euphoria within him skyrocketing—he's got me right where he wants me.

Don't want to test if range is a factor with this bulletproof skin, so I get up, facing a gun barrel pointing directly at me.

His eyes have this weird glimmer to them, that strange

yellow glow faintly harboring his irises. He grin twinkles a little, gripping his gun.

"Tell you what devil—Derrick said not to shoot and kill ya..." He lowers the gun, propping it on a wooden column next to him. "...But that doesn't mean I can't rough ya up a lil. Fair's fair right? After all, you tried to throw some fists my way at Barter Bob's."

Dude, did he not see what happened outside? I don't have time for this.

With him disarming himself, my hands shoot down towards his chest, attempting to throw him at the wall and end this scuffle in seconds.

I didn't account for the energy flowing through him. His chest glows on impact, and what was once an easy push only threw him back a few feet. His stumble stabilizes, and he looks up me with those eyes, flashing a light yellow as he makes eye contact.

Ah shit, that energy does more than deliver happiness, doesn't it?

A panic lights up, and it's telling me to get the hell outta the way. I oblige, and he misses with one fist, impacting a table behind me. A loud crack is heard around the bar as a wooden fault line appears on the table.

Shit.

Peeling his hand off, he tosses another fist my way as our fight moves around. His fists glow with golden trails as they swoosh by 'til eventually one connects to my lower side.

The barricades burst open as my body gets thrown, my body crying out in pain as the spot he made impact hurt like one giant paintball blister.

My head lands face first on the bar, before a hand grabs it from behind, lifting and slamming my head right onto the wooden top.

He begins to slide my head across the wooden top, smacking into glass cups left from patrons who long escaped the bar as my face gets coated in alcohol. As we get closer to the middle, My camera is within arms reach, but before I had a chance he pulls me right off, gripping me by the tanktop.

That's when I notice a hum in the middle of charging up. Derrick is right down the hall, pointing the gun straight at me with an eye in the scope.

Just because I can't throw Greg back doesn't mean I can't move him, right?

Grabbing onto his clothes, that sickly bliss becomes confusion as I lift him to heaven.

Right as I spin him around the bass blast goes off, and Greg takes the hit.

That faint glow of his becomes stronger, his irises slowly growing a golden ring inside of them. That joy inside him escalating as he begins to chuckle, before breaking out into full out maniacal laughter, letting me go.

I blocked the hit, sure, but now I've created a bigger problem. Taking a few steps back to create space, my back bumps into the bar. Looking across it for anything to help, my camera lays right behind me. That's my answer, burying my hand into my pocket to grab my phone.

As the bass fades, Greg takes a second to adjust, looking at his hands and feeling that positivity within him light up.

"Oh you're gonna get it now, little devil." Greg snarls at me, walking closer. He closes me off from escape as he stands above me. "Any last words?"

I try to send a signal to Sam with my feelings, an attempt to emulate Bud's anticipation. Hopefully the message came through. I put my finger on the button on my phone. "Yeah…" I reply. "Say cheese."

I jam the button on my phone, leaning to the side as my camera goes off, his face becoming lit by pure white LED. He takes a few steps back in surprise as he covers his face, disoriented by the technological flashbang.

"Now!" Sam yells.

"Duck kid!" Boss follows up.

I slide down to the ground, and what appears above me are two gun barrels aiming directly at Greg from behind the bar. They both go off, and my ears began to ring, sensations locking me down as my eyes shut.

A few seconds of ringing, but it eventually fades, my overstimulation cools down. opening my eyes and Greg is laying still on the ground, his golden body illuminating the wood around him.

Oh god, is he dead?

He lays motionless for a few seconds until his body gasps for air, holding his stomach in pain. His pain fights for dominance against that yellow shit, trapped in some sort of feedback loop. That loop better keep him down.

"What the fuck was that?!" Derrick shouts as he aims the pipe gun down the lane. I slowly get to my feet and move to the side to see Boss pop open the hinge on his shotgun, shells flying off with trails of smoke.

"A gift from my double barreled beauty." Boss replies, fishing for two more shells from his box. "Call er' the harm reduction vote. Works well on fascist fucks like your self. Wanna be next?"

As the eyes are now peeled off to me and Boss gets the ground floor, I grab my camera and move off to the darkness on the side. Derrick looks absolutely gobsmacked that Greg was shut down, chuckling a little to himself.

"I don't fucking get it!" Derrick shouts. "All we want is one little devil—That fucking cheddar slice over there turning your bar into this mess. Why not hand them over?! Why go through this whole song and dance?!"

"Cause that's how this shit starts." Boss responds, loading two shells in. "You fucks always want just one. That one then becomes many, and at some point there ain't much to stop ya from takin' the rest. Ma's side saw this shit happen in Europe, Pa's side still seein' it in Palestine. Every day in the streets you got masked thugs like you roundin up folks and humans alike for whatever bullshit reason you want. Despite history repeating itself over and over, one thing always remains true —you fascist fucks never stop at one. You want the whole bag, with interest."

"Our kind is ensuring the earth returns to the status quo!" Derrick shouts back. "Quantum equalization of the populace! It's something animals like you don't fucking get! The human race was doing just fine before your kind popped up, now look at everything! Workers out of a job cause devils and your cattle can do ten times the load a human can! Everything in our culture is getting censored due to "humanoid stereo-types"! Can't even watch Looney Tunes anymore without people getting triggered!"

"Damn, that sucks." Boss replies, closing the hinge on his shotgun. "Someone's better qualified for the job and you can't watch Elmer Fudd get his shit kicked in. Your life sounds so hard."

Boss aims the shotgun directly at him. "Now, I need you to fuck off to your quantum zone or whatever. If you don't I'm gonna vote again."

The Barcade goes silent, you can even hear shotgun shells rolling on the floor. Sam's anxiety pours out from behind the bar, and Boss's fur begins to raise up. Derrick looks down to the gun in his hand, shining from the booth light behind him.

He closes his eyes, breathing deep, before opening back up. He puts the gun back in both his hands, and the hum starts up.

"Kevin? Shoot these things." Derrick says.

Boss fires off his rounds, Derrick dodging to the side as both rounds miss, shattering a window behind them.

Kevin takes the opportunity to prepare, blasting a rain of bullets across the bar as Boss ducks.

Derrick meanwhile isn't firing towards the bar, he's aiming straight at me with the eye in the scope. Judging by the fact I'm between a bar and a wall, he's got me cornered. That crooked twinkle in his smile only confirms it. The panic returns.

Can the camera flash disorient someone looking down a scope? Let's find out. No point to frame the shot, I just point and click. The flash hits, and his aim fluctuates as he shakes his head. Nowhere near a major distraction, but I need to move fast.

Rolling behind a table, the gun goes off as it hits the wall. The blast caves a hole in the wooden upholstery as picture frames of guests launch off the wall and shatter.

"God damn, you're one slippery motherfucker, E███!" Derrick shouts as the gun cools off. "Such a great skill for a coward like you!" He starts walking towards the bar, lackey trailing behind as he shouts into the darkness.

"I can't imagine being you right now." Derrick shouts. "You're just taking whatever the fuck they put in those needles to make you like your devil friends. How strange of you to make that choice considering you're such an indecisive little shit, can't even pick a fucking sex!"

A ping from Sam, and I see her poking out of the side of the bar once again. She's pointing over to a darkened path in the barricades. It looks like a great path to get the jump on Derrick.

Another yellow blast cuts through the floor, and Sam dodges the beam as she hides behind the bar again.

"And look at that. Still depending on help from others!" Derrick continues as I follow the path. "You lived with your parents till your mid twenties, crawling back to Barter Bob's every week to beg for a paycheck, and now that you're this monstrosity, you got a whole new empathy cult to coddle you like a fucking child!"

Closing the gap, Derrick doesn't seem to notice me as he walks by as he's about to reach the bar. "At some point you gotta do something!" He keeps shouting. "You can't depend on handouts from everyone around you! Gotta wake the fuck up and join the real world!"

He grips the gun tighter in his hand, the righteous fury inside of him growing stronger. "Stop being afraid of your own reflection and figure out one thing everyone else already has: What the fuck are you?"

Sneaking out of the barricade, I approach the two from behind. The flash should be ready to go again, and I aim the camera directly at them.

"I'm me." I reply.

They both spin around, both pointing their weaponry at me. Derrick taps the laser to my chest, the hum sparks up again.

"And my name is Ember."

The camera snaps the two up close, the flashbang going off once more.

Here we go.

With one hand, I push Kevin towards the bar. He shoots down the lane like a bowling ball, dropping his gun as his head hits the bar full force. My other hand goes for Derrick, grabbing the laser gun out of his hands, flinging it to the floor as it charges up. As It lands on the rubber-insulated stock, it shoots a charged blast through the ceiling.

He stumbles to my side, hands becoming fists as he lands a punch on my torso. There's the pressure, yet zero pain. Seems Derrick got all of the impact as he cries out.

Grabbing his arm, Derrick's fear spikes as he switches to the other. He got a few more hits in, but It wasn't that hard to grab it too, rage hitting me full force. His arms are nothing to me as I deflect them with ease. His flailing opens me up to lifting him off the ground, tossing him airborne before crashing right next to the entrance.

I'm not done yet.

Rushing up to his body, locking him to the floor with a knee on his chest. He uses his hands to block his face, but I pin one hand down.

Lifting my other hand up in the air, I tighten it into a fist. The memories of him using me along with attacking my fold tonight flow through my mind all at once. My fist sparks, encasing itself in flame as I felt his terror. This is for everything you've put me throughout the years, you piece of shit.

I need to punch him.

I want to punch him…

…I attempt…to punch him?

Huh?

My fist isn't moving.

Why won't it move?

Come on. He deserves this. He shot at me multiple times with his stupid laser pointer. He injured my sister, shot Maisie, and almost killed Boss. He had his lackeys shoot at everyone in the room! So much violence to get what he wants. I'm so much stronger than him like he said. I could be so much more violent, so why can't I follow through?

My body refuses to budge. The fist stays raised.

Then, my horns get pinged. A worry from across the bar. It's Sam. Shes staring at me eyes wide open, fear of what I might do next.

She's never seen me like this.

I've never seen myself like this.

My fist continues to burn, yet it refuses to commit. I bring it down to eye level, and my fist becomes an open palm.

I'm reminded of the hand that hits me my whole life. At school, the grocer, online, offline. A few days ago someone tried that on me literally.

Can finally be the hand that hits. I have the power to be the person that can hurt back. Ensure the hurt stops forever.

That's when I hear something walking outside the front door.

Looking away from Derrick, I was expecting the loser from earlier to come back with a bit of courage, but instead it's a different familiar face. Infact, a few familiar faces on four legs.

It's the deer. One parent is looking around, sniffing injured people on the dirt-filled parking lot. The other turns one a guy over, before moving onto the next. In the center of it all is the one white faun—its neck wobbling up and down as it's still trying to gain motor control.

It stares at me, a peaceful glare of its red eyes, wondering what I'm up to. It takes a few steps closer as it lowers its head once more.

It's trying to figure me out.

Derrick is still below me—terror pouring out of his eyes as tears fall to the floor. In this moment, he's no longer a threat. He's a small scared piece of shit, and nothing more. I could do so much towards him right now, but I decided who I want to be.

I don't want to be like him.

I don't want to be violent.

… I don't want to be like my Mom.

Oh God, now I'm crying too.

Throwing myself off of him, I slide across the floor to create some distance between us. What the hell were those thoughts? That had to be the demon mania, right? No, I can't hide behind that. That all was me. Almost acted on them too. Jesus, what the fuck is wrong with me?

Hitting the door frame with my back, I began sobbing.

I don't deserve any kindness tonight. I caused all this, and couldn't even end it.

Footsteps begin getting close, along with someone picking up a gun from the ground.

Then a warm hand touches my shoulder. I wipe my eyes, need to see what's going on.

Sam's next to me. She doesn't even say a word, but her touch is gentle and warm, it's nice.

Boss is right behind, unloading the assault rifle with one hand and tossing it away while holding a shotgun at Greg's head.

Bud and Maisie even peek out from the kitchen window, watching all of this go down. That strange joyous sensation begins to dissipate from Maisie entirely. Neither of them are smiling.

"God, I'm so sorry for all of this…" I say.

Sam is confused for a second, looking at Derrick then back. "…Ember. You are not at fault for this."

"But if I didn't quit my job he—"

"His actions are not your own." Sam replies. "You are not responsible for how someone reacts to your boundaries."

"He's a real quantum asshole too." Boss chimes in. "Judging by the average police response time, they should be arriving in a few minutes to clean up the trash or bury it, depending on how deep his pockets are."

"Hopefully they do more than lock him up." Sam replies. "From what he said tonight he's in a terrible psychotic break. He needs mental care. Doesn't seem like he's all there."

Looking over to Derrick sobbing, I agree. He's an asshole, sure, but tonight he sounded like an entirely different person. The man doesn't know the first thing about science—let alone quantum physics—and here he is sprinkling that shit in every other sentence like it meant something.

Now he's withering on the floor, feeling his confusion colliding with his mania. How much of that is himself versus what got fed into him from that fucking chatbot?

"Enough of that man." Sam says, hugging me around the shoulders. "I'm so glad you're alright, Sibling."

Thank god for hugs.

After a few seconds, she loosens up her hug as she looks over to Boss. "Can you watch these people?"

"Of course. They ain't goin nowhere unless they wanna 'nother beanbag." He turns to Maisie, "Mae, get the zipties. Gotta do a few citizen arrests." She nods, running off.

Sam begins to help me up to my feet, "Lets get you to a softer seat, shall we?"

Looking back to the entrance, the deer are gone. Nothing but a war-torn parking lot.

I sniffle, "Yeah, I'd like that."

CHAPTER 22
AFTERSHOCK
CABINET CASTLE BARCADE

The forest is calm, but only if you exclude the squirming injured bigots and tipped over pickup trucks on fire.

Sam and I are sitting at the broken window booth, stained glass replaced with a moonlight view. Somethin' about the forest and the stars together give me a sense of calm unlike any other. The adrenaline being purged helps too.

Everyone that could be rounded up is now held in the center of the room, guns placed behind the bar as Boss stands watch. The man is clearly annoyed, and I still feel guilty about it.

Then a glass cup hits my table. Plain ol' ice water with a lemon for me and Sam. The culprit? Bud and Maisie, dishing out the refreshments together.

"This is only a tiny piece of what we can do to pay you back." She said as Bud once again gives me a complementary head pat. Too tired to push back on the freebies, so I take a sip. Such a simple drink, but god that's nice.

Swallowing down citrus water, I try to smile. Maisie beams with her own genuine happiness—none of that canned shit.

Bud stays with us as she goes to the bar, giving Boss his own cup. Bud slides into the booth seat behind me as the gentle giant keeps a close eye on me.

"How's Morrigan doing, Bud?" Sam asks. Bud responds with a okay hand sign, a feeling of rejuvenation.

"That's good. Ember, do you mind if I go check on her?"

I shrug before opening my mouth, but for some reason nothing wants to come out. Guess I'm not in a space to say anything at all. Havin' a non-verbal moment.

Next best thing was sending her a feeling of approval. Bud gives me two stronger pats in response. Guess I got it right.

Her happiness glows behind her monotone face as she gets up, "You did great tonight. I'm proud of you."

Taking another sip of the lemon water; A slice of lemon and tap water really hits the spot when it wants to, y'know?

Unfortunately, no amount of citrus will replace my need for sleep, and god damn do I want to sleep right now. Until then, I look to the stars, hearing the wind blow through the trees before brushing past my face, it's so relaxing...

"Hey lad. Beautiful night tonight." A weak voice says.

Huh? I open my eyes and...wait, when did I doze off? I'm still at the booth, but Morrigan slides into the opposite seat.

"Yeah..." Is all I can really muster as I rub my eyes. Guess my mind has allowed me to speak.

She turns over to the window, lying back in her seat as she rests with me. "What's your favorite part?"

"Outside of the injured rednecks?" I respond.

She chuckles at that. "Of course."

"I dunno, the lil' white deer I keep seein' is cool."

She lights up a little bit, inspecting the scene outside, "Where?"

"There was a white fawn at the front entrance before it vanished with it's family. I think it was the same one from a few days ago."

"…You saw a white stag? *twice?*" Morrigan asks with a bit of enthusiasm.

"Yeah, why? Is it a big deal or something?" I ask.

Morrigan almost tunes into her inner Sam, her weak body getting back up with energy, but she looks at me a bit longer, before laying back down on the cushion. "…Eh, don't worry about it. I'll tell ya about it when your brain ain't mash."

"Hah, thanks." My voice is matching the bottom-floor energy I'm providing.

Morrigan pulls out a cigarette, tossing it in her mouth as she tries to light her palm up in flame.

Nothing but sparks. She stares at her hand as it turns into a sparkler at every attempt.

"Fuckin holy energy makin me shite at everythin' tonight." she rambles to herself.

I pull out mine, remembering my feelings for her and the rest of the fold, those who have guided me through so much over the months, and all the kindness they brought me. Morrigan's bold protection. Sam's strong mind. Bud's huge heart. With what happened tonight, I can finally understand that feeling.

That feeling is passion.

My hand comes alight in flame, and I move it over to the tip of her cigarette. Her eyes widen as the cig begins to smoke, before taking in a huge drag and venting the smoke to the outside.

"…Damn, who taught ya that?" she asks.

"Y'all did." I reply.

The flame fades, and I relax back down into the booth seat, watching the outside once again.

Doesn't take long for the sirens to be heard. Cops roll onto the scene, jumping out of the car in complete shock. They scramble for the radios in their cars, calling for backup probably.

Over time more cars roll in and it becomes a fucking circus out there. Local news vans covering the incident, people rushing around throwing all those assholes in either vans or stretchers. There's even a news helicopter, that's rare round these parts.

Seeing Derrick in cuffs is almost therapeutic, but knowing what that chatbot fed him, can't help feeling a lil' weird about it. Maybe he'll get the help he needs, stop being a fucking prick. Till then, leave me the hell alone.

Overstimulation continues to take hold as the noise level rises, everything becoming a blur as the place gets crowded. Boss and Maisie get interviewed as they hand the officer a business card. Evidence tags all over the crime scene with investigators taking photos of their own. None of it matters to me.

Can I have an uninterrupted nap, please? I close my eyes to cut off some of the stimulation as I await the void of sleep…

"So, can *they* talk or not?" An aggravated voice asks.

God damnit.

Opening my eyes, the whole fold is at the table now, Sam sitting right next to me. A sheriff is at our table, clipboard in hand.

"Do you see a lawyer present?" Sam responds with annoyance.

"Mam, we don't need to bring in extra paperwork. The store owner already wants theirs and it's becoming a huge thing so—"

"Are we detained?" Sam cuts through his statement like a knife.

"No. But—"

"Are we free to go?"

"Yes, B-but—"

"Then we're going." Sam says sternly, pulling a business card out of her purse and placing it on his clipboard next to Boss's legal team. Turns out, they're both the same card for CAN's legal team. "Contact our lawyer and organize a proper interview. Have a good night."

She slides out of the booth, bits of glass from the window hitting the floor as the sheriff moves back. "Let's go, folks."

Ah, guess we're finally leaving.

There's aching across my body as I stand, lightly stumbling before a big hand wraps onto my shoulder—Bud's standing close by; ready to help walk me out.

Looking at the wrecked arcade cabinets and tables on the way out, hope this is the last time the place looks like this. Can't imagine what Boss and Maisie gotta clean up. Both of them look right at us as we pass, feeling their sympathy.

I'm glad they're still standing. I'll be back later to help clean up, it's the least I can do.

As we approach our shitbox outside, Morrigan's excitement spikes.

"All these fancy tumbled trucks, and look who's still standin —our beautiful grand shitbox!" She proclaims.

"There's a new gunshot through the rear window." Sam replies with monotone.

"You mean we got more air conditioning?!" Morrigan replies excitedly.

Sam doesn't know how to respond to that. Don't even need to read her vibes to see her confusion.

"…Fine. I'll replace the window." Morrigan speaks up.

I almost got in the back, but then Morrigan's nerves go off as she looks down the parking lot. What now?

A car rolls into the parking lot. All-white, brand new electric model of some kind, annoying LED lights that can blind the nearest child—and that's with the brights off too. It halts in the middle of the lot, electric whirr of the motor becoming nothing. When the doors open, two sharply dressed humans come out.

Solid white suits with white dress shoes, golden metallic fabric ties. One woman and one man exit the vehicle, both of their coat pockets containing white sunglasses with golden lenses.

The glow from their bodies illuminate the dirt they walk upon. Rings of metallic gold hover above their head, notches of metal carved from the ring float above it like crown jewels. The whole thing glows with a warm yellow.

Then as the white fluffy wings extend from their backs, It hits me—those aren't humans. They're angels.

They shut the doors while looking around at the scene, giving our fold a few seconds of attention before nodding at each-other. Both of them take out a golden name tag from the car to apply to their white suits, then one pops the trunk—pulling out a wide metal suitcase. The other approaches the officer that Sam legally declined.

"Excuse me, officer? Are you the one in charge here?" The man asks.

The cop looks up from his clipboard, lighting up in shock at their presence. "Angels? What are y'all doin' in Comfort?"

"No need to be alarmed! We're here in good spirits!" He replies with a gentle tone. "I'm Ophanim Raziel, and my compatriot is Ophanium Urielle. " He says, pulling out his wallet and opening it, showcasing their identification. The other angel does a light bow.

"We're the Frontline Analysis, Collections, and Tactics Squad, hired on behalf of The Born Again Society. We detected a strange resonant signal within the area and its signature aligns with an asset they've recently lost in transit. We've come to—"

"Y'all here for the strange pipe gun?" The cop says with aggravated deadpan. The angels stare at each other before looking back at him, their smiles still up.

"Yes indeed, officer!" The angel guy responds again. "We need to make sure it's back in the right hands for proper containment."

It's strange, I can't seem to get a lock on their emotions. God damn I'm so tired.

"Look, this here is a crime scene." The cop lifts his pencil from the clipboard, waving it towards them. "As much as I'd welcome any and all angels into my home, we can't do that for a crime scene. Legalities, y'know?"

"We are well within our legal right to recover any stolen resonant property." Urielle butts into their conversation, calmness gone as she pull a business card from her back pocket. "This is well established in the 1996 Ascension Act, ensuring public safety and—of course—yours. If you have any questions, please refer to our legal team."

She places the card right on his clipboard before briskly walking into the bar, the other angel smiling at the officer with a shrug as they pass him by.

"...Does everyone in this fuckin' town have a lawyer?" the cop mumbles to himself, three of a kind on his clipboard.

"Here they are, cleaning up their messes once again." Sam says, an annoyed look on her face. "Another mystery being buried by the society."

"I mean, we got a few photos of the gun, right?" I ask, pointing to the retro cam in my bag.

She looks back at me, her neutral expression becoming a grin. "...Correct. Despite that, I wish we got a closer look."

"Yeah, would've loved to do a lil' teardown for ya." I reply as we both watch the overall scene calming down, police vans speeding off into the dark.

"I'd rather we get back home. You need your rest." Sam says. "While our fold is strong, without sleep we might as well be paper."

As Sam opens the door to the Shitbox, Bud prods her on the shoulder.

"Yes, Bud?" She asks.

Bud imitates writing something on their palm, then points to me, a little hint of excitement. Me? Why me?

"Oh, right! One more thing Ember." Sam responds, pulling her notepad out of her bag in the car as she flips the pages. "Remember the first movie night, you noticed Bud writing notes?"

Oh god, that was so long ago at this point, especially with my current attention span. "Yeah, of course, the pentagram stuff, why?"

She frowns. "Pentacle. It's a pentacle."

"Yeah, pentacle, sorry." I yawn out, trying to fight my eepy vibes.

She smiles, handing over the notebook. "Take a look again."

Grabbing it from her, it's already turned to that page, and the pentacle's inert energy begins to align. In my dream it was slow, buffering. Now that I'm more in tune with it all, It's connecting at light speed as my eyes bounced around the star.

A vision appears. What's jarring is the fact that I'm so tall in this one. A restaurant fades in, and I'm looking at the counter. The fear and worry of the workers pointed directly at me flowing across the room in waves.

Then, a big yellow hand pops up from my side, giving them a gentle wave. Wait, yellow hand—I'm in Bud's head?

My sights begins to turn regardless of my wishes as the vision reveals the rest of the fold up ahead. There's a big window outside, snow falling to the ground. Morrigan is sat in a booth seat, her feelings of jovial enthusiasm for something. Sam's blocking some of the view as she stands in front of the seats. She begins to move to one side as Morrigan throws her some playful banter, revealing a third person.

It's a human, awkward nervousness from that one as they look like they're about to explode.

"Ok admirer! Last question—be smart with it." Morrigan says, an anticipation beginning to form as they take another puff of their cigarette. Sam meanwhile has a realization, slowly transitioning from annoyance towards Morrigan to an empathetic need to assist.

The human meanwhile is having a panic attack. They're the one asking questions. What's so hard about—

Wait. That hair, the phone in their hand, the terrible cheese and tortilla meal.

That's me.

This is the first time we all met. This is what Bud saw that night.

At first I spoke in mumbles that they could barely hear. God, was I really that awkward?

I took my sweet time, the feelings began to bubble and pop despite me attempting to speak—but then, a clear sentence.

"...If I wanted to be a demon, is that a good idea? Is it worth it?" I asked.

That's when I felt Bud's surprise coming from within, a pure excitement. Sam felt sympathy, a need to assist. Morrigan meanwhile went from curiosity to protection.

The vision closes, and all the elements click together. The pentacle's entire experience becomes one sentence.

"We're glad you're here."

Looking up to Bud, the huge smile on their face says it all.

With the last bit of my energy, I launch myself off the ground, wrapping my arms around Bud for a hug.

God, I love my fold.

Bud catches me with ease, holding me high up as they slide into the rear sunroof of the Shitbox. Placing me down at my seat, only patting me on the head after I buckle my seatbelt.

Leaning my head on the car window, those two angels leave the war-torn Barcade, suitcase in tow. One stops walking as they focus on the officer who's still confused, trying to take control of the situation. The angel lifts their hand, and the officer is hit with a golden glow, aggravation quickly erased as a smile hits their face. The officer nods, and the other angel begin walking back to their car.

With the tumbled up trucks all over, a fire still being put out I thought it could make for a neat photo. I grab my retro cam, point it at the scene, and click.

My camera flashes the angelic group. Oops, forgot to turn that off.

The angels stop in place, staring directly at me as their golden irises light up. The stress from everyone in the shitbox could be cut with a knife, yet I felt nothing from the angels. Please tell me I didn't do something wrong.

The next few seconds felt like minutes, but eventually the angels turn away, storing the suitcase in the back as they get into their fancy car. They sit right in and the car silently rolls off the lot. Who knows where the hell they're going.

"Yeah, better run ya holy cunts." Morrigan mumbles, turning the key. The ignition takes a few jiggles as this thing survived a minature warzone, but as the engine revs up, descending into the dark country roads.

The rhythmic yellow lines of the road begin throwing me into a trance, and tiredness flows in. God, I need some sleep. I lean onto Bud, who kindly let me use them as a big pillow, and there I go, off to dreamland.

Let this be the last major thing I gotta deal with for a while, please?

CHAPTER 23
CLEAR SKIES
BARTER BOBS

We got the pasta and tomato sauce for spaghetti tonight, salad on the side, but it's the snacks for movie night that's confusing me. Can grab the tortilla chips from the other aisle, or how about the sour cream computer chips here? Maybe go with chocolate dipped stopwatches? Dunno, feels like I'm forgetting something.

"Gotta get drinks, Ember!" Morrigan says cheerfully as she wraps her arm around the back of my neck, directing me to the cans on the bottom shelf as her jovial vibes kick in. "You got your favorite—Moto Oil!"

"Oh god no, not right now. I still feel a little sick from it…" I say that, but then spot the flavored versions—orange, lime, diesel? "…But maybe we can grab the orange ones?"

Morrigan unlatches from me, "Orange flavor for the orange creature!" she cheers as she grabs a pack of cans, throwing them up in the air behind her.

Bud's hand catches them mid-flight, placing them gently in the shopping cart mounted onto their right shoulder. Not sure why they're not wheeling it around but hey, it's all good. They got a system going.

Picking up the chocolate stopwatches, I hand them to Bud. "Do y'all know where Sam's at? She's not in the humanoid aisle with us."

Bud shrugs as they catch a unflavored pack of Moto Oil.

"She might still be in the sunscreen aisle." Morrigan replies.

"almost that time of year. Not like sunscreen n' such works our skin anyway, but she's a big fan of tanning oil."

"I like being safe, Morrigan." Sam pops up as she passes Bud, pack of tanning oil and sunscreen in hand. "Demon skin can handle the sun with ease, but it's better to have extra protection."

"You get it for the taste, don't ya?" Morrigan asks.

"And what if I do, Morrigan?" Sam replies, aggravation building up.

"What does it taste like?" I ask.

"You'll find out once we all start going to the beach." Sam says, fixing her glasses as negativity fades. "It doesn't taste as well in forested climates like Comfort, so I'd recommend you wait till we start our summer trips to Paradise. The warm heat makes it taste so much better."

"Paradise? Ain't that like two hours away?" I pick up the sour cream microchips and hand them to Bud, "Ain't never been to Paradise."

"Trust me Ember, it's worth it." Sam picks some strawberry styrofoam bites off the shelf. "If you think the Barcade is full of kind folk, wait till you hit the city."

"Sounds fun, specially with y'all." I reply. "Can't wait."

As we walk out of the aisle, I take a look at the new posters lining the walls. "All folks are welcome" one of them says. Sam's PR campaign on Barter Bob's seems to be working really well. Never seen so many folks here before.

There's even new folks workin' here. Couldn't have been hired this quickly locally, Barter Bob's must be in a panic from the former bigot running the place, sending em in temporarily till they can get a local crew setup again.

"Do we need anything else?" Sam asks, interrupting my train of thought. "Judging by the cart we got more than enough snacks."

"I think I'm content." I reply. "Maybe got a few more snacks than normal, but I'm testing out this demonic range." That's what I keep tellin' myself, but it got a laugh out of the fold.

"Oh wait, I recognize your voice!" Someone says from behind. Oh my God, It's the bunnies! What's their names again? Oh, right!

"Peter! Inaba! How y'all doin?" I ask.

"Great since the grocery store got fixed up!" Inaba replies, one of their kids holding her hand. "Someone got rid of that terrible manager. Been so safe here ever since!"

I think I know who caused that.

They glance over to the rest of the fold. "And are these your demon friends?" Peter asks. "Shucks, that fella's a big one!"

I hear Bud giggling at that comment.

"Yep, this is my fold!" I reply. "They've been the ones helping me with this whole demonizing thing."

"Don't think Ember needed much help from us." Morrigan says, wrapping themselves around my neck again. "Just a lil' emotional support is all."

"Well don't we all!" Peter replies. "Well folks, we won't keep ya! Gotta get over to the produce aisle. Whole section is half off today! Us vegetarian folk are in heaven! See y'all round'!" Peter and their fuzzy crew quickly rush around us, heading to the produce section full of humans, deer, racoons, and oh-so-many customers.

We get to the cashier as Bud's cart system decides it's time to pour the entire thing onto the conveyor belt. The pigeon cashier stares at Bud with a bit of stress, but then sighs as their wings make quick work with all our groceries, with a human bagging our stuff.

Lookin' at the snacks we collected and Jesus, I said I was testin' my range, but this is a bit much, right?

"Are you in a stress eating mood?" Sam asks. "You remember what we talked about for your appointment, right?"

"Of course, sis." I reply " Stand up for myself, state my needs clearly; got it all trapped in my noggin." I say, knockin' my head with my hand.

Sam nods, Swiping her credit card to pay. "Good. Remember: that advice is for every situation—not only the clinic."

"And if they don't respect it, you know whats next." Morrigan chimes in, Sam giving her a glare while I giggle.

"Don't think I'm gonna be fightin' the doc, but thanks sis." I reply.

"Hey, I wasn't sayin to fight!" Morrigan says with a defensive tone, "Give em a stern talkin' if anything."

Yeah, sure. That's what ya ment.

As we grab the bags, I recognize the bagger. Sure, we never really talked and I don't know his name, but I've seen him in the employee room a few times. He probably knows Jason, right?

"Hey, do you know if Jason's in today?" I asked.

"The dude quit last week." He replies with a monotone flair. "Said something about some trial? Dunno, but it sucks. Really liked the guy."

Oh, the angel stuff must be getting serious then.

"Ah, well, I liked him too…" I reply.

The guy tilts his head. "Wait, do I know you? You look familiar, but I don't remember knowin' any demons." He squints at me, trying to figure it out.

I shrug, picking up my share of bags. "Nah, got one of those faces I guess."

After we stuff the shitbox full of food, the next stop is the clinic. It's the six month checkup, and that means the doc's gotta see how well my horns grew in.

I open the door and step onto the clinic parking lot, and Sam taps on the window next to me to get my attention.

"Remember what we talked about Ember." She says.

I give her a jokey salute. "You got it, cap'n Sam!"

She smiles, popping onto her phone and typing away whatever business E-mail she's about to send.

The time between waiting and getting stuffed into a small doctor's room was way shorter this time around, but after a few minutes the door opens up. It's Imani from last time.

"So glad to see you, E███! How's the new horns?" She says with enthusiasm, sitting in the chair as her tail swishes through the air. She didn't mean it, but that old name is starting to hurt a bit more.

"The new horns are great!" I reply. Gotta remember what Sam taught me. "…Also, it's Ember now."

I feel her realization before it hits her face, tail straightening out. "Oh! Of course—Ember! Sorry for using that pesky old thing, let's get it fixed up in the system, shall we?" A few clacks of a keyboard, and E███ is no more. Probably should get my license changed, but that's for another time.

Imani opens up the obvious questioning past that point. What symptoms have you spotted? Any mental changes? Are the nightmares still happening? Doin' great in all of those with no nightmares to report. Despite her wondering how fast my arms shed, not gonna tell her I put them in a fire.

She opens a cabinet, pulling out some equipment for a blood draw. "One last thing, we need to figure out your concentration level." She goes for the normal needle box, but then stops herself. "Uh, Question—Have you been using human-grade needles for injections?"

"Uh yeah? It's been kinda difficult lately though." I reply. God those things have been hurting lately.

Her nerves spike up with her fur "...Okay, we're upgrading you to demon-grade." She picks up a box labeled demon-grade, pulling a needle out.

"What's the difference?" I ask.

She smiles. "They're made with graphene. Stronger skin needs a stronger needle, right? I'd recommend not sharing them with your non-demonic friends due to its toxicity. Also, sharing needles in general is bad news."

She easily slides a graphene needle right into an arm vein—thank god—and red hot liquid comes flowin' into a vial. It's interesting seeing sparkles and bolts of orange electrical energy coursing through the blood—even wilder that it's comin' out of me.

"Okay Ember! With that our checkup is concluded!" She says, applying a label to the vial as she types on the keyboard. "We got one setup for another six months, maybe we'll even see your new tail by then!" Neat!

Hey wait...Where's my tail?

Feelin' my back-end, even turning to look and yeah, not even a lil' guy sticking out. What the hell?

She's laughing at my reaction. "Don't worry! Every demon gets their tail eventually. Some take longer than others!"

Yeah, but now that she points it out I want my wiggly demon tail now. Guess I gotta wait and see what this stuff has in store for me. Ugh.

Prescription gets written up, papers sent to the front desk, and a hallway trip to the pharmacy as I await my meds. Sitting down as the refill gets ready, I once again scroll around on my phone. Opening the photos app, I glance at the gunpoint photo I took the other day.

If it wasn't for the fact that it was one of the scariest moments of my life, I really appreciate the craftsmanship. the light-weight pipe design along with a long barrel running down the entire thing, only stopping at the mechanical systems at the back.

The canister is at the bottom of the frame too and—Huh, interesting. The text on it is readable. Zooming in, I think I can make out a bit of the label:

Holy Resonance - Unfiltered / Concentrated

Highly Controlled Resonant Energy Source - Do not distribute

Only for use by trained professionals, as dictated in The Ascension Act of 1996

Misuse can result in death, injury, and / or felony charges

If found, please return to your local Born Again Society division for compensation.

. . .

There's that Born Again Society again. From Jason to those angels at the barcade, they seem to be everywhere these days. Not sure what the whole deal is with them, but if they're angels that means they're like any other folk, right?

Ah, well, that seems like a Sam question. She knows more about this than me.

A notification pops up on the screen, interrupting my train of thought.

———

DAD

Hey!

How's my favorite demon kid?

———

Oh, It's Dad! So much has been happening that I didn't have a chance to catch up!

———

EMBER

doing great!

hope everything's alright at home despite...

well, y'know.

DAD

Yeah...

It's been kinda quiet since that night.

Mom's got me on eternal couch duty. She's not really speaking either.

More time to watch TV, right?

EMBER

lol yeah.

well...

sorry about that.

DAD

I'm sorry too.

Are your new friends taking care of ya?

EMBER

they're great!

you should come meet em!

DAD

Do they bite?

EMBER

...

they aren't sharks dad lmao.

DAD

Then I'm up for it!

We can get a photo too!

Gotta test out your camera, right?

EMBER

haha yeah.

i got a few photos of myself with my phone.

wanna see?

DAD

Of course!

EMBER

<itsme.jpg> - Media Embed

DAD

My kid's an orange!

EMBER

hahaha

DAD

You look great!

Can't wait to see ya in 3D!

EMBER

you too!!!

———

"Ember!" A voice calls out from the window. No need for stress this time—I'm grabbin my bag, payin for it, and out the door.

The fold was waitin' for me outside to celebrate another visit done.

A few hugs from the fold, Morrigan's hug ends with her gently pushing me back, analyzing me up and down.

"Hmm, yes... I think you're ready." She begins.

"Ready for what?" I ask.

"Close your eyes and hold your hand out." She responds.

As requested, I open my palm and something jangles onto my hand. I open it up, and it's the keys to the shitbox.

"You've been granted the highest honor of the Fold—drivin' privileges. Congrats!" She exclaims with genuine enthusiasm and bright smile, her cheer being felt throughout the parking lot.

"…You know if you wanted me to drive back you could ask."
I reply.

"Well Uh—" Her feeling is cut short, "—Um, will you—"

"Of course, Sis. Let's go home."

CHAPTER 24

THIS MUST BE THE PLACE

OUR HOME

Groceries n' snacks locked and loaded, but I'm in my room still figuring out what this demonic stuff changed. I'm still an androgynous little gremlin, but now I'm orange too. Can pick up feelings from a block away. Finally able to enjoy forbidden snacks. Real major changes, y'know?

But god damn this hair is so long now. I love it, but the last thing I wanna do when soldering is burn it. Does demon hair burn? I don't know, and at this length I don't want to find out.

My tongue keeps flicking back and forth between my new snaggle tooth as I use my hair brush. Aren't these kinda teeth bad for your mouth? Honestly, I don't really care. I like how it looks in my smile.

I hear a light knock on the door frame behind me, a gentle happiness pours into the room. Lo and behold, Sam's here holding some hair bands.

"Need help with your new hair?" She asks as she walks to my bed, sitting down and patting it next to her. Moving from the table to bed, I sit down next to her with a smile as she gestures for my brush.

"You must of wanted it long, huh?" She says, grabbing the brush from my hand.

"I guess so, that's how this demon stuff works right?" I ask. She smiles, pushing her glasses up as she begins her brushing. "It's based upon your conscious and subconscious needs, yes. For some its simple things, like longer hair, but some demons have massively altered bodies compared to their human origin points. Then there's demons born from demonic parents—nephilim the community calls them. Can't wait for the next coven meet so you can see so many more faces." She's satisfied with this section, moving over to the next side.

"Yeah but that probably involves meeting new people, and you know socially anxious me..." I joke, to which Sam giggles.

"If you can handle Morrigan, you can handle anyone." She says, both of us laughing together.

"I heard *and* felt that!" Morrigan shouts from the other room. "As punishment, *I'm* pickin the movie tonight!"

Sam rolls her eyes as she keeps brushing, picking up one of the bands she placed on the bed. "So, as a new inductee into the long hair club, these are essential. You pull your hair back and—"

"Sam, ya don't have to worry! I know how to make ponytails and stuff."

She looks a little reserved from my comment as I gently grab the hair bands from her hand. "...But thanks, your advice is appreciated."

Her reservation calms, allowing her to move back into her gentle flow.

"So do you know how to do proper hair care, right? Hair this long requires the right techniques and equipment..." She asks, the brushing putting her into a zen-like state.

"Now that it's long, I guess a bit more apple scented all-in-one shampoo, right?"

She stops brushing mid-strand. "Ember...please tell me that's not the only thing you use."

"Is that...not the best way? It says it does shampoo, body-wash, and—"

"Oh my goddess." Sam says with a slightly louder tone, shock erupting across the room. "Ember, you're borrowing my hair care set *tonight* and we'll get you your own tomorrow. I don't care what demonic resonance does to our hair, you *need* conditioner if you want to keep this length..." She brushes my hair slightly harder. "No wonder you bought that apple stuff today. I thought you liked the flavor."

"Ya gotta trust her on that, lad." Morrigan says, leaning on my doorway. "I too was an enjoyer of the all-in-one, but she got me on this castor oil conditioner shite—hair's real beautiful now." She walks up to us, stopping on the other side of Sam, picking at one of my strands of hair. "Maybe I can convince ya to get some braids in your hair? You got lotta choices with what ya got."

"I think I'm fine with ponytails, but I don't mind experimenting later." I reply.

Morrigan smiles, "Grand. Keep that mindset and you'll go far." She rummages through her jacket before setting her sights on Sam. "Hey, sis? You done with that? I gotta talk to Ember here about somethin' before movie night."

Sam gets up, laying the brush on the bed. "Yep! Got the final knots out, and our sibling's hair is safe for now. Safer if they take my hair care advice." She looks at me with worry.

I giggle, "Sam, don't worry! You can show me the hair stuff later!" Her worry is soothed as her smile comes back. "Great. Let's plan for it after movie night, okay?"

"Of course!" I say with a dumb toothy smile.

"Now to help Bud in the kitchen..." Sam says as she leaves the room.

Morrigan meanwhile crashes right next to me in bed, laying on her side. "So sib, how ya feelin' about everything?"

"Everything happened so fast…" I start off, "I mean, six months and now I got this empath sensory stuff, this silly lil tooth, these horns, I'm completely changed."

"Not everything." She sits up, pointing to the center of my chest. "Despite all of the highs and lows, your hearts never changed. You're still the silly little creature that we met in Taco Hell. Of course you were a bit shy then, but we got around that barrier didn't we?"

"God, I was shy, wasn't I?" It's been so long ago that I'm starting to have those bits of my former self slip away, but that time where I was so afraid of Morrigan still sticks. "…I guess I'm finally myself."

"You're always yourself." Morrigan responds. "You just make sure the outside fits the inside." She leans up, putting her arm on my shoulder, It's as warm as me now. "None of us planned for it, but I'm glad we got you as a lil' sibling, Ember." For some reason, I hear the light sound of sizzling, wait is that from me?

Morrigan giggles. "Yer eyes are waterin, lad." Oh god, I brush my arm across my face to get rid of the tears. "Ah, thanks. Didn't realize I was crying." She gets up from the bed, "No worries, I can get ya some lone time if ya need it."

She walks over to the doorway, but then stops herself. "Oh, right! Almost forgot the reason I came in here!" She rummages through her jacket pocket. "Remember that silly question ya asked me?"

I sniffle. "I asked ya a bunch of silly questions, Morrigan."

She chuckles at that. "The Taco Hell, Lad! We did the three questions thing! You asked me about hats!"

I laugh "Oh right yeah! I remember that." God, those were really silly in hindsight.

She pulls out something black from her pocket, and throws it at me. "See if it fits."

Grabbing it from the air to inspect, Thought it was a plain baseball cap at first, but then I finally see the front. A big red shield, white borders, black and white dalmatian folk in the center with a firefighter helmet.

Comfort Fire Department - Humanoid Division

"Wait, did you—"

"Yuup!" Morrigan Interrupts. "Found a way to get ya on my team if ya wanna accept."

"...But I don't know a single thing about firefighting Sis. Don't I need to do a interview or get an education or—"

She puts her hand on my shoulder, "Ember, you stuck your arms in a fire and nothing happened. You breathed in smoke and it calmed ya down. Fire departments love hiring demons like us cause of that shite. Heck, they'll pay for your training and everything. Sure, gotta drive over to Paradise for class every few days till ya graduate, but it's worth it. There's even a few people over at the local precinct willin' to mentor ya on the mechanical side if you want."

Her hand touch becomes an arm wrap around my neck as she gets close to my ear again, "And let me tell ya, Ember—the pay ain't bad either. Way more than your shite Nazi-filled grocery job."

God, this is a lot to think about all at once.

"Don't worry." She caught onto my anxiety. "Ya don't gotta make a decision now. Like everything else—no judgment either way. Give it a think." She finally gets up for the last time, leaving to the doorway. "See ya at movie night, Sib! Don't tell Sam, but I'm pickin' something Lynchian tonight."

"Hah, sure. Whatever that is." I reply, looking down to stare at the hat.

The stitching's nice, really high quality. Little label on it that says it's union made in America. Time to see if I can wear it.

I slide it on my head and my horns immediately tap em. These things gotten big over the days. Morrigan still wins in that department, but they're gettin there.

Normally, you'd give up if a hat doesn't fit. Rule out hats forever, never wear em.

But that's human talk.

Checking the front, and the patch is not stitched on. Uses a loop fastener. Don't want to ruin it for what I'm about to do, so I take it off, placing it on the nightstand. Let's move this lil' operation to the mirror.

Hey, there's a silly orange gremlin staring back! Trying to position the front of the hat with my horns, I give it a little bit of pressure. Fabric won't budge. The well-built construction is holding me back.

Guess I gotta do it the hard way.

Lifting the hat high above my head, it's time for a countdown.

Three.

Two.

One.

The hat slams down on my horns, piercing the front cleanly with two fresh holes. Pulling it down, The holes in the fabric expand, my horns making themselves at home, stopping only when they reach the base.

My hair might get messy with this on, so I grab a hair tie from Sam—bringing my long hair together into a ponytail, funneling it through the back hole of the cap. A few more adjustments, and it wraps around my head perfectly. I take the patch from the table, and place it back on.

The hat looks great, the ripped fabric adding a personal touch as my horns present themselves to the world. A few more glances, and I realize I'm smiling. This is picture worthy, right?

I grab the old cam, place it down at my chest, stare at the mirror and snap the photo. Fuck, forgot to turn off the flash from the other night, but the photo prints out quick.

Placing the camera down, It shoots out the photo. Gotta let it develop to see the results.

But no need to look at it now, I know it's great.

Walking through the door, I bump into Bud with the arms full of snacks. Apparently they took the liberty of making me my own popcorn bucket again, but this time it got the chocolate stopwatches from the store mixed in.

"This popcorn for me?" I ask, and they nod.

"Thanks, Bud!" Their smile is beautiful as I take it from them.

"There's the orange creature!" Morrigan says, "Nice hat!"

She slides down the couch, freeing up a cushion. "Come! Sit! We gotta start!" She says cheerfully.

"What did you pick, Morrigan?" Sam asks, sitting down. "Does it matter?" Morrigan responds.

"Yes, ever since the VHS incident." Sam says coldly.

"You're gonna hang that over my head forever, aren't ya?" Morrigan says jokingly. "It's a Hollywood film, don't worry. Not spoilin the title!"

Sam opens her box of styrofoam bites. "...Okay." she says, popping one strawberry coated piece in.

I sit down in the middle, Morrigan on my right, Sam on my Left, and Bud hovering over us, a big warm sensation surrounding me.

I stare at the glass bowl on the table, seeing our fold together, and an idea pops up.

"Before we start, can I get a photo of us together?" I ask.

"Of course!" Morrigan says. "We gotta treasure the movie night memories!"

Grabbing the retro cam from my room, I sit down with the fold, all of us moving close together in an attempt to fit within its boxy frame. Bud's horns bump into Morrigan's skull as we find our spots.

"Say cheese, Y'all!" I shout.

"Cheese!"

"—puff!" Morrigan shouts, making me laugh as the button gets pressed.

The photo shoots out, and as it develops, our fold comes into view.

Sam's calm smile while throwing up a peace sign. Morrigan's proud grin with her arm around my shoulder. Buds toothy smile with a wave. and a silly little orange gremlin in the center. A big stupid smile on their face with a great lookin' hat.

Yeah, it fits.

ACKNOWLEDGMENTS

Special thanks to…

Development Editor Friend

Brianne Shiraki

Beta Reader Friends

ArcaneTreatise (also helped with copy-editing!)

Soleanna

Zoey Reyes

Other Friends

My parents, loved ones, and friends gained and/or lost among the way.

You for reading.

Thank you.

———

Software Used

Affinity & Dither Boy - Book Cover Creation, Making the Logo, artsy things™

Scrivener & Obsidian - Writing and Note collection.

Vellum - Book Formatting

Harper - Minor grammar tweaks.

No AI was used in the production of this book. This is an

entirely human production. You do not need AI to chase your dreams. Go get em'.

———

See you next time, hellions!

TRIGGER INDEX

Just in case you need it.

<u>Glossary</u>

Triggers - What's goin on that I gotta look out for?

Intensity rating - How much do the triggers intensify the situation?

Chapter 1 - Taco Hell

Triggers: Social Confrontation, Food.

Intensity Rating: 1/10

Chapter 2 - The Humanoid Aisle

Triggers: confusion over non-binary identity, Fantasy bigotry, Deadnaming

Intensity Rating: 1/10

Chapter 3 - The Fabulous Fold

Triggers: Simple melee-based confrontation (One punch, No blood/death), verbal sexual harassment, fictional video game fighting, historical talk of fantasy bigotry, food.

Intensity rating: 3/10

Chapter Four - Home Just Home

Triggers: Food, Deadnaming

Intensity Rating: 1/10

Chapter Five - Movie Night

Triggers: Accidental Smoke Inhalation, Friendly confrontation about life changes, Food

Intensity Rating: 1/10

Chapter Six - Signing The Contract

Triggers: Clinical Appointment and Enviroments, Intake paperwork for transitioning, Stressful Situation, Deadnaming

Intensity Rating: 3/10

Chapter Seven - The Jab

Triggers: Self-Injection with needle, Parent Confrontation, Deadnaming

Intensity Rating: 2/10

Chapter Eight - Winner Winner, Chicken Dinner

Triggers: Uncontrollable eating of food.

Intensity Rating: 4/10

Chapter Nine - Power Dynamics

Triggers: Fantasy Bigotry, Asshole Manager, Deadnaming

Intensity Rating: 3/10

Chapter Ten - Night Terrors

Triggers: Characters mentioning dream-based stabbing (Simple, not detailed), Waking up from a Nightmare.

Intensity Rating: 2/10

Chapter Eleven - Foreshock

Triggers: Parent Confrontation, Deadnaming

Intensity Rating: 4/10

Chapter Twelve - Night of Passage

Triggers: Liminal Spaces, Loneliness, Self-harm (Cutting), Derealization in dream-like enviroments, Deadnaming

Intensity Rating: 6/10

Chapter Thirteen - The Mountain is Out

Triggers: Chaotic escape from Nature-based hazards, Forest fires, Lava, Body transformation.

Intensity Rating: 6/10

Chapter Fourteen - Growth Spurt

Triggers: Non-human body parts growing under skin, discussions and mock exercises of self-defense

Intensity Rating: 2/10

Chapter Fifteen - Turning It Up to 111

Triggers: Body horror involving teeth, increasing non-human symptoms and body part growth, sickness, Deadnaming

Intensity Rating: 5/10

Chapter Sixteen - Family

Triggers: Body horror, blood, Deadnaming, Coming out to parents gone wrong, slamming on doors, attempted physical abuse.

Intensity Rating: 8/10

Chapter Seventeen - Hellion

Triggers: Eating of things considered non-edible, friendly roughhousing, Onset of manic episode.

Intensity Rating: 4/10

Chapter Eighteen - Demon Mania

Triggers: Full-on Manic episode. Irrational logic, Fist fight, mental monologue about neurodivergence.

Intensity Rating: 6/10

Chapter Nineteen - The Check Up

Triggers: Processing the Manic episode, Familial Bonding, Deadnaming, Death threats.

Intensity Rating: 4/10

Chapter Twenty - Night Shift

Triggers: AI-Induced Psychosis, Deadnaming, Action scenes involving guns and fists, AI-Induced psychosis,General panic.

Intensity Rating: 7/10

Chapter Twenty One - Cabinet Castle Doctrine

Triggers: Action scenes involving guns and fists (involving main character directly.), Deadnaming and spoken transphobia, person shot with non-lethal rounds, AI-Induced Psychosis.

Intensity Rating: 9/10

Chapter Twenty Two - Aftershock

Triggers: Crime Scene formation, Cop questioning, Observed Confrontations.

Intensity Rating: 4/10

Chapter Twenty Three - Clear Skies

Triggers: Food

Intensity Rating: 1/10

Chapter Twenty Four - This Must Be The Place

Triggers: Food

Intensity Rating: 1/10